# WHO R U REALLY?

# WHO R U REALLY?

MARGO KELLY

MeritPress | fw

Published by
Merit Press
an imprint of F+W Media, Inc.
10151 Carver Road, Suite 200
Blue Ash, OH 45242. U.S.A.
www.meritpressbooks.com

ISBN 10: 1-4405-7276-3
ISBN 13: 978-1-4405-7276-0
eISBN 10: 1-4405-7277-1
eISBN 13: 978-1-4405-7277-7

Printed in the United States of America.

10 9 8 7 6 5 4 3 2 1

Library of Congress Cataloging-in-Publication Data
Kelly, Margo.
Who R U really? / Margo Kelly.
pages cm
Summary: When the boy she likes at school disappoints her, fourteen-year-old Thea connects with
a fellow player of the online game, *Skadi*, but although he claims to love her she becomes more and
more uncomfortable with him and has to cover up their relationship.
ISBN 978-1-4405-7276-0 (hc) -- ISBN 1-4405-7276-3 (hc) -- ISBN 978-1-4405-7277-7
(ebook) -- ISBN 1-4405-7277-1 (ebook)
[1. High schools--Fiction. 2. Schools--Fiction. 3. Internet games--Fiction. 4. Family life--Fiction.
5. Online identities--Fiction. 6. Online sexual predators--Fiction.] I. Title. II. Title: Who are you
really?
PZ7.K296393Who 2014
[Fic]--dc23
                                    2014013255

Cover design by Frank Rivera.
Cover images © Aliaksei Lasevich/123RF; Cathy Yeulet/123RF.

*This book is available at quantity discounts for bulk purchases.*
*For information, please call 1-800-289-0963.*

For Katie,
because you amaze me.

# Acknowledgments

I have been blessed to be surrounded by wonderful people during the process of creating and publishing this story. A big thank you to the team at Merit Press, especially Jacquelyn Mitchard for her editorial insight, Frank Rivera for an amazing cover, and Diane Durrett for her polishing expertise.

When it comes to agents, I snagged the best one. Brianne Johnson has been an unparalleled advocate in my corner. Her insight and enthusiasm for this story took it to a whole new level.

My gratitude is endless for my personal cheerleaders and early readers: Wannetta Cooke, Kevin Kolditz, Brooke Hofhine, Lara Leigh Hansen, Jill Koudelka, Gary & Nancy Kelly, Jami Harris, John Cooke, Artemis Grey, Shelby Engstrom, Mary Buersmeyer, Katharine Cecil, Shannon Eckrich, Lisa Terada, Alison Miller, Holly Barnes, and Natalie Malm.

Melissa Dean was my first critique partner, and I loved her from moment one. We had the opportunity to meet in person at a writers' conference, and we were instant friends. She has been a huge support along this path to publication. Christi Corbett was my second critique partner, and she never hesitated to call me out on plot and character details that needed improvement. These ladies have been the best critique partners in the world, and I truly appreciated all of the time they spent helping me improve this story.

And finally, huge thanks to my family: Christopher, Mitchell, Jacob, and Katie. I struck gold when they came into my life; their encouragement and love means the world to me.

# CHAPTER 1

When Tim's eyes, bluer than an Idaho sky, met mine, my mind turned to mush. He towered above everyone else at the bus stop, and on this cold January morning he looked cuter than ever with his bomber hat and rosy cheeks. He shoved his sidekick, Josh, jokingly, and a cloud of white air escaped Tim's mouth.

My best friend, Janie, whacked me on the hip. "Omigosh, Thea. Here they come. Smile." Her words bounced in rhythm with her black ringlets. She adjusted her new fluffy snow-white parka. Even though it had a hood, she would never smash her perfect curls simply to stay warm. The crisp air made the tip of her nose red, but the rest of her face remained alabaster white. We'd been best friends for years, and now at fourteen, having a friend made the ninth grade bearable.

Janie hoped Josh and Tim would ask us to the Winter Solstice dance, but I just hoped to speak to Tim without sounding like a complete idiot. Tim walked in our direction with Josh right on his heels. They stopped in front of us, and everyone else hovered to watch the show.

"Thea," Tim said.

I wanted to reply, but no words came. Josh approached Janie, and I fidgeted with my favorite fuzzy pink scarf.

"Jan-eee," Josh said, dragging out the last syllable of her name. He eyed her up and down. "You look like a giant fat marshmallow."

Janie's smile dissolved, and her cheeks flushed.

"What did you say?" My voice cracked, and heat spread from my chest to my ears. I stepped in front of Josh.

"Get out of my face." He loomed over me and the veins in his thick neck swelled . . . but it would take more than words and a threatening look to scare me off.

I stretched up closer to him. "Not until you apologize to my friend."

He moved toe-to-toe and leaned nose-to-nose with me. "Back off, toothpick." His breath reeked of sausage. He jerked his hands upward and faked a lunge toward me.

I stumbled backward and landed on my butt. Gasps echoed. I sat dazed, too angry for tears but too humiliated for retaliation. I tugged at my scarf, and it tightened like a noose around my neck. A couple of girls from the crowd helped me stand up.

Janie found her attitude and shoved Josh. "You jerk!" With a little head sway from side to side, she said, "I ain't no marshmallow. You have marshmallows for brains. Didn't your mama teach you not to hit girls?"

The girls in the crowd chimed in with a "Yeah!" and many of the guys positioned themselves behind Josh and Tim. We stood divided. Tim's mouth hung open, and he did nothing to help.

"I didn't hit her," Josh said. "I can't help it if she's a klutz—"

Tim lifted his hands. "Stop, before this gets out of control."

"Josh is the one out of control," I said. I wanted to do more than fake a lunge toward him, but he was bigger and stronger. I didn't stand a chance.

"Oh, come on, Thea. He was joking," Tim said.

"No . . ." I dusted off my jeans and rearranged my scarf. "Josh is a disgrace to the human race, and you're guilty by association."

"Whatever." Tim motioned for Josh to follow him. As they walked away, Josh glared over his shoulder at Janie and puffed out his cheeks like a blowfish. She flushed again. So much for getting asked to the dance. That yelling match also ruined my chance with Tim, not that I particularly wanted to go with him anymore.

The bus ride to school was endless. Janie's cell phone chimed, and she pulled it out of her pocket. She fingered the phone, and her shoulders sagged. She flung it into my lap. A video was playing on the small screen, starting with me landing on my butt and ending with Tim saying, "Whatever."

The bus pulled into the lot. People clambered off, leaving us behind. We were glued to the seat, staring at her cell. Suddenly, the bus radio seemed louder. The smell of vinyl and residual body odor made me want to gag. I needed off the bus. I grabbed the edge of the seat in front of me, to hoist myself up, and my fingers stuck in a wad of already-been-chewed gum. Great. I plopped back down and pushed against Janie.

"Move," I said.

She stepped into the aisle and let me climb out.

■

For the rest of the day, people turned traitors and yelled, "Whatever!" I was mortified, but not like Janie. Guys shouted "Marshmallow!" at her over and over. Even though cell phones weren't allowed in the classrooms, people snuck them out and kept sharing the video. Bullies like Josh needed to be put in their place, but I was clearly incapable of doing anything without humiliating myself in the process. Janie and I walked home.

■

Later that night, I headed down the hall from the bathroom to my bedroom. I tapped the portraits on the wall as I went. Mom hung our school pictures here, but she also included special family events, like when we planted the dogwood and maple trees in the backyard nearly ten years ago.

Mom stepped next to me in the hall. "Are you all right?" She pulled the reading glasses off her nose, and when she propped them on top of her head, gray roots peeked out from beneath her short copper hair.

"Yeah." I shrugged.

"Did something happen today?"

Only if you count the whole world coming to an end. After a slow sigh, I moved toward the end of the hall. Mom followed after me, and I wondered if I should tell her. Maybe she could help. Once in my room, I crawled into my bed and crushed my pillow. A tear escaped, and I wiped it away with the pillowcase.

"You can tell me," Mom said and sat next to me. She stroked my hair, and my heart ripped open. I blubbered like a baby until I'd finished telling her every last detail.

"Josh ruined everything," I said, "and I don't know what to do about it. Plus, he could have pummeled me if he wanted, and I wouldn't have been able to stop him." I curled around and rested my head on her thigh.

She rubbed my back and said, "If it will help, I can call Josh's parents tomorrow, and I can drive you to school."

"Or you could just punch him for me. That would help."

Mom grinned. "Well, I don't think I can punch him. His parents wouldn't like that very much."

"I'd like it. Doesn't that matter?" I smirked. Mom rested her hand on my cheek.

"Thea, you do not have to tolerate that kind of behavior from any guy." Mom's face paled, and she held her breath for a moment. "Maybe we should take a self-defense class together at the rec center."

"So I could learn the best way to kick Josh in the nuts?" I asked.

Mom scrunched up her face. "I'm serious, Thea. It's important to know how to protect yourself."

"Have you taken one of these classes before?" I asked.

Mom nodded. She twisted a ring on her finger, and then a tear fell from her face.

"What?" I sat up and gripped her hand.

"I was attacked in college—" We locked eyes. "—I'm fine, but it was terrifying. If I'd known some self-defense moves, maybe I could have fought for myself, but I didn't know anything. And when this guy came at me from behind, I had no idea what to do. Fortunately, for me, some other students came along and chased the guy off. But anything could have happened to me that night. Later, as a part of my recovery from the trauma, I took a self-defense class . . . and I've never needed to use the skills I learned . . . but I think it would be good for both of us to go and take the class together. Knowledge is power."

"And I could probably punch something," I said, trying to make Mom smile.

"Probably." She grinned. "I'll check into it and figure out when we can take a class."

"I'd like that."

She wrapped her arms around me. "I love you, Thea, and I'd do anything for you. And if it was up to me, I'd cocoon you and keep you safe forever."

"But you have to let me grow up," I said.

"I know, but not yet." She pulled me tighter.

■

The next morning, I pulled my massive comforter up to my neck and dreaded facing the day. Even after confiding in Mom, I still spent hours crying during the night because I was so angry. By morning my eyes burned; they were probably red, raw, and puffy. Yesterday's events still haunted me, and I repeated the nightmare over and over in my head. I grabbed my cell from the nightstand and replayed the video. I tossed my phone on the floor and tried to gather my determination, but instead, I yanked my blanket over my head and hid in the safety of my bed. I promised myself I would never cry over a guy like that again.

About thirty minutes later, I gave up. I rolled over and switched on my lamp. I tore off the top page of my Quote of the Day calendar—my annual Christmas gift from Mom—and read the day's quote.

*The roots of education are bitter, but the fruit is sweet.—Aristotle*

Whatever. I ripped off the page, crumpled it, and threw it across the room toward the trash can. Missed. I read the next quote.

*Men cease to interest us when we find their limitations.—Ralph Waldo Emerson*

Nice. That one made sense. Who needs them? I patted the quote and swung my legs over the side of the bed. Warm air blew from the vent in my floor, and the fuzzy fibers of my pink scarf danced ever-so-slightly as it hung on the back of my chair. My thighs still ached from the forty-five minute trudge home yesterday. We had nearly frozen to death, but it was better than climbing onto that bus after school.

I enjoyed a long, lazy shower, shaved my legs (even though hardly any hair had grown since last week), and plucked my eyebrows. As I wiggled into my newest pair of jeans, I thought of Janie's cool clothes from Abercrombie & Fitch. My parents believed jeans were jeans, and that a pair from Walmart would do just fine. I usually agreed with them, but I had to tug these jeans down a smidgen at the waist to add length at the ankles.

I finished my outfit with some black flats, a white T-shirt, and a cherry-red sweater—which looked great with my puffy eyes. Not. But it could serve as a bright distraction instead. I checked in the mirror to make sure my hair hung perfectly straight. Mom always said it was a gorgeous dark auburn color, but it's red. And red is red. The freckles don't help the situation. I rubbed foundation over the pesky spots, and then I applied olive colored eyeliner and black mascara to help camouflage my swollen eyes.

"That's the best it's going to get this morning," I said to my reflection. I headed down the hall and around the corner to the kitchen for breakfast with my family. Sunshine flooded through the windows, and I squinted at the bright sparkles bouncing off the sliding glass door.

"Good morning, baby-girl. Feeling better?" Mom poured herself a glass of orange juice.

"No."

Dad downed a bowl of cereal while leaning over the granite counter. He licked milk from his lips and said, "Cynthia, we adore you. That's what matters. Besides . . . no dating until sixteen. Family rules."

I huffed at Mom. "You weren't supposed to tell the whole world."

"I only told your dad."

"I've got to go." Dad snagged another bite of cereal. Then he grabbed his coat and cell phone, kissed my head, told Mom he loved her, and gave a short salute to my older brother, Seth, who sat at the table near the windows. Dad left in a flash.

"Would you like some scrambled eggs and toast?" Mom asked.

"Sure." I plopped onto the barstool.

"Today will be better. I'm sure everything has blown over." She cracked eggs into a bowl as she spoke and dropped the shells into the trash. "It's not the end of the world, and you'll find out boys do dumb things all the time."

"Hey! Boy sitting right here," Seth said. He acted offended for about five seconds and then went back to reading the comics. Seth, two years older than me, was a junior and already a star player on the football team. No one cared that his hair was as red as mine. He slathered it with gel and spiked it a bit in front. Everyone worshipped him. So annoying.

Looking back at Mom, I said, "Seriously. This is so not funny. Everyone saw that video."

Mom came around the edge of the counter and set her hand on mine. "Oh sweetheart, I know it isn't funny. I can still call Josh's parents and talk to them."

"Don't. That'll make it worse." I twisted a napkin into a ball. "I just want to be liked."

Seth snorted.

"Shut up!" I threw the wadded napkin at him.

"What?" he said. "I'm reading the comics here. They're funny." I glared at him until he shrugged and went back to the newspaper.

"Besides, you are well liked," Mom said. "You've got lots of friends, Janie, Emily—"

"Stop. I get it." But those are all girls. I longed for a boyfriend who would confide in me and need me. I wanted him to say the three most beautiful words in the world to me: I love you. A slow sigh escaped my lips, and I rested my chin on my hands.

"Okay, honey," Mom said and beat the eggs with a fork.

∎

I avoided Tim over the next several weeks, which was an epic challenge considering we shared a bus stop. Janie and I showed up as late as possible and waited on the opposite side of the group from him and Josh. And yet, whenever Tim came within fifteen feet of me, my heart sped up.

Two days before Valentine's, Janie ran through the cafeteria waving her cell phone.

"Omigosh! You'll never believe this!" she shrieked, bouncing up and down.

"What are you talking about? Calm down!" I gripped her shoulders to mollify her.

Janie took a deep breath and then spoke as fast as a bullet shot from a gun. "Tim wants to go out with you!" She sprung up like a coil and bounced again; a huge brace-filled smile overtook her small face.

"Go where?" I knew what she meant, but I was too stunned to believe it.

Janie flinched. "Are you a complete moron? Not go some-where. Go out. As in, be your boyfriend!" Janie shoved me. "Say something!"

"How do you know this?"

She pushed her phone in my face, and I read:

*Will u ask Thea if she'll go out with me?—Tim*

I gawked at it. "Why would he text you instead of asking me himself?"

"I don't know! But it's for real!" She started bouncing again. "Isn't it awesome? Aren't you excited? We have to hurry and reply *yes*. I almost did it for you, but figured I should let you."

"No."

Janie halted. "No?"

"I will not be his girlfriend."

"Are you crazy? This is what we dream about. We want a boy-friend. This could be the start of something huge for us. He could be your soul mate. We have to say yes!"

"Don't you remember the agony he and Josh put us through?"

"Oh, Thea, last month is old news. He likes you!"

"No." I scanned the cafeteria and spotted Tim in the lunch line. I pulled out my cell, tapped in Tim's number, and typed a reply.

*No way! Plus u didnt even ask me in person!—Thea*

I pressed the Send button and watched him across the room. He was by far the tallest guy in our class. Rumor was he'd started shaving three years ago. I wished I could touch his skin to see if it was true. And how he remained tan in winter mystified me. The fluorescents overhead brought out the natural highlights of his honey-colored hair. He moved forward in the line, balanced his tray with one hand, and pulled his cell phone out of his pocket with the other.

Oh no. What had I done? My eyes began to sting, but I remem-bered my promise: I would not cry over a guy. Ever. I counted the tiles in the ceiling and willed the tears to recede. Crying equaled weakness. I took a deep breath and wiped my eyes. Stupid.

Tim swayed in the lunch line. His brows creased together as he looked at his phone. Josh leaned in and looked at it, too. Then Josh raised his voice loud enough for me to catch him calling me a stupid shrew and telling Tim to forget about me. The lunch lady waggled her finger at Tim and pointed to the phone. He slipped it back into his pocket and proceeded through the line. I needed fresh air. I clutched Janie's arm and pulled her outside to eat, even if it was thirty degrees.

■

At the kitchen table that evening, Mom forced a family conversation. Frankly, I prefer the clanking of forks to a pointless discussion, but there was no way I could stop her.

"Seth, what was the best part of your day?" Mom asked.

Through a mouthful of spaghetti he said, "Found a great new computer game called *Skadi*."

"Is it one of those violent first-person shooter games?" Mom asked.

Seth cocked an eyebrow. "Not at all, Mom. It's totally tame."

Mom glanced at Dad. He shrugged and tucked a napkin into his collar.

"Thea, what was the best part of your day?" Mom asked.

I could only come up with the worst part. "A guy asked me to go out with him."

Seth stopped shoveling food. "Seriously?"

I tightened my eyes into tiny slits. He took the hint and went back to shoveling.

"Go out where?" Dad asked and twirled his noodles with his fork. "Cynthia, you're not old enough to date."

"Oh, Robert . . ." Mom rubbed a fingertip along an eyebrow, and I wondered why she didn't color the gray in her brows to better match the copper color of her hair. "It's a term kids use. They don't actually go out. It is more of a status symbol."

Dad grimaced—which emphasized his sagging jawline—and then folded his beefy arms across his chest. Long past his prime, Dad used his extended hours at work as an excuse to not exercise. But his appearance didn't matter to me. I just wanted him to be proud of me like he was of Seth.

Mom continued the conversation. "Well, that's exciting, Thea. What did you tell him?"

"I told him no way."

Dad's eyebrows shot up. "Way to devastate the poor boy's ego."

"You said I'm not old enough to date. So I told him no."

"Yes, but you could've explained to him that you're simply obeying your parents' rules."

"Right." I struggled to control my irritation. My hand twitched, and I doubted my decision of rejecting Tim. I held my breath to reinforce my determination.

"Cynthia, I know you are still trying to figure things out," Seth said, "but if you want guys to ask you out when you're sixteen, you need to do ground work now. You need to gently say no so you don't crush the guy. Otherwise, they won't come near you. After that video last month and now this . . . you need to learn to be friends with guys before you can ever hope for them to date you."

"Well said, son." Dad gave Seth a thumbs-up.

"Shut up, Seth, and don't call me Cynthia. It's Thea."

And with that, I was sentenced to my room.

■

A few weeks later, just before spring break, a new guy named Taylor moved into town. He didn't waste time. He came straight up to me before English class. "Hey Thea, you want to go out with me?"

Taylor had brown eyes, not blue like Tim's, and they had no effect whatsoever on the rate of my heartbeat. I recalled Seth's advice and said, "My parents won't let me date until I'm sixteen."

"Okay." Taylor slid into the seat next to me. His casual reply surprised me.

The teacher started class and wrote a quote by Dr. Martin Luther King Jr. on the board. Something about the family being the main educational unit of mankind. If that was true, why was I stuck in school all day? I decided to write the quote down on the last page of my notebook along with the rest of my quote collection.

After school, I didn't bother telling my parents about the newest guy interest. What was the point? Sixteen seemed so far away. Besides, I'd already ruined my chances with the one guy who made my heart race.

# CHAPTER 2

In our front yard, tender daffodils opened wide to the spring sun. I knelt in the flowerbed and tugged a weed from the dirt. But before pulling another, I lifted my chin to the sunlight and enjoyed the warmth.

A car door slammed. Marcus, one of Seth's drop-dead-gorgeous friends, approached me.

"Hey, Thea. Your bro home?"

"Yup." I hopped up and led Marcus to the front door. Our family lived in a single level house, just like everyone else on the street. Inside, we had a small entryway that led to our family room on the left, a guest bathroom down on the right, and the rest of the house through a hallway straight ahead. We found Seth back in the kitchen, eating a piece of pizza while staring out the sliding glass doors.

"Hey," Marcus said. Seth spun on his heel and inhaled the rest of the pizza.

I should have left them alone, but instead I followed them around the corner to Seth's room. He slammed the door in my face. I pressed my ear to it and caught a few words when Marcus raised his voice while complaining about his dad. I could've been preparing for tonight's school dance, the Spring Fling, but no one had asked me. I'm sure Dad would never have let me go anyhow. I wondered if Tim had asked someone else. I hated the idea of his arms draped over another girl. To distract myself from my insurmountable social problems, I followed Seth and Marcus when they left the bedroom and moved to the family room.

"Knock it off!" Seth said. He and I had the same parents, but that's where our similarities ended. Well, except for our red hair and the fact that we both annoyed the crap out of each other. Seth poked his finger in my shoulder. "Go away."

Marcus came to my rescue. "It's okay."

Marcus was older than me, but I was mature. He could fall for me. Sure, he didn't make my heart accelerate like Tim did, but Marcus ranked high on the cuteness meter. He had a deep voice, dark eyes, and self-confidence that must come with age. He and Seth played football and basketball, and they went skiing every winter. I could settle for someone handsome and considerate like Marcus.

"Do you like computer games?" Marcus asked me.

"Sure. Who doesn't?"

"Don't be nice to her," Seth said and poked me again. I batted his finger away.

"Let me show her *Skadi*. It'll keep her busy for days." Marcus winked. Was the wink intended for me or my brother? Not sure.

We headed down to the end of the hall to my room and huddled around my desk. Small, with barely enough space for my keyboard, monitor, and mouse, the desk leaned against the same wall as my bed and opposite from my door. Luckily, I had been motivated earlier to straighten my bed and pick up my laundry. Who knew a hot guy would be in here this afternoon? I moved the mouse while Marcus directed me how to log in to the game on the Internet.

*Skadi*, a multiplayer online role-playing game, allowed gamers to create characters and join guilds. After joining the guilds, the characters worked both independently and together to accomplish quests. It was fun, easy, and free. Plus, if Marcus was interested, so was I.

"Do you play this game a lot?" I asked him.

"Sure! It's fun."

"Can I join your guild? Help you with quests?"

"Kamikaze is in charge of our guild. You'll need to ask him." Marcus wrote down the bizarre name, and next to it he wrote two more character names, CharlieHorse and MightyPegasus. "If you see either of my guys, open a chat box and say hey."

"Why do you have two characters?" I asked.

He shrugged. "I play a lot."

"And what's with the crazy usernames?"

Marcus flashed his pearly whites at me. "It's fun to pretend and come up with extreme names. Online you can be anything you want." He locked eyes with me, and after a few seconds, I glanced away to the keyboard. He touched my wrist, and I willed myself to meet his eyes again. "You'll like it," he said. "Come up with your own outrageous name, and let me know what it is!" He cocked an eyebrow, and I felt faint.

He explained more about the game, but his hand near mine was a terrible distraction, and I hardly heard a thing he said. I wondered what would happen if I reached out and touched his fingers. Could Marcus be my one true love? Maybe someday he'd whisper sweet romantic verses to me and gently hold me in his arms. Marcus stood to leave and smiled . . . and like those crazy gum commercials, a bright spot sparkled on his teeth.

"Have fun!" he said. My stomach fluttered. I wanted him to stay, but he and Seth left without another word. Hopefully, we could talk again later.

*Skadi* wasn't hard to figure out, but I wanted Janie and Emily to join so I'd be able to chat with people I knew while playing.

Mom leaned into my room. "Want to help with dinner?"

"Dinner?" I looked at the clock. "It's already six?" The afternoon had flown by.

"Yes, and thus the reason for dinner." Mom moved to my desk and peered at the monitor. "What's this?"

"*Skadi.*"

"Is this an online game?"

"Yes."

"I'd rather you wait and let your dad check it out and make sure it's safe."

"Seriously? Seth already plays it."

"Seriously." Mom bugged out her eyes. "And watch your attitude." She left my room, and I followed her out into the hall.

"I don't understand what the big deal is." I shook my head. "It's just a game."

■

Two days later, Janie, Emily, and I discussed *Skadi* during lunch. "My dad gave the website his thumbs-up approval," I said and fiddled with a french fry. "He explained to my mom that it was a role-playing game."

"My mom thinks it will poison my mind," Janie said.

"Whatever. I think it's cool."

"Because Marcus thinks it's cool . . . right?" Janie fluttered her eyelashes.

"Maybe at first."

"You know," Emily said, "they held him back in kindergarten, like twice."

Janie grimaced. "What?"

"Really," Emily said. "He's like way older than everyone else in his grade."

"How could I not already know that?" I asked. "He practically lives at our house."

"And his mom died—"

"I thought his parents were divorced?" I said.

"Nope." Emily shook her head. "She died a long time ago."

What else did I not know about Marcus?

"It's old news," Emily said. "At least your parents let you play *Skadi*. My stone-age parents let me use the computer thirty minutes a day—for homework."

We huffed and shook our heads in unison. I dipped a french fry into some ketchup and passed the tray to Janie, but she waved it off. I popped the fry into my mouth and wished our parents would just let us grow up.

# CHAPTER 3

Finally, spring break was about to start. Mom had enrolled us in a four-week series of self-defense classes at the rec center. She pulled into the parking lot and drove past a million open spots. Apparently, few people exercised on Saturday nights. Mom ultimately parked at the far end of the lot. I never understood why she always did that, but it didn't matter. I just wanted to start the class, because once I learned some skills, I'd be able to protect myself if Josh ever got in my space again.

Mom checked us in at the front counter, and we headed upstairs to Studio Four. A mirror covered one wall of the classroom from floor to ceiling while windows made up the other three sides of the room. An indoor running track bordered the outside of two of the glass walls. The third, along with the door, faced an area where people stretched. I would have preferred if the walls were constructed of wood instead of glass. The idea of someone watching me from the outside made my skin crawl.

The instructors, both male, pulled mats out onto the hardwood floor. Mom hustled over and offered her help. Not me. They could do the work. The polished floorboards reflected the florescent lights from overhead. In the far corner stood some blue kick-boxing-punching-bag things shaped like men with rounded bases. I stepped toward them and caught a distinct whiff of Windex, probably from cleaning the excessive amounts of glass.

"What are you doing?" Mom startled me from behind.

I pointed at the blue men. "Are we going to punch these?" I asked her.

"Probably," she said.

"Time to start!" one instructor called out.

But it was the other one, who looked like he must be on steroids, who spoke to the class. "Welcome everyone," he said with a low rumble in his tone. He pointed to the mats, and we followed his silent command to sit down. "I'm Jackson, and this is my assistant, Keith—" He motioned to the other instructor, who stood about a foot shorter than Jackson and half as wide. Keith stuck out his chin and widened his stance, but he was still a dwarf next to the super-sized Jackson. "Tonight, we will discuss situational awareness and learn a few basic defensive moves. Next class, we'll learn escape techniques, punch-n-go tactics . . ." Jackson went on and on, explaining why our attendance was so important and how long he'd been teaching, but I found his deep husky voice way more interesting than the actual words he spoke.

He towered close to six foot six and wore a tight black shirt that revealed every curve of his six-, no, eight-pack along his stomach. His arms hung wide because his biceps and triceps bulged so much they couldn't lay flat against his sides. His shoulders extended three times the width of his waist, forming an upside-down triangle. If I poked him with my finger, would those muscles be hard like a rock or would they give a little? For an old guy, he was pretty buff. His salt and pepper hair was cropped short and styled with gel. And although his jawline was clean and smooth, he had a long mustache that stretched out to the sides with curled ends.

Mom nudged me. She tapped her ear and then pointed up front.

"Trust your instincts," Jackson said. "When you're in danger, you may feel a tingle along your spine. Maybe the hairs on the back of your neck will stand up and itch. Or maybe goose bumps will pop out along your arms. Pay attention to these signals. This is your body's survival system kicking in. These instincts alert you to look around, protect yourself, and get out of the situation. Any questions?"

Mom raised her hand, and Keith, the assistant, nodded at her. "Go ahead."

"How do you teach a teenager to be aware of these things?"

Oh crap. Seriously? In front of these people? I glared at Mom. Then I pulled up my knees and buried my face in my legs.

"A teenager will listen to you when you listen to them first," Jackson said. "Thea, what safety issues concern you?"

I lifted my head. It concerned me that he knew my name, but how was I supposed to say that to the instructor? Instead, I shrugged and said nothing.

He advanced toward me. "Surely, there's something. What concerns you, Thea?"

"Well . . ." I avoided looking at him. "It concerns me that you know my name when I didn't tell it to you."

"Good," he said and caught my eyes. His mustache lifted, revealing bleached white teeth. "Alertness will save your life. Don't spend time wondering how a stranger knows a detail about you. Ask."

Maybe this guy was okay. He didn't humiliate me in front of everyone.

"If your instincts are speaking to you, don't take time to ask, just get away. So, Thea, is your gut warning you right now?"

"No."

"Why not?"

"Because we're in a self-defense class with lots of people around. You wouldn't risk your job by doing anything to me."

"So, it's a safe environment?"

"Yes, but I'd still like to know how you knew my name."

"Don't be rude," Mom said.

My cheeks lit on fire.

"She's not," Jackson said, defending me. "Thea, your assertiveness is good. I know your name because your mom and I spoke before class, and she told me. I'm glad you're here this evening."

He directed the next comment to Mom. "She's listening, and she's smart. Ask her questions and be sure to listen to her answers. All you moms here tonight should make it a point to have a conversation with your daughters on the way home. Next week, we'll explore this topic more. But for now let's hop up and do some exercises."

We followed Jackson's lead and stretched. Then Keith took over.

"I need a volunteer to help demonstrate a few basic stances." Keith glanced around the room and then locked on me. "Thea, come help me."

I hesitated, but Mom urged me forward.

Keith showed me how to stand. He set his feet apart, his hands raised. I tried to mimic his pose, but he shook his head, reached down, and tapped my calf. I moved my foot forward a few inches.

"Better," he said, "now lift your elbow more." His fingers grazed my bare skin, and a tickle ran along my forearm. "Just like that," Keith said and turned toward the group. He walked around the room and checked everyone's stance. Then he taught us some deflecting shots. We worked muscles I'd never used before, and I knew right away that I was going to be sore tomorrow.

At the end of class, we grabbed our things and headed for the studio doors.

Jackson and Keith held the double doors open for everyone.

"So, Thea, what did you think of the class?" Keith asked.

"It was fine." I waved Mom forward. "Let's go."

"Just fine?" Jackson angled his chin downward.

"Yup." I got a close-up of his crazy mustache. I wanted to ask if he trimmed it every day.

"Don't mind her," Mom said. "She's anxious to get home to play her online game."

Really? She talked about me like I wasn't even there.

"What game is that?" Keith asked.

"Strange name: Skay-dee," she said, mispronouncing it.

"Mom, it's Ska-die."

"Oh, yeah," Keith said. "I've heard of that. Great game, Thea."

"So you think it's safe?" Mom asked.

Oh. My. Gosh. She was killing me.

Keith nodded his approval to her, but then spoke to me, "Do you have a crazy username like everyone else on there?"

"ImmortalSlayer," I said. Mom pursed her lips, but before she could spout her disapproval, Jackson chimed in.

"That fits you," he said, "and by the time you're done with this class it will be more true than ever." His mustache wiggled, and I couldn't help but smile.

As Mom and I left, I said, "I can't believe you talked about me before class."

# CHAPTER 4

Monday night equaled family night, and while I enjoyed playing cards (hated board games), I sat at the kitchen table, distracted. Milton Bradley or Hasbro most likely created game night as a lame marketing scheme, and my parents fell for it. I stared out at the blooming dogwood tree in the backyard as the setting sun cast shades of orange and pink across the sky. I anticipated getting back online to chat with Kit more. At the end of spring break, we had connected online and had become good friends while playing *Skadi*. But now that we were back in school, we didn't have as much time together.

In *Skadi*, belonging to a guild appeared to be more fun than playing independently. I had tried for over two weeks to get into one, but the leaders said no when I requested to join. I even tried Marcus's guild, but he said Kamikaze had to approve it first, and Kamikaze was never online. Maybe Marcus just didn't want me in his guild. I knew Seth would never let me into his. So frustrating. But it didn't matter anymore, because Kit had accepted me.

He held the second-in-command position in his guild, and he allowed me to join. He showed me the tricks to mastering the different quests, and I enjoyed chatting with him. He confided in me and teased me.

One of the first things Kit had said that caught my attention was that girls shouldn't play tough sports like football. I argued the point, saying that we girls can do anything we set our minds to. We debated for quite a while, but it never got mean. I had a blast, and he listened to my opinions. We also enjoyed discussing sports like basketball and downhill skiing. I was excited to find out that he liked music, too. We both had dads who didn't have enough time for us, but his dad was an alcoholic, and his mother had died when he was younger. Kit needed a friend, and I was happy to be there for him. Kit was his nickname because his full-length character name was Kitsuneshin. He said it was a Japanese term that meant "young fox." Figured.

"Earth to Cynthia!" Seth leaned forward and waved at me.

"Do not call me Cynthia."

"What are you daydreaming about?" Mom asked.

"Nothing." I placed a card on the table and the game continued, until my cell rang.

Mom held up her hand. "It's family night." But I had already pushed the Talk button.

"Hello?"

"Are you free?" Janie asked.

"Sure, what's up?"

"You have to log onto *Skadi*. Kit is totally flirting with some other girl. He's cheating on you." I hurried from the kitchen and down the hall to my bedroom.

I lowered my voice. "He is so not my boyfriend. Therefore he cannot be cheating on me."

"Come on, you like him a lot. I see your chats when we do quests together."

She would whack me if she found out Kit and I had private chats outside of the quests. I considered admitting the truth to my best friend, but hesitated because I had promised Kit I wouldn't say anything. He worried that he could get in trouble since he was nineteen, and I was fourteen.

"Tell me what he's saying. It will take me a few minutes to log on." But before she could fill me in on the details, Mom stepped into my room.

"Off the phone," she said.

I continued to hold the cell to my ear.

"Now! We are in the middle of family time."

"But Janie and I have a homework assignment we have to finish. It will affect our final grades." I surprised myself with how easily the lie came.

"You can call her back after we finish our card game."

"I heard," Janie said. "You're a liar. Call me back." I pushed the End button, set the phone next to my computer, and followed Mom back out to the kitchen table.

"Nice of you to rejoin us," Dad said.

"Can't your little friends survive five minutes without you?" Seth smirked.

"Shut up!" I slugged my brother in the shoulder. He rose and grabbed my fist.

"Don't hit me." He hung over me to emphasize his point.

"Or what?" I had learned enough in my first two self-defense classes to know I shouldn't antagonize a thug, but I couldn't help myself.

"You are so immature," he said and released my fist.

"Sit down—both of you," Dad said.

"No hitting. Ever. We're having family time. Sit down and enjoy it," Mom said.

Both my brother and I slouched in our chairs. I wished he would disappear. Life would be easier as an only child.

■

After our fun-family-time had ended, I checked my phone. Janie had already sent several messages urging me to hurry up. She was the only person who ever texted me. I dialed her number.

"You missed it all," Janie said without even a hello.

"Is he still online? I'm logging in."

"No point. He left about thirty minutes ago."

"Tell me everything."

Janie spoke as fast as ever, detailing the events of how Kit brought a new player, named Red, into our guild. I finished logging into *Skadi* and extended my fingers out straight. I'd painted my nails yesterday, and they were already chipped. I grabbed my bottle of blue nail polish, left the computer, and stretched out on the floor. I leaned against the bed frame and put the phone on speaker. Then I opened the bottle and touched up the flaked spots while I listened to Janie.

"They totally dominated the chat by giving personal information about themselves," she said. "Red is a fifteen-year-old girl that lives in Hawaii. Did you know Kit is nineteen and lives in Georgia?" I tightened the lid on the bottle of polish and considered my answer. Yes, I knew.

"Really?" I said.

"Thea, be careful. He is too old for you."

"I can handle it. Besides, we're just friends. And it doesn't sound to me like he flirted with her."

"No, Thea. They even exchanged a couple of sex jokes."

My heart sank. I chewed on my lip while I struggled to reply.

"Tell me you're not giving him personal information," Janie said.

"Don't be silly."

"Thea, he left right after Red. I'm telling you, they were hooking up."

"Whatever. Why would he flirt right in front of you? He knows you'd tell me."

"You know . . . you could log in as a new character and try to trick him . . . see if he's lying," she suggested.

I was tempted. "No. It doesn't matter. Are you going to play for a while?"

"I'm going to study for tomorrow's math test. I need summer to get here sooner."

"Agreed. See you tomorrow."

I ended the call and heard Mom talking to herself as she walked the length of the hall toward my room. I hopped up, sat at my desk to collapse the game screen and open a Word document, and smudged my wet nails in the process. Mom came in without knocking.

"When was the last time you vacuumed in here?" she asked.

I raised my eyebrows. No point in answering. We'd had this conversation before, and my room was never clean enough. Yes, I had a few dirty clothes behind the door, but other than that I kept my room spotless. Mom expected everything to be perfect.

"How's the homework coming?" She perched on the extra chair near my desk and clasped her hands in her lap.

"Fine."

"What else do you have open on your computer?" Mom squinted at the tiny words at the bottom of the monitor. "Are you playing *Skadi*?"

"I have it open, but I'm not playing it."

"Log off *Skadi*," she instructed. I did as she said. "I let you play a lot during break, but now you need to refocus your priorities." Mom picked up my dirty laundry and left.

I got ready for bed, and then I told my parents I'd finished my homework and wanted to read for a while. They said their goodnights, and I headed back to my room. Once there, I closed the door and shoved a large blanket at the base of it. If my parents came to check on me, the barricade would slow the process long enough for me to shut off the monitor and slide into bed. They didn't check, and Kit was online.

# CHAPTER 5

Kit and I lingered online, chatting and completing quests. No one else from our guild was playing, so we didn't censor our comments. Well, except for the fact that I couldn't bring myself to ask about Red, and he didn't mention her. Instead, we debated song lyrics.

**Kitsuneshin:** DeathTomb's CDs r the best.

**ImmortalSlayer:** Never heard of them. Are they some sort of Heavy Metal band?

**Kitsuneshin:** *head slap* RU kidding me? American Alternative Rock - ranked #1 on Billboard

**Kitsuneshin:** You have to listen to them. Their lyrics nail how I feel.

**ImmortalSlayer:** Ok. Next time I'm at the library I'll look for them.

**Kitsuneshin:** Library?

**ImmortalSlayer:** Ya. We don't buy CDs. We borrow them. *eye roll*

**Kitsuneshin:** That's smart!

**Kitsuneshin:** Plus, u can always watch the videos on YouTube.

**ImmortalSlayer:** Which one should I watch first?

**Kitsuneshin:** I'm listening to Broken right now

**ImmortalSlayer:** *opening YouTube*

**Kitsuneshin:** "I try to protect myself, but with you I'm wide open"

**ImmortalSlayer:** Is that from the song?

**Kitsuneshin:** Yup . . . I suppose you're a fan of that country-pop-crossover chick, Lauren Harper?

**ImmortalSlayer:** Yes!

**Kitsuneshin:** LOL How can you possibly like her?

**ImmortalSlayer:** Hey! Don't be hatin' on my music!

**Kitsuneshin:** LOL . . . jk . . . Besides some of her songs have great lyrics.

**ImmortalSlayer:** Which ones?

**Kitsuneshin:** Short Romance . . . *clears throat and sings*

**Kitsuneshin:** "Baby, someday, we'll make history"

**ImmortalSlayer:** *sings too* "Together, we'll sing, we'll laugh, and we will dance"

**Kitsuneshin:** "Because . . . baby . . . this is more than just a short romance."

**ImmortalSlayer:** Hah! *high five* Nicely done! You must be a closet fan of Lauren Harper!

**Kitsuneshin:** Must be! *peeks out of closet*

**Kitsuneshin:** LOL—u have a great voice!

**ImmortalSlayer:** Thank you! *takes a bow*

**Kitsuneshin:** Ha! We are great together!

A shiver ran up my bare legs. I hopped up to grab my robe from the closet for extra warmth, and that's when I realized I'd left my window blinds wide open. My bedroom window faced the backyard, and sometimes I liked to stare at the stars, but not right now. I reached over and closed the blinds before I returned to my desk.

**Kitsuneshin:** I just wish my friends wouldn't give me crap for hanging out with you.

**ImmortalSlayer:** Why are they giving u crap?

**Kitsuneshin:** Our ages

**ImmortalSlayer:** Ignore them—our ages don't matter

**ImmortalSlayer:** We connect. That's what matters.

**Kitsuneshin:** UR right . . . besides five yrs isn't that much

**ImmortalSlayer:** When u are 25 I'll be 20 *counts on fingers*

**Kitsuneshin:** I can picture us then . . . but . . . how old would be too old for u?

**ImmortalSlayer:** IDK . . . maybe age shouldn't matter

**ImmortalSlayer:** Watching Broken on YouTube . . . so sad! ☹
**Kitsuneshin:** Ya.
**ImmortalSlayer:** RU sad?
**Kitsuneshin:** Sometimes, but my days r better when I talk with u.
**ImmortalSlayer:** Ah . . . thanks! Me, too! *hugs*
**Kitsuneshin:** *hugs back*
**Kitsuneshin:** We should swap cell numbers so we can chat during the day
**ImmortalSlayer:** No . . . I'll get in trouble for texting during school
**Kitsuneshin:** RU sure? I hate waiting until *Skadi* to talk with you.
**ImmortalSlayer:** I know . . . but I can't.
**Kitsuneshin:** What about e-mail?
**ImmortalSlayer:** Maybe . . . but it's almost midnight here. I should go.
**Kitsuneshin:** LOL it's 2am here in Georgia!
**ImmortalSlayer:** Then we should both get some sleep LOL see u later
**Kitsuneshin:** I'll miss u. *tucks u into bed*
**ImmortalSlayer:** ☺ nite
**Kitsuneshin:** Sweet dreams!

■

The next morning, I had a hard time dragging myself out of bed. I lingered on the edge for a minute and rubbed the sleep from my eyes. Once I could focus, I grabbed my Quote of the Day calendar. The date said June, even though it was only April, because if I didn't like the assigned quote for the day, I tore off pages until I found a good one.

*Whatever is good to know is difficult to learn.—Greek Proverb*

That sounded like a bad omen. I ripped it off, crumpled it, and chucked it toward the trash can. Swish. I read the next quote.

*If women want any rights they had better take them, and say nothing about it.—Harriet Beecher Stowe*

I wasn't sure what that meant, but I liked it. I wrote it down in the back of my notebook with the rest of my quote collection. The front half served as my diary. Sometimes I detailed the events of my day, and other times I analyzed my favorite quotes and tried to figure out what they meant to me. Not today, though. I needed to get moving. I slipped the quote notebook into my backpack—because I usually took it everywhere with me. Once I had made the mistake of decorating the cover with bright papers, ribbon, and glitter. It was gorgeous! But it attracted attention, and people asked questions about it . . . questions I didn't want to answer. My notebook was private. So I stashed that pretty one, and I've used a plain black and white composition book ever since. No one ever commented on it. They probably assumed it was just schoolwork.

I pushed off the bed and grabbed my hairbrush. I pulled it through my hair until all of the knots disappeared, and then with my fingers I drew my hair back into a ponytail. I grabbed a pink T-shirt from my dresser and pulled it on, shoved my arms into my white hoodie, and looked in the mirror as I zipped it up. I'd messed up my hair already. After readjusting my ponytail and ensuring no stray hairs stuck out, I wiped off yesterday's makeup and put on some fresh eyeliner and mascara. I picked up the bottle of foundation, but set it back down without using it. I had confessed to Kit last night that I hated my freckles. He said he loved freckles. I examined my splotchy skin in the mirror. I guess it didn't matter. It wasn't like he'd be at school anyway. I left off the foundation for a change.

The doorbell rang.

I checked the clock. I couldn't remember Janie ever arriving on time, let alone early. I grabbed my backpack and hustled to the front door to greet her, but Seth reached it before me.

His voice rang out loud and clear. "Holy crap, Janie!"

I shoved him out of the way and halted midstep. "What happened to your hair?" I asked.

Janie pushed past us and ran to the guest bathroom off the entryway. I was right behind her.

"Omigosh, it's awful. I don't know what to do." She dropped her bags and leaned into the mirror. She pinched and pulled at the short bangs—her long black curls gone—and spoke to our reflections. "My sister and I tried to give each other highlights yesterday. Epic Failure. Mom ran us over to her hair salon. They stripped the color, and our hair was fine. But then Mom freaked and told her lady to cut it all off. Both of us. We look so stupid." Tears streamed down her cheeks, and my heart ached for her. "How can I go to school like this? I tried to fake sick this morning, but that was a failure, too."

"Why didn't you tell me last night?" I drew my friend into a hug. "It's not that bad."

"Don't you lie to me, Cynthia." She pulled back and swayed her head from side to side. "I know you. I even know your middle name. So, don't you dare lie to me. Not ever. Understand?"

"Got it." I stepped back and examined her hair. "It's not good, but with the right products and styling, we can improve it. Besides, I'll kick anyone's butt who dares to say something to you. Okay?"

"Thanks."

"And you should've told me last night."

"I guess I was in denial. Or maybe shock." Janie wiped her tears.

She and I moved to my room at the end of the hall. We added mousse, paste, and hair spray—lots of hair spray—and styled her hair the best we could in the limited time available. We grabbed our bags and linked our arms. Together we could handle anything.

The crowd at the bus stop was too surprised to say anything. Well, except for Josh, of course. "Did your dad take a weed whacker to your hair?"

I stepped toward him and considered which new self-defense move I should use, but Tim blocked me.

"Ignore him," Tim said.

He smelled like aftershave lotion, and he stood so close I could see his pores. I wanted to touch his smooth skin. My hand lifted, but I stopped myself. Tim seemed to move in slow motion, and his lips curved as he spoke to Janie.

"Sorry, Janie," he said. Then he placed a hand on Josh's shoulder and pushed him to the other side of the group. Tim still affected me. Would that ever change? He looked back toward me and smiled. Crap. Then he turned away again.

I caught my breath and said to Janie, "Ignore him. How a dim-witted tool like Josh can play sports and not hurt himself amazes me!" The girls around us giggled.

Janie attracted a few confused stares throughout the day, but when she was with me I put a single finger in the air and cocked an eyebrow. The smart ones clued in and withdrew. The dumb ones called names, but when I took a step toward them, they cowered and left Janie alone. While I felt bad for her, I appreciated being needed, and the distraction of defending her made the day go faster. That was a good thing, because lately the hours at school dragged on forever.

I could hardly wait to return home and check for Kit online. Summer break needed to arrive sooner so I'd have more time to devote to him. He'd asked for my cell number and e-mail, but I wasn't ready. Not yet. I was probably being paranoid.

After school, I went through the usual motions of a snack and chores. Then I used the excuse of homework to retreat to my room. It was about half the size of Janie's huge bedroom, but I liked it. I pulled up the blinds on my window, to allow the sunshine in, and admired the huge trees in the backyard. My twin bed—positioned just to the right of the window—sat higher than normal, because last year Dad and I put it on risers. He even built a small step stool for me to climb up onto the bed. He and I had gone shopping, and he let me pick out the comforter, bright pink, and other new bedding. We painted the walls and assembled the desk together. My computer was a hand-me-down, but it worked fine, and it was my own. I didn't have to share it or worry about anyone lurking over my shoulder while I used it.

I took a break for dinner and then disappeared back to my room. Kit didn't come online until almost eight, which was ten o'clock for him. I could do the math fast, because I did it constantly. He lived in Georgia, and I was in Idaho.

My heart beat faster when his name appeared in the guild box. I set my hand on my chest. This was the first time since Tim that my heart raced at the idea of talking to someone else. Maybe I was finally over Tim.

I typed hello to Kit, but before he could respond, Red's name appeared also. Kit said hello to both Red and me in the same line. We're just friends, I reminded myself. They made some irrelevant comments about which quest we should do. I texted Janie and told her to log on and join us. Flashfire, her online name, appeared moments later. Red and Kit picked a quest. Janie and I followed like little puppies.

During the quest Red and Kit chatted about where they lived. Red in Hawaii. Kit in Georgia. They described the weather, the scenery, the special events, blah blah blah. Janie opened a private chat box with me and asked if I felt left out. As though Kit read her mind, he typed into the guild box:

**Kitsuneshin:** Slayer, what state are you in?

Janie told me not to answer him. It was easy to keep the conversations separate, because the private ones were colored blue, guild ones purple, and the general *Skadi* boxes were black. When someone opened a private chat with another person, a tiny blue square blinked next to their username. The full chat box wouldn't open until the user clicked the square.

I read Kit's question again, but before I could decide what to do, I heard Mom coming down the hall. I quickly typed:

**ImmortalSlayer:** The northwest

Mom knocked on my door. I closed the private chat box and collapsed the game before she moved in direct view of my monitor.

"Did you finish your homework?"

"Yes."

"Then why did you collapse *Skadi*?"

"I don't know. I just did."

"Pull it up."

"Fine." What was she up to? I enlarged the game screen and typed:

**ImmortalSlayer:** My mom says hi.

"Thea! Why did you do that?"

"I thought you wanted me to." I stole a quick peek to gauge her reaction.

She took a deep breath. "Show me how you play this."

I explained it in the best monotone I could muster. I knew she didn't care about the workings of *Skadi*. Why would she? Mom never played on the computer. I kept my eye on the chat box, but since my friends knew she was watching, they kept the conversation moving with game-related nonsense.

Mom interrupted my tutorial. "Are you missing important things? The comments seem to fly by pretty fast."

"I can always scroll back if I miss something—" The words spilled out before I realized what I said. I rubbed the back of my neck.

"Show me."

I scrolled back through the comments, to the point where I identified Mom's presence.

"Further," Mom said. I sighed and complied, moving line by line.

"Far enough?" I asked.

"No."

"Are you looking for something?"

"Not necessarily."

The pressure in my skull increased like a vice tightened down on it. I scrolled up to the point where Kit had asked where I lived, and I had answered.

"You gave him personal information," Mom said.

I cringed. "I didn't tell him Idaho, and I didn't tell him Nampa." I twisted in my chair and studied her.

Mom scrunched her bare toes along the surface of the carpet. She stiffened her back, and her lips tightened. The computer hummed in the speechless silence. Mom switched her weight from one foot to the other. "Thea, I'm concerned you're spending too much time with this game and this Kit character."

She didn't trust me. My jaw clenched so fast that I bit my tongue. Pain shot through my mouth. "I'm not doing anything wrong," I said while massaging my jaw.

"Then don't collapse your computer screen when I enter your room."

"Okay."

"Will you type that I left the room, and let me read what they say afterward?"

Fuming, I was certain flames would shoot out of my fingertips at any second, but I typed anyway.

**ImmortalSlayer:** My mom wants me to tell u she left the room.

"That's not what I meant, and you know it." The chat box was still. "If you want to keep your Internet privileges, work with me."

"Fine."

**ImmortalSlayer:** She's really gone let's just finish our quest

**Red:** A good surfer doesn't get wet.

"What does that mean?" Mom asked.

"She likes to quote people and old sayings." I tapped on the keyboard.

**ImmortalSlayer:** Nice one, Red.

**Red:** Mahalo.

"Is she from Hawaii?" Mom asked.

"I haven't asked her." Truth.

"But can you see how simple things like saying, 'Mahalo' can give away personal details about where you live?" I didn't respond. I had to keep my lips closed or I would blurt out something rude. Mom didn't wait long before she started yammering again.

"Why would you choose such an awful username?"

I struggled to control my facial expressions. She folded her arms across her chest. I took a deep breath and tried to sound calm. "It's a name. That's all. Online you make things up. That's part of the fun."

She remained motionless. I refocused on the game, and Mom pulled over a chair to stay and watch. I participated in sterile conversations in the chat box about the game. After about fifteen minutes, she left in silence. I phoned Janie and told her everything.

"Are you kidding me?" she asked.

"Nope. I'm just glad she didn't walk in when I had a private chat box open with Kit."

"What do you guys talk about?"

I wasn't sure how much to reveal.

In her angrier deep voice she asked again, "What are you saying in private chats?"

"He tells me stuff about his dad and his friends. He asked me to keep it quiet. That's all." I'm sure she knew I was holding out on her, but she didn't push it and changed the subject.

"I don't know what's wrong with our mothers. I hate my hair. I feel so ugly now."

"I'm sorry . . ." I'd been so concerned about my own situation I'd forgotten about her awful hair. "What can I do to help you?" I wanted to be supportive. I did. But I was distracted by Kit. He was all I could think about.

"Stay away from Kit," Janie said. "That's what you can do to help me. I have a bad feeling about him, and I have too much to worry about right now with my mom. I can't deal with this, too."

I wondered if she was right about Kit.

# CHAPTER 6

Mom and I stepped into Studio Four of the rec center, and my chest tightened. The stink of perspiration filled the thick air, and class hadn't even begun yet. Mom and I had been concerned about passing the test tonight at this, our final self-defense class. I had no idea everyone else would be just as apprehensive. No one said a word because the sign taped to the door read, "No talking."

Jackson and Keith waited at the front of the room. With their feet apart and their hands clasped behind them, they were sculpted mercenaries. Tight clothing and mirrors revealed their perfect bodies, front and back. When the last students arrived and took their places, Jackson spoke. His deep raspy voice filled the room.

"Law number one: You will be assaulted by someone larger and stronger than you. That's because bullies intentionally select smaller people. They think they can intimidate you. After tonight, that will be the last mistake they ever make. Over the last month, you have learned to use your core strength and body mass against vital kill zones. No matter how big or strong, you know the skills to knock a predator out cold."

Kill zones. Knock a predator out cold. Sheesh. I only wanted to be able to stand up to Josh. I didn't really want to hurt anyone. But over the four weeks of this class, I realized strength, psychology, and confidence were all necessary if I wanted to defend myself. I hoped I could do it.

My palms started to sweat when a man in padded gear entered the room. Duct tape patched multiple spots on his protective equipment. His helmet was already in place, but he tightened the chin strap as he walked. He stepped onto the mat, and then he pounded his fists together. My breath caught.

Keith picked up a clipboard that must have held a list of our names, because after he looked at it, he studied us. I prayed he wouldn't say my name first. He locked eyes with me, and I almost panicked. He gave me a reassuring nod and called someone else's name. A grandma. Seriously. She had to be like fifty or something. Surely, they wouldn't actually hurt her.

Jackson turned her away from the padded attacker, and then he addressed the group. "No more silence tonight. No more letting others hurt you. No more intimidation. No more good girls. Tonight, you will fight. Fight for your lives. And, as you watch your friends fight for their lives, you will yell for them. Cheer for them. And give them your strength."

He left the grandma in the center of the mats by herself and moved over next to me. He glanced at me, smiled ever-so-slightly, and then faced back to the mats. His body radiated heat, and his triceps flexed when he grasped his hands behind his back.

A bead of sweat rolled down my right temple.

The padded assailant ran up behind the grandma and grabbed her shoulders. She screamed, flipped around, and shoved the heel of her hand up into his jaw. The room erupted in cheers; the circle of students screamed their support. My throat clenched. I was paralyzed with fear. I knew it wasn't real. But it seemed wrong for this man to attack her. My cheek quivered when a hand touched my back. To my left, Mom bent forward and screamed with viciousness I'd never before seen in her. To my right, Jackson whispered to me, "You're all right. You're safe." He rubbed his hand across my back until his arm wrapped around my shoulders. My skin tingled. This caring Goliath was different from the tough mercenary I'd met in the first class. I leaned into him, grateful for the comfort he provided, but at the same time, ridiculously embarrassed. I was the only one not yelling and screaming to cheer on the grandma. She finished knocking her assailant down and raised her arms, a champion. Everyone in the circle ran onto the mats and embraced her. Jackson pressed against the small of my back and urged me forward to join the group. Reluctantly, I did as he indicated.

Person after person fought off the padded attacker, and it became easier for me to watch and eventually to cheer and clap as well. About halfway through the group, Mom's name was called. Her face, flushed from the adrenaline and the yelling, showed no hesitation when she ran out onto the mat. I wished I had her strength.

Before I could blink, the padded attacker picked Mom up and slammed her down on her back. He straddled her across the waist, and instinctively I stepped out on the mat to help her, but Jackson grabbed my wrist and restrained me.

"She has to do this," he said. He pulled me back to the edge of the mat, and a sour odor, like mildewed clothes or milk gone bad, clung inside my nose. I wasn't sure if the smell came from Jackson or someone else. I snuck a quick sniff of my shirt. It wasn't me, so I ignored the stink and yelled for Mom.

"Go Mom! You can do it!" I wiped sweat from my forehead and continued shouting for her. Soon, she wrapped her legs around his upper body, pinned his arms, and used her lower body strength to drag him backward toward the mats. And then . . . in an instant . . . she balled up her fists and pounded him in the groin. She darted out from under him and jumped in triumph. Everyone cheered and ran in to congratulate her. I threw my arms around her and hugged her tighter than I had in years. Her wet face rubbed against mine as she kissed my cheeks.

We took our places around the mats again, and Keith called more names. Finally, he summoned me to the center.

"Thea Reid."

Keith watched me without blinking, and I stepped forward.

At that point, I had so much adrenaline pumping from the energy of the other women that I knew I could do it. I had to. I couldn't be the one to fail, and I didn't want to disappoint anyone. I took my place in the middle with my back to the padded attacker and rocked from foot to foot. The buzz of the florescent lights amplified, and I started to count nervously. One . . . Two . . . Three . . . And then his arms locked around my torso.

Even though protective gear covered the majority of his body, the bones of his forearms pressed into my ribs as he pinned my arms against my sides. I struggled for each breath. I knew it wasn't real. I wasn't actually in danger. The grandma didn't get hurt. But yet, I froze. And the room became silent. The women in front of me still yelled and clapped, but I could no longer hear them. The padded assailant lifted me from the mat, the glare of the overhead lights temporarily blinded me, and I blanked. For the life of me, I could not think fast enough to figure out what I was supposed to do.

As the attacker threw me, everything moved in slow motion. I caught a glimpse of Jackson with his fist balled. I focused on him and remembered what he and Keith had taught us. First step, I went limp and let go of my fear. Jackson's handlebar mustache twitched, and I smashed onto the mat. With determination, I took a deep breath. Second step, I recalled an escape technique. I concentrated my power and shoved the heel of my hand into the attacker's chin as he hovered over me. Pain shot from my wrist to my shoulder. I winced and licked my lips, tasting salt from the perspiration that plastered my skin.

Then, the events snapped into full speed and I refocused. The hit to his chin had thrown him off balance. I spun on my side and swept my leg against his feet, knocking him to the mat. Then, without delay, I kicked the ball of my foot into his neck. He rolled to his back, and I used my lower body strength to wham the heel of my foot into his chest.

Energy surged through me, and I jumped up, ready to kick him again and again, but before I could unleash more fury, the women surrounded me and screamed my name. I'd almost forgotten I wasn't alone. I threw my arms in the air and yelled with them, but it ended too suddenly, and I wasn't sure what to do with the pent-up adrenaline that still pumped through my body.

Mom found me through the throng and wrapped her arms around me. "I'm so proud of you," she yelled. My hands shook, and my stomach clenched, but I also felt empowered. Like I could beat anyone. Do anything.

Before Mom and I walked back to the edge of the mat, the padded attacker said, "Good job, Thea."

Across the circle, Jackson gave me a thumbs-up and mouthed, "Way to go!"

I smiled, and my face dripped with sweat.

■

To celebrate, Mom and I went out with the majority of the class, and the two instructors, to a local coffee house. With Italian sodas and scones in hand, we mingled and chatted about our victories.

The adrenaline had emptied from my system. I yawned, tapped Mom on the shoulder, and pointed up to the wall. "Is that clock broken? Or is it really that late?"

Before she answered, Keith and Jackson stepped over. "Fantastic job tonight, Thea!" Jackson squeezed my shoulder. "I'm impressed with how far you've come."

"I agree," Mom said and looped her arm through mine. "You did great!"

"Together, you two will be a hard team to crack," Keith said. He stuck his chin out in his usual way and the muscles in his jawline tightened.

"That's right," Jackson said. "Be sure to say hello whenever you're at the rec center." We agreed to do that, and both instructors walked away to join another cluster of people.

"Let's head home," Mom said.

"Yes, please."

I could hardly wait to get online and tell Kit about the evening. Problem was, by the time I dragged myself into my room, I wanted to sleep. I kicked off my shoes and climbed into bed without even changing my clothes.

■

After a late Sunday brunch and quick shower, I logged into *Skadi*. Kit was already online. He opened a private chat box and typed hello to me.

**ImmortalSlayer:** Hey!

**Kitsuneshin:** I waited online for u last night. How was your final class?

**ImmortalSlayer:** Omigosh!

**Kitsuneshin:** I waited for hours.

**ImmortalSlayer:** Sorry. I was exhausted last night and crashed!

**Kitsuneshin:** If you'd let us text we wouldn't have to wait until you got home.

**ImmortalSlayer:** I know. I am sorry! Do u still want to hear about the class?

**Kitsuneshin:** Yes. How'd it go?

**ImmortalSlayer:** Scary . . . I thought I was going to fail. But I didn't!

**Kitsuneshin:** I couldn't imagine u failing at anything! UR so amazing!

**Kitsuneshin:** Should I take you out to dinner tonight to celebrate?

**ImmortalSlayer:** If there are candles! *smiles*

**Kitsuneshin:** Candlelight, soft music, and holding hands across the table . . .

**ImmortalSlayer:** Sounds perfect! ☺

**Kitsuneshin:** Agreed. *calling restaurant for reservations*

**ImmortalSlayer:** LOL . . . if only!

**Kitsuneshin:** We can fantasize . . . right?

**ImmortalSlayer:** Absolutely.

**Kitsuneshin:** Did you get hurt last night?

**ImmortalSlayer:** A few bruises, but I'm ok

**Kitsuneshin:** RU sure? *wraps arms around you*

**ImmortalSlayer:** Ah! You're so sweet!

**ImmortalSlayer:** But I'm ok. And still kinda pumped from the excitement.

**Kitsuneshin:** I couldn't think of anything but u last night.

**ImmortalSlayer:** ☺ Thanks!

**Kitsuneshin:** I wish u could know who I really am.

**ImmortalSlayer:** Why? Who RU really?

**Kitsuneshin:** I just mean . . . sometimes I feel like the distance between us makes us strangers.

**ImmortalSlayer:** But we're not strangers. We've connected and gotten to know each other thru our conversations.

**Kitsuneshin:** I'm still skeptical. But I want to be with you; our love is unconventional.

**ImmortalSlayer:** Uh. Oh. I guess we need to watch the Broken video again on YouTube! LOL.

**ImmortalSlayer:** *slugs shoulder* Shake it off! We're good! ☺

**ImmortalSlayer:** —brb—mom coming

Mom sang off-tune and moved down the hall. I closed the chat box and moved away from the computer. She entered without knocking.

"Are you playing *Skadi* already?"

"Yes." I figured the truth was easiest for now.

"I'd rather you do something else."

"Mom . . . please?" I needed to spend time with Kit.

She pulled a chair over and sat next to me. "Why is this so important to you?"

"It just is."

"I need more than that."

"It's fun. I've made new friends. Janie and I like to play it together."

"What about this Kit character?"

"He's a nice guy."

"You can't know that," Mom said. "He could be up to no good—"

"Why would a bad guy waste his time playing a kid's game?"

"Because that's where the kids are," Mom said. "It's a sure bet he'd invest time there."

"If you'd give him a chance, you'd see that he's great. He's a lot like Marcus. Who knows? Maybe it is Marcus, and he's just too embarrassed to say so—" I couldn't believe I said that out loud . . . to my mom! But I knew she liked Marcus, and her approval still mattered to me. I needed to redirect the conversation. "Besides," I said, "didn't I prove last night that I can take care of myself?"

"Yes." She studied me like she was trying to read a map of a foreign land. "I suppose you can keep playing *Skadi* today, but only if you promise to keep your door open, and promise to not collapse the screen when I walk in . . . and promise to not announce my presence to your friends when I observe you."

"Sure thing, Mom," I said.

"Have fun." She set the chair back where it belonged and headed out.

Success. I breathed a sigh of relief and hopped up. I dropped my dirty clothes from last night outside my room and closed the door halfway. I knew if Mom came to check on me, she'd see the pile first and complain aloud about it . . . which would serve as a perfect early warning system. I opened a new chat box with Kit.

**Kitsuneshin:** What took so long?

**ImmortalSlayer:** Mom lecturing me about Internet safety LOL

**Kitsuneshin:** Yikes! Anything I should know?

**ImmortalSlayer:** Well . . . she wants to pop in and observe chats unannounced . . . what are we supposed to do about that?

**Kitsuneshin:** Do u always know she's coming before she gets there?

**ImmortalSlayer:** Nope

**Kitsuneshin:** Let me think about it for a few minutes *taps finger on desk*

**ImmortalSlayer:** Ok . . . hey . . . what did you do last night?

**Kitsuneshin:** Besides sit and wait and worry for u?

**ImmortalSlayer:** Seriously! Spill . . .

**Kitsuneshin:** Oh . . . nothing fun . . . Dad was drinking so there was a lot of yelling

**ImmortalSlayer:** Sorry! I wish there was something I could do to help you.

**Kitsuneshin:** UR doing it right now! Listening and being here.

**ImmortalSlayer:** ☺

**Kitsuneshin:** I really appreciate our relationship.

**ImmortalSlayer:** Me too!

**Kitsuneshin:** I feel like I can tell you things and you won't make fun of me.

**ImmortalSlayer:** Same here! ☺

**Kitsuneshin:** So . . . what's the Quote for the Day?

**ImmortalSlayer:** *jumps up and grabs calendar*

**ImmortalSlayer:** *clears throat and tries to sound important* "In the moment of crisis, the wise build bridges and the foolish build dams."—Nigerian Proverb

**Kitsuneshin:** Oooohh . . . I think that means we need to build up our characters more in *Skadi* today! *rubs hands together*

**ImmortalSlayer:** Haha! Sounds good!

We started a new quest. Red and Janie never got on, which let Kit and I chat privately for hours. I was no longer jealous of Red. I knew they were only friends. Besides, she loved quotes. How could I not like her?

Kit and I came up with a system of codes to share with Red and Janie so we'd know when someone's parents were watching us. We also came up with a plan for the private chat box. Since I was sure Mom had no clue about these, I could close the box when I heard her coming down the hall. But, to be safe, I regularly closed it. Kit knew if I didn't respond in a private chat, it was because I couldn't.

We also agreed on other codes. If he suspected Mom was watching, he'd ask in the purple guild box if I liked a certain CD. And likewise, if I wanted to warn Kit of Mom's presence I'd type about the most recent CD I'd borrowed from the library. With this system, we could keep everyone happy.

# CHAPTER 7

Summer arrived and school finally let out. Janie and I spent a ton of time online with Kit and Red, and we all became a lot closer. Janie even shared personal stories with them . . . like how her hair got chopped off. I also let Janie observe some of my private chats with Kit. She started to agree he was a good guy who just needed friends.

Kit had been promoted to Guild Leader, and I'd even advanced my character quite a bit in the game, clear up to level seventeen. I was so close to the next level I could taste it. However, today, *Skadi* would have to wait because Janie and I planned to go to the water park, Rapid Shores.

I pulled my swimsuit from the back of a drawer and inspected it. I wanted a new one, but only my legs had grown longer, not my torso. So, the one-piece still fit, and Mom figured it was fine. Oh well, at least it was bright pink.

Examining myself in the full-length mirror, I noticed the suit fit snugger around my chest. I looked over my shoulder and checked out different angles of my reflection. I lifted my arms to see if I should've shaved my pits, but not a single stubble of hair showed.

I moved over to my computer, hoping Kit had come online. I wanted to chat with him before we left. His name appeared, and I typed:

**ImmortalSlayer:** O Yay! I was worried u wouldn't get on before I had to leave! How RU?

My toes tapped with anticipation. He might be five years older, but he understood me and I understood him. I had finally found somcone I could talk to and confide in; someone who would love me, for me, alone.

**Kitsuneshin:** Good. How RU? I've missed you.

**ImmortalSlayer:** It's only been since last night, how can u miss me already?

Kit switched to the private chat box. A small blue square appeared next to my username. I clicked it and a secondary blue screen appeared on my monitor.

**Kitsuneshin:** How can u even ask that? *nearly falls off chair* You are the world to me. Every minute I can't talk to u feels like an eternity. I love spending time with u, and I don't want you to leave.

**ImmortalSlayer:** I love spending time with you, too, but I have to go. Mom thinks I spend too much time on the computer.

**Kitsuneshin:** Where are you going?

**ImmortalSlayer:** Swimming at Rapid Shores

**Kitsuneshin:** RU going to wear a bikini? ☺

**ImmortalSlayer:** No! *blushing*

**ImmortalSlayer:** I couldn't wear a bikini. I don't like how much skin shows. I would feel naked in it.

**Kitsuneshin:** Naked wouldn't be a problem from my perspective! LOL

**ImmortalSlayer:** Not funny! *shakes head*

**Kitsuneshin:** JK—UR the most beautiful person in the world to me!

**ImmortalSlayer:** How do you know? You've never even seen me!

**Kitsuneshin:** Send a picture to my cell. And then we could text . . . we wouldn't have to be apart!

I wanted to give him my cell number, because then we'd have the freedom of texting, and he could send me a picture. I'd finally know what he looked like. Nervous flutters rose from my gut, and I realized I was free to choose. I drummed my fingers on the desktop and pictured my parents discovering I'd given out my cell number. It would be certain death. I could give him my e-mail address, but my parents monitored the family e-mail accounts just like they did our Facebook accounts. There was only one thing I could do. I reached for the keyboard . . . but I had taken too long to decide.

**ImmortalSlayer:** —mom coming—brb

I closed the chat box as Mom knocked and opened the door. I lifted my hands away from the keyboard, and Kit typed a bunch of *Skadi* lingo into the purple guild box to make it appear we'd been discussing leveling up and what quest we'd pursue next.

"Are you ready to go?" Mom asked.

"Yup."

"Really? Looks like you're playing *Skadi*." Mom peered at the monitor and read Kit's previous comments. I reached forward and typed.

**ImmortalSlayer:** We should do the dungeon next . . . but later cuz I'm going swimming now.

**Kitsuneshin:** Ok. Have fun.

"Why do you always play with this Kit character?" Mom asked.

"Because we're in the same guild and his character is at a super high level. It's easier for me to level up with him."

"Is there a reason you're in his guild?"

"When I joined *Skadi*, he was the only one accepting new members."

"Okay . . . shut it down and grab your stuff. We need to pick up Janie. Sunlight's a-wasting!"

■

Mom pulled to the curb near the water park's entrance and handed me cash. "For admission and food," she said.

"Thanks, Mom." I shoved the money into the side pocket of my bag and turned toward Janie. "Let's go!" We bolted from the car, and our flip-flops smacked our feet as we ran to the water park's entrance.

"I won!" Janie proclaimed and touched the ticket window first. I bent forward and braced my hands on my knees to catch my breath.

"Too bad you both run like girls."

We spun around to see who had insulted us. Josh.

"What are you doing here?" Janie asked. Tim and Taylor walked over and joined their partner-in-crime.

"Uh, it's a water park." Josh bugged out his eyes. "We came for the slides. What did you come for? Shopping?"

"Very funny." Janie gave her usual angry head sway, which looked much better since her hair had grown a bit. Instead of short spikes, she now had cute little flips in the back and on the sides.

Josh brushed against my shoulder. "You babies are probably too chicken to plummet down the big slides," he said and started to walk away.

"Too bad you forgot your deodorant," I said. He stank like a bad onion. He lifted an arm and smelled his pit. Then he glared at me before cutting in front of us to pay for his admission. His friends joined him, and they acted like the Three Stooges entering the water park.

"And we're not babies," I hollered at him as he moved out of earshot. "We're fifteen just like you."

Janie lifted her sunglasses and peeked at me. "Actually, I'm fifteen. Your birthday isn't until August."

"Whatever," I said.

Janie and I paid our admission, and then we searched out the best spot for our base of operations. We spread our towels on the lounge chairs and plopped down to discuss strategy.

"Can you believe Josh is here?" Janie said and fiddled with her hair.

"Let's ignore him and have fun." I fished out a bottle of sunscreen from my bag and began to slather my legs. Janie pulled off her navy A&F T-shirt and wiggled out of her super cute blue and white plaid shorts, but then she snatched her towel and wrapped it around her.

"I can't do this, not with Josh here." She slumped next to me.

"What are you talking about?" I smeared lotion onto my cheeks. The sun's ultra-violet rays would make more freckles pop out, and I needed protection.

"Thea, I can't let people see me in a swimsuit. I'm fat."

I stopped applying sunscreen. "If by 'people' you mean Josh, forget him. He's just a brainless pizza-faced toad." I had to shield my eyes from the sun as I spoke to Janie, because I had forgotten my sunglasses. "And, that's beside the point. You are so not fat. You're skinny. You're gorgeous. And you wear the cutest clothes. Now put on some sunscreen, and let's go hit our favorite slides."

"Are you sure I look okay?"

"Yes." I handed her the bottle.

"No, thank you." She waved it off. "My skin doesn't react to the sun like yours does, and I need a tan." She moved back to her seat, and I finished applying the lotion. What she said was true. She tanned in the summer. I burned, peeled, and freckled.

■

Our favorite slide was the Colossus. After plummeting ninety feet, a park camera snapped our photo with our hands stretched up and our hair flying out. At the picture booth, a hefty employee, old enough to be my dad, offered to e-mail the shot to us for an additional two dollars.

Janie eyed the guy up and down. His shoulders drooped, his uniform was untucked, and his hair was disheveled.

"Well?" he asked.

She shifted her focus back to me and said, "Let's do it. We can forward the picture to everyone we know."

I ran my fingers through my wet stringy hair, and an idea popped into my head. I snatched the form out of the guy's fingers, wrote an e-mail address, and handed it back to him with my money.

"Whose e-mail did you put?" Janie asked.

"Kit's."

"How do you know his address?"

"He gave it to me." And it was easy to remember, because I'd thought about it ever since. His e-mail was the initial of his first name (real name): D for Derek; followed by his last name: Felton; at georgiasouthern.edu. Derek Felton lived in Georgia, and I was sending him my picture because he wanted to know what I looked like. But he didn't want me to tell anyone we'd exchanged real names. He worried one of us would get in trouble. So, I kept it to myself.

"Thea!" Janie shoved me.

"What? He's been asking me to send him a picture. This is perfect. Plus . . . this way there's no record of it on my computer. My parents will never know I sent it to him."

"Sneaky . . . and still not a good idea." She raised her eyebrows and shrugged. "Your choice," she said and filled out her own form. When she handed it back to the attendant, he smirked, and a bit of mustard flaked off his lower lip.

We waited for our prints, and Tim slid in next to us. "Nice picture." He pointed to our photo, still displayed on the monitors with other pictures of swimsuit-clad kids.

"You are in my bubble." Janie used her hands to define an imaginary space around her.

Tim recoiled in mock horror and stepped closer to me; his toes touched mine. I had to bend my neck backward to look up at him. He'd grown even taller since school let out, and his honey-colored hair glistened with water droplets in the summer sun.

"Do you have a bubble, too?" he asked.

"Where you're concerned, yes. Back off."

"Why are you so cruel to me?" He lifted a hand to his bare chest.

"Why are you so dramatic?"

"I can't help myself when I'm near you." He rocked back and forth. His blue eyes shined brighter when he smiled. "Come on, Thea, go out with me. We'd be great together."

Janie's mouth dropped open and her eyes just about popped out. She stood behind Tim, listening to every word. Maybe a month ago my eyes would've popped too, but I was over Tim. My heart beat faster for someone else now.

"Sorry, I already have a boyfriend," I said.

Janie mouthed the word, "What?"

"Who?" Tim's shoulders sagged.

"Oh, nobody you know. He's older."

"What's his name?"

"Yeah, what's his name?" Janie asked, clearly upset hearing headline news this way.

"Kit."

"Kit?" Janie asked.

"Kit," I said.

"Kit? What kind of stupid name is that?" Tim asked. "Are you making him up?"

"No, he's real," Janie said.

"Then why didn't you know about him?" Tim asked her.

"I knew about him. I just didn't know it was an official boyfriend-girlfriend situation." She emphasized each word making it clear she was mad.

"Where did you meet him?" Tim shot the words at me.

Janie answered before I could. "On *Skadi*."

"That online game?" he asked. Janie nodded. He popped his knuckles and took a step back. "Okay," he said and then jogged toward his friends on the other side of the pool.

Janie whacked me on the shoulder.

"Ouch! What was that for?"

With both hands on hips, she said, "I've asked you a million times if you were serious with Kit and you've always said you were just friends. What's up with that?"

"Sorry. It's gotten more involved. I think he really likes me." I grinned.

"What about Red?"

"What about her?"

"He totally flirts with her when you're not online."

"Maybe he did that to make me jealous . . . to see if I was interested. Besides, Kit gets me. He cares about everything I do and think."

"But do we know him? He's like way older than us."

"He's barely nineteen. And we know a lot about him. He's an only child. His mom is dead. He lives with his dad. He has a summer job, and he's trying to decide if he should go to a college closer to me so we can see each other."

"Does he know where you live?"

"Not specifically."

"Have you seen a picture of him?"

"No, but he could text me a picture if I—"

"Do not give him your cell number!" She stuck her finger in my face. "I mean it!"

"Okay. I won't."

She relaxed; then with a spark in her eyes she said, "You could have him send a picture to my e-mail, and then we both could see what he looks like. And your parents still wouldn't suspect anything."

Her change in attitude surprised me.

"Look, you're going to find a way to do this whether I help you or not," Janie said. "So, I might as well help and keep an eye out for you at the same time." She lifted one eyebrow, and we both smiled.

"You're the best friend ever!"

The rumpled attendant cleared his throat and slid our prints across the counter. We grabbed them and ran back over to our lounge chairs to admire our pictures.

"I love them!" Janie said. "But that guy was creepy. Did you see the way he gawked at us?"

"Well, you were kind of staring at him first," I said.

"Only out of morbid curiosity," she said. "You'd think he'd get fired for being a slob."

"Appearances aren't everything," I said. "Maybe he's a hard worker."

Janie cocked an eyebrow.

"Maybe he's a really nice guy on the inside," I said.

"Are you nuts?"

"Fine," I said. "You're right. He should've at least combed his hair."

We slid our pictures into our bags and bolted for the next slide.

The line stretched for a mile, so we diverted to the water fountain. After I took a drink, I stepped too quickly and slipped, landing hard on my rear. A hand reached down to help me. I shielded my eyes from the sun and discovered the hand belonged to Josh.

"No, thank you." I stood on my own.

"Hey," Josh said, "Don't be all hateful."

"What do you want?" I asked.

Janie squeezed her lips together and then practically hid behind me. Josh's swim trunks clung to his hips, and a trail of hair ran from his navel to his waistband. I prayed he'd tied that drawstring tightly enough. His skin pulled across his chest, stretching his dark nipples wide and exposing the curve of his muscles.

"I just want to talk to you."

"Hurry up," I said.

He rubbed his chest. "Look, you've got to stop crushing Tim. Why can't you just go out with him?"

"Uh . . ." I started but couldn't come up with a reply. Janie poked me from behind.

"I know I can be a jerk," Josh said, "but don't take it out on my man Tim. Reconsider. He's a good guy, who for some unknown reason wants to be with you."

"Right. For some unknown reason." I accidentally snorted. "Well, maybe when you've got the reason figured out—"

"Fine. I'll give you reasons. You're funny. You're tough—"

"You're starting to freak me out, Josh. You should leave now."

"Give him a chance." Josh lowered his head and walked away.

"Oh. My. Gosh." Janie clutched my shoulders and spun me around. "What the heck was that?"

I shuddered in disbelief.

"Maybe if you reconsider going with Tim, Josh will reconsider going out with me," she said.

I didn't want to crush her hopes, but I was over Tim. "Maybe," I said, "but why are you even interested in Josh?"

"I can't help it. I just am." She let out a long sigh. "And maybe we've misjudged him. We have to look past his tough exterior and give him a chance."

"Right," I said, but I wasn't convinced. I grabbed Janie's hand and pulled her toward the next slide.

# CHAPTER 8

The August sun broke through my bedroom window. I stretched in bed and let out a long sigh. My birthday. Fifteen. Somehow it sounded so much older than fourteen. Plus, it put me closer to Kit's age. Obviously, I wouldn't ever catch up to him in years, but I was getting closer to a point where our age difference wouldn't matter.

The night before, Kit had told me on *Skadi* that he'd have a surprise for me today. I wondered what it would be. He said he had to work this morning but he'd be online this afternoon at three o'clock. How could I wait that long? I glanced up at the framed picture of Janie and me splashing down at the water park—the same photo I had e-mailed to Kit. He never did send one of himself to her e-mail address. He didn't like the idea of Janie being involved in our relationship. But if I gave him my cell number, he assured me, he'd send a picture. A knock on my door startled me out of my thoughts.

"Come in," I said and sat up in bed.

"Good morning, birthday girl." Mom carried in a platter of steaming french toast, crispy bacon, and sparkling apple juice. Yum. She set the tray on my lap, and the sweet aroma of maple syrup drifted through the room.

"Thanks, Mom!" I snatched a piece of the thick-sliced peppered bacon and bit off a chunk. "Mmm," I mumbled while chewing.

"So, are we going out on our annual shopping binge?" Mom perched on the edge of my bed, and I stopped chewing. Usually I couldn't wait to go shopping, but Kit had suggested I do something different this time. I struggled for an innocently worded excuse, because I didn't want her to suspect my reasons.

"Thea?" she asked.

"Well, what if, instead of our annual shopping trip, we spend the money on a class, which we could take together, at the rec center? And . . . there's another thing I'd like . . ." I wondered if she'd ever agree. "A door knob that locks."

Her face wrinkled, more than usual. "A lock?"

"I need privacy. I need to change my clothes without you or Dad barging in on me."

"We knock—"

"Not always."

"Okay, maybe," Mom said. "Let me discuss it with your dad, but why take more exercise classes when volleyball is going to start soon?"

"Yoga might be fun." In fact, Kit had suggested both birthday items. He knew a locked door would offer us privacy, and he thought I'd enjoy yoga.

"I will call and see how much it costs," Mom said. I'd already checked online, and it would use up the majority of my birthday money to get a punch pass for the rec center, but Kit would be pleased to know I was doing it.

Mom patted my knee. "Enjoy your breakfast while it's warm, and then we can discuss what you want to do today." She got up and headed for the bedroom door.

"I think I'd enjoy a quiet day at home." And an afternoon of chatting online.

Mom turned toward me. "Really?"

"Yeah. I've got a couple of books I wanted to read this summer, and school starts next week already."

"Well, it is your birthday. You get to choose. Maybe I'll read a book, too . . . or, we could run out to the rec center this morning and then come back and relax."

I shoved another piece of bacon into my mouth. "I like that idea."

"Thea, I can't understand you."

I finished chewing, swallowed, and then said, "Can we go after I eat?"

"Sounds good."

Relieved after she left, I took a deep breath, grabbed another piece of bacon, and reached over to tear a page off my Quote of the Day calendar. The next one, October 14th, read:

*Honesty is the first chapter in the book of wisdom.—Thomas Jefferson*

Whatever. I shoved the rest of the bacon into my mouth. Then I twisted my shoulders and reread the official quote for today, August 10th, which I had already taped to my wall:

*Love has nothing to do with what you are expecting to get, only with what you are expecting to give, which is everything.—Katharine Hepburn*

Completely satisfied, I grabbed my notebook from the nightstand. I knew exactly what I needed to write in my diary today. I had finally found love, and this quote was a perfect sign that this relationship was meant to be. This was going to be a great day. After I finished writing, I set the notebook down and enjoyed the rest of my breakfast.

◾

Mom and I walked through the main doors of the rec center and headed over to the counter to purchase punch passes. We stopped in our tracks when Marcus turned around to help us.

"Marcus?" I rested my elbows on the countertop. He was his usual drop-dead-gorgeous self, and I was drawn to him like a moth to flame.

"Hey, Thea!" He leaned in, closing the space between us. I caught a whiff of soap—like he'd just stepped out of the shower—and I imagined him with a towel wrapped around his waist. I bit my lower lip and indulged my dreamy desire. I remembered what Emily had said and wondered how old he truly was.

"Since when do you work here?" I asked.

"Summer job," he said.

"Do you like it here?" Mom asked, interrupting my fantasy. Marcus dragged his eyes away from me and straightened up.

"Yes. It has great benefits." He glanced back at me and winked. Dang. He was cute. I stepped back and stuck my hands in my pockets. What else was I supposed to do with them? Reach out and grab his beautiful face? Too bad he was friends with my brother.

Mom cleared her throat. "Well, we need to buy two punch passes, and do you have a schedule for the yoga classes?"

"Mrs. Reid!" A man's voice boomed out from behind us. I whirled around. "Thea!" Jackson, our old self-defense instructor, thrust his hand out for a shake. I took it, and with his firm grasp, he pulled me into a hug. Without even asking. And with Jackson's chest, a hug equaled smashing into a brick wall.

"Can't breathe," I said.

"Sorry!" He let go and stuck out his hand toward Mom. "Mrs. Reid, how are you? I haven't seen you since class. Things going well?"

"Fine. Today's Thea's birthday, and we've decided to sign up for yoga classes." Why did Mom always volunteer too much information? I grinned, or grimaced, I wasn't sure which. Didn't care. I wanted to get back to Kit, and I felt a little guilty for flirting with Marcus.

"Perfect!" Jackson said. "The yoga instructor is Keith from our self-defense class."

"Is he good at yoga?" I asked.

"Oh, yes. I've taken his class a couple of times," Jackson said.

"Perhaps we'll see you in class," Mom said.

"That'd be great! Right now, I've got to run, but it was nice to see you again!" He hustled to the stairs and took them two at a time.

"I cannot even picture him doing yoga," Marcus said. "It'd be like a Mack truck twisting into a pretzel."

I couldn't help but laugh and agree. Mom finished paying, and we headed back home.

■

The rest of the day moved too slowly. I caught myself reading the same page of my book over and over. I slapped it closed and stared at the time. One o'clock . . . Watching the minutes tick by turned torturous. I let out a slow groan and rolled off my bed. I needed a distraction from my misery.

I pulled my bicycle out of the garage and headed toward the nearby cupcake shop. At first, I pedaled as quickly as possible, and then I pedaled as slowly as possible. I resisted the urge to look at the time. I picked up an eight-pack of red velvet cupcakes for my family and returned home. I parked the bike in the garage and strolled in through the front door.

"Hi, Mom," I said and passed through the archway to the family room. She looked up from her book, her reading glasses slanted on her nose. I lifted the bag. "I got cupcakes for dessert tonight."

"Sweet," Mom said.

"I'm going to my room to read." Not.

"Okay baby-girl," she said.

I closed my bedroom door, and set a book next to the computer for good appearance and logged into *Skadi*. Kit typed hello as soon as my screen name appeared in the game.

**Kitsuneshin:** Finally! I've been waiting a lifetime for you.

**ImmortalSlayer:** LOL. ☺ You have not! *rolls eyes*

**Kitsuneshin:** Ok, just years then. Now that I know u, my life can finally begin. *nearly faints*

**ImmortalSlayer:** Whatever. Stop teasing me.

**Kitsuneshin:** *tickles tummy and laughs*

**Kitsuneshin:** Ha. Should I sing Happy Birthday to u now?

**ImmortalSlayer:** No. But you can tell me what your big surprise is!

**Kitsuneshin:** Man, I wish I could be there to celebrate your birthday in person with u.

**ImmortalSlayer:** I wish u could be here too, so I could see your face and hear your laugh and see the light in your eyes.

**Kitsuneshin:** *sigh* I would wrap my arms around you and hold you close.

**ImmortalSlayer:** You make me smile ☺

**Kitsuneshin:** I also wish u could be here for my birthday in October.

**ImmortalSlayer:** Yes! And u could show me the sights of Georgia!

**Kitsuneshin:** Oh . . . someday we'll be together!

**ImmortalSlayer:** Yup . . . someday.

**Kitsuneshin:** So . . . what's the special quote for your birthday?

**ImmortalSlayer:** Oh. It. Is. A. Great. One!

**Kitsuneshin:** Tell me! *shakes computer so you will hurry up*

**ImmortalSlayer:** "Love has nothing to do with what you are expecting to get, only with what you are expecting to give, which is everything."—Katharine Hepburn

**Kitsuneshin:** *takes breath away*—That is a great one!

**Kitsuneshin:** What's the quote for my birthday?

**ImmortalSlayer:** Can't tell you.

**Kitsuneshin:** Why?

**ImmortalSlayer:** That would be cheating. We can't look that far into the future. We can only take one step at a time. ☺

**Kitsuneshin:** Right. I already know you read ahead and find quotes u like on your calendar.

**ImmortalSlayer:** I guess you will have to check back with me on your birthday. LOL

**Kitsuneshin:** Can you believe we've only known each other for five months? I feel like we've known each other forever.

**ImmortalSlayer:** I know! Right?

**ImmortalSlayer:** I guess it's a good thing u let me join your guild!

**Kitsuneshin:** Right! Otherwise, we wouldn't even know each other now!

**ImmortalSlayer:** I'm glad I found *Skadi* . . . so I could find u . . .

**Kitsuneshin:** I totally agree.

**Kitsuneshin:** Are you ready for your bday present?

**ImmortalSlayer:** Ya! Ya!

Kit went on typing step-by-step instructions for me to log into a private online e-mail account he had set up for me on Yahoo! The account used my *Skadi* screen name, ImmortalSlayer, for my address, and Kit had chosen "together-forever" as the password. Accessing the account was easy, and my parents would never know about it. But that wasn't all. My real present was something else. He had already sent me my first e-mail, and in it he wrote:

*Dear Thea,*
*Many miles and years separate us, but my heart is so close to yours, I can feel it beating when I think your name. Thea, I love you.*
*Happy Birthday,*
*Derek*

This was the first time he had actually said it to me. I had been pretty sure he felt that way, but reading those three most beautiful words in the world on my computer meant everything to me. It was the best birthday present ever. I clicked Reply and typed my response:

*Derek,*
*I love you, too.*
*Thea*

# CHAPTER 9

The first day of school arrived too soon. Why school started at the end of August, I never understood. Janie showed up to my house an hour early so we could make sure our hair, makeup, and outfits were just right. Of course, Janie looked perfect when I opened the front door, but even when I told her that she never believed me. Her beautiful black hair had grown quite a bit over the summer, and she styled it in ringlets again. It still needed to grow more, but it looked so much better. I ran my hand down my own smooth auburn hair, hoping my straightening products would hold out.

It was going to be a hot day, and Janie had dressed appropriately. She wore brand new A&F crop jeans, a navy and white pinstriped top that opened in a wide V-neck and had short gathered sleeves, a white cami peeking out from underneath, and leather flip-flops that showed off her new pedicure.

Mom came to the entryway and greeted Janie. "I have fresh donuts from Krispy Kreme. Come on back to the kitchen and have some."

"Seriously?" I asked. Mom rarely splurged on unnecessary things.

"Seriously. It's the first day of school. We need to celebrate."

I grabbed Janie and pulled her down the hall and around the corner to the kitchen. I snatched a melt-in-your-mouth donut and leaned over the counter so it wouldn't drop icing on my own new A&F navy T-shirt. Janie and I had gone to the mall together last week, and I shopped the clearance racks. I found an A&F T-shirt, skinny jeans, and a braided belt—all at a steal. I had to admit, sporting trendy brand names on my first day of tenth grade was a lot of fun. Plus, I bought a bra with frilly trim. Derek had asked once what kind I wore, and I was too embarrassed to tell him that I only had a plain white cotton bra. But now I had a satin one with lace. The edges made my skin itch, but it made me feel more adult. I took a second bite of my donut and noticed Janie was just standing there, gawking at the box.

"Grab one," I said through a mouthful. I continued chewing and used my other hand to wipe icing from the corner of my mouth. I tilted my head back. "Oh, Mom, these are so good."

"Donuts!" Seth and Marcus yelled as they strolled into the kitchen. Seth pushed past me and grabbed two, while Marcus wrapped his arm around my shoulders and pulled me tight.

"Looking fine!" Marcus said.

I pulled away and whacked him. "Don't be a creeper."

He pouted for a few seconds. Then he laughed and grabbed a soft donut, keeping his eyes on me. I looked away first.

"Seth, do you want to drive the girls today?" Mom asked.

"Uh, no. Why would I?" he asked and then inhaled half a donut.

"Because I pay your car insurance," Mom said.

"I planned to hitch a ride with him." Seth jerked his thumb toward Marcus.

"We can give them a ride," Marcus said, and Seth elbowed him in the gut.

"It's okay," Janie said. "We'll ride the bus."

"Good." Seth grabbed Marcus by the shirt, and they darted from the kitchen.

"Janie, don't you want a donut?" Mom asked.

"Oh . . . no, thank you. I'm on a diet," she said and moved away from the counter.

"Since when? You are so not on a diet. You could eat five and gain nothing." I shoved the remainder of my second donut in my mouth and went to the cupboard for a glass.

"Yeah. You're right," Janie said, but she sounded hesitant. She gingerly lifted a donut, but then ate it faster than I ate mine. She didn't even notice the fact she was dropping crumbs and icing on her shirt. I pointed at the mess she'd made.

"Crap." She ran toward the guest bathroom, and I followed, but before I caught up, she locked the door. I intended to wait, but then I heard her throw up. I leaned closer to make sure I wasn't imagining it. She threw up again. I tapped my knuckles on the door.

"Are you okay?" I heard the faucet running, but she didn't answer me. I knocked again. "Unlock the door."

"I'm fine," she said and opened the door. "The donut didn't sit right."

"Do you have the flu? Should you go home?" I knew she wasn't sick, but I wasn't sure how to ask her why she vomited.

"No," she said with her don't-mess-with-me head sway. "I am not missing our first day." She had cleaned off her shirt and looked more like herself again.

"Fine." I grabbed her arm and led her to my room. We finished getting ready, and then walked to the bus stop. Less people were waiting for the bus than last year. The Three Stooges, otherwise known as Tim, Josh, and Taylor, were nowhere to be seen. Fine by me. Less drama was a good way to start our year.

The bus arrived on time, and we climbed on. Pop music blasted from the radio, and the bus smelled like fresh vinyl. We took a seat near the front, and I couldn't resist the urge to lean against the window and peer between the seat and the wall. No wads of gum. The bus had to be new. I slid my hand along the wall, knowing that this would be the only time I'd be able to do such a thing. It was fresh and clean. Too bad it wouldn't stay that way for long.

A second before the doors closed, the Three Stooges barreled onto the bus, panting. Josh let his backpack whack Janie in the shoulder, and Tim shoved him down the aisle. Taylor brought up the rear and plucked one of Janie's ringlets.

"Some things never change," Janie said and rolled her eyes. I grinned and stole a peek over my shoulder. Tim looked right at me, and I quickly faced forward.

"Yeah, some things never change."

# CHAPTER 10

School had been in full swing for two weeks. I was so busy that time was flying. Volleyball practice ate up a lot of those hours. I wanted Janie to try out for volleyball, but she refused to be seen in those super-short, super-tight shorts. I didn't understand her sometimes. And while I loved sports, that was time I could've spent online with Derek. I was torn, and I was tired of trying to keep up with everything, including my grades. Purely exhausted, I needed to go straight to bed at night, but I never did. I would be sad if I didn't check in with Derek. I closed my bedroom door, shoved my comforter behind it as an obstacle, and logged onto *Skadi*. Derek was waiting.

**Kitsuneshin:** Hey! Glad you made it.

**ImmortalSlayer:** Me too, but I am really tired. VB is wiping me out.

**Kitsuneshin:** I'm sorry! But UR tough and VB is important to you.

**ImmortalSlayer:** But so are you.

**Kitsuneshin:** Ah, thanks! But I support you in whatever u want to do!

**Kitsuneshin:** If you'd let us swap cell numbers, we could text during the day and not have to wait until so late at night.

**ImmortalSlayer:** Can't text during school.

**Kitsuneshin:** Before or after?

**ImmortalSlayer:** My parents would kill me if they knew I gave out my cell number

**Kitsuneshin:** Well . . . I certainly don't want them to kill u! *gasps*

**Kitsuneshin:** But maybe they don't need to know.

**ImmortalSlayer:** IDK

I stretched backward in my chair and caught my reflection in the mirror. My hair was snarled in some places and stringy in others. I attempted to finger comb it, but it was a lost cause. I looked awful, and I was so glad Derek couldn't see me right now . . . but I still wanted to know what he looked like. I turned back to the monitor. Derek had typed another message.

**Kitsuneshin:** *kneels and begs* . . . please?

**ImmortalSlayer:** Will u send me a picture of you if I give you my number?

**Kitsuneshin:** Why do want a picture of an ugly guy like me?

**ImmortalSlayer:** *shakes finger* I need a picture. Besides . . . what does ugly even look like? Are you the Hunchback of Notre Dame? A serpent covered Gorgon? A mangy mutt?

**Kitsuneshin:** I'll send u a pix right now if u tell me your number ☺

**ImmortalSlayer:** Promise?

**Kitsuneshin:** *crosses heart*

**ImmortalSlayer:** If I give u my number, we can text but no phone calls.

**Kitsuneshin:** Why?

**ImmortalSlayer:** Too risky. I'll get caught.

**Kitsuneshin:** Deal.

**ImmortalSlayer:** Ok—let me think about it for a few min

I hopped up and grabbed my hair brush and began to work on the knots in my hair. I needed to take a shower and wash it, but then I wouldn't be able to chat with Derek. So the brush would have to do for now. I sat back down and read the next message.

**Kitsuneshin:** I'm just glad you logged on tonight. I've been really bummed

**ImmortalSlayer:** Why?

**Kitsuneshin:** My dad's been drinking a lot lately. He gets mean.

**ImmortalSlayer:** Why does he drink so much?

**Kitsuneshin:** IDK He probably misses my mom.

**ImmortalSlayer:** Probably. It must be hard.

**Kitsuneshin:** I miss her a lot too.

**ImmortalSlayer:** Do you want to talk about it?

**Kitsuneshin:** Not really. Too depressing. I don't understand why she had to die.

**ImmortalSlayer:** Don't worry . . . I know you will see her again.

**Kitsuneshin:** Everything's harder. Dad drinks more. He never talks to me. Sometimes I wish I could die too.

**ImmortalSlayer:** Don't say that.

**Kitsuneshin:** I've already tried twice.

**ImmortalSlayer:** Tried what?

**Kitsuneshin:** Suicide

**ImmortalSlayer:** Are you joking?

**Kitsuneshin:** No. But I couldn't even do that right. Failed both times.

**ImmortalSlayer:** What did u do?

**Kitsuneshin:** First time, I tried to cut my wrists, but I chickened out after the first small cut because it hurt so freaking bad. I put a bandage over it and didn't tell anyone . . . well, except for u now. Please don't tell anyone else.

**ImmortalSlayer:** I won't. Don't worry *hugs*

I turned my wrist over and traced the veins with my fingertip. I tried to imagine what it would feel like to cut into my own flesh, but just the idea sent shivers up my spine. I could never intentionally cut myself. I couldn't imagine the pain or loneliness that Derek must have felt.

**Kitsuneshin:** Second time, I took a bunch of my dad's pain pills and drank his whiskey. I woke up the next day with a splitting headache. My dad didn't even notice I was passed out on the couch all night.

**ImmortalSlayer:** I am so sorry! Please don't ever do that again! Promise me!

**Kitsuneshin:** With u, I have a reason to live.

**Kitsuneshin:** I love you so much.

**ImmortalSlayer:** I love you too ☺ *wraps arms around you* I don't want you to hurt anymore.

**Kitsuneshin:** Thanks

**Kitsuneshin:** I have your picture posted on the wall right next to my computer.

**ImmortalSlayer:** What picture?

**Kitsuneshin:** The one from the water park.

**ImmortalSlayer:** Oh!

**Kitsuneshin:** I love it. UR gorgeous. I love ur smile, ur hair, ur face *kisses cheek*

**ImmortalSlayer:** Ah! UR so sweet!

**Kitsuneshin:** I love you.

**Kitsuneshin:** Our hearts have gotten to know each other before our bodies.

**ImmortalSlayer:** Is that a song lyric?

**Kitsuneshin:** No. It's how I feel about us.

**ImmortalSlayer:** *melts* I love u

No hesitation remained in my mind. I sent him my cell number. I needed a picture of him. And I needed him to know he could contact me anytime. The idea of getting caught still terrified me, but the idea of Derek attempting suicide frightened me much more. I didn't know how to help him, except to try to be there for him, and listen.

He kept his promise and sent a photo to my phone, but it was of him on a ski slope—decked out in goggles, hat, gloves and more. Not good enough. I texted him.

*That's cheating!—Thea*

*LOL—Derek*

*Send a real one!!!—Thea*

*Okay! I was just teasing u! But that really is me!! I love skiing.—Derek*

He sent another, but it was out of focus and in black and white. I tried to zoom in on it, but that didn't help much.

*Why is it black & white?—Thea*

*I snapped a shot of my HS senior picture from my yearbook—Derek*

*It's blurry! Can u try again?—Thea*

*No point. My camera phone is a piece of crap. Sorry—Derek*

*Why not take one of u tonight?—Thea*

*Thought you'd like me in a tux better!—Derek*

I studied the photo again. He was in a tux. His hair was longer in the back than I had imagined in my mind, and something about the angle of his chin or the muscles in his jaw seemed familiar, but the image was too blurry for me to figure out how I knew those features. Besides, I'd gone to sleep so many times dreaming of him, maybe I had imagined some of his characteristics correctly. I didn't push him for another picture. He was obviously worried that I wouldn't like what I saw.

We chatted awhile on *Skadi*, because it was easier to type out messages there than on a cell phone. Then I told him I had to get some sleep. It was already 3:30 A.M., but he still didn't want me to go. Derek had no one in his life to care about him except for me. I loved him. I did. But sometimes the burden was heavy. Finally I said goodnight to him and logged off, but I couldn't fall asleep right away . . . and Derek texted.

*Love u—Derek*

*Love u too—Thea*

*Wish I was holding u in my arms tonight—Derek*

☺ *nite—Thea*

I lay in bed for at least another hour visualizing our future. What if this worked out? I tried to imagine falling asleep in his arms. If we got married, my last name would be Felton. That would be nice. I smiled and hugged my pillow.

■

Derek made me promise I wouldn't tell anyone about the suicide attempts because he was ashamed; however, when Janie and I walked to the bus stop the next morning, I recounted the details and swore her to secrecy. I said nothing about the fact we'd exchanged real names, cell numbers, and e-mailed each other privately. Keeping track of what I'd already told her and not told her was becoming a chore.

"He's too old for you," Janie said.

I glared at her, a silent we've-already-had-that-discussion expression. Then I said, "I can't break up with him. He might try to kill himself again."

"Omigosh! That cannot be your job."

"It's not, but I'm the only good thing in his life."

"Dump him and forget about *Skadi*." She raised her eyebrows in a question mark.

"I can't. I have to at least be there for him until he's stronger."

"How long will that be? You seriously love him that much?"

Instead of answering, I counted the cracks in the sidewalk. I wished I could explain my love for Derek to her, but I wasn't sure I could explain it to myself. Janie linked her arm through mine, and we walked to the bus stop in silence.

■

Later that afternoon at volleyball practice Coach Gavyn yelled at us. "What do you think this is? Recess? Get the air out of your heads and focus. Thea!—"

My heart stopped. Why was he singling me out?

"—I expected more out of you! Pull it together," he said and turned away.

One of the girls giggled. He whipped back around, and we all hushed.

"If you can't get the ball over the net, you can't win the game. Do the drill again!" He waved for the next girl in line to serve and stomped over to the side of the court. Another girl giggled.

The cackles spread like a crashing wave, and Coach Gavyn yelled more, but that made it worse. We tried to stop. Really we did. But as we attempted to bottle up our laughter, we served the balls into the net. As a result, Coach made us run stair laps. My thighs lit on fire. We pounded up—and then down—hundreds of steps. We didn't learn to serve any better. But we sure laughed . . . even through the first five stair laps. During the last five, we became quiet. It wasn't funny anymore. In the locker room, we threatened to quit the team. Of course, no one would, but we felt better by complaining about it.

Most of the girls' parents were already parked and waiting in front of the school when we walked outside. I waved goodbye to them and shook out my aching legs. The area emptied, and I waited alone. Off in the distance the guys finished up football practice on the field.

I considered texting Derek, but my thighs were throbbing. So, I parked myself on the curb and extended my legs out straight. I leaned into the stretch, extending my fingertips toward my toes, and a long shadow fell over me. I glanced up and found Tim towering above. His backpack was slung over one shoulder and his hands hung at his sides.

"Hey," I said.

"Hey." Tim set his backpack down. I pulled my legs out of the way, and he sat next to me, but gave me plenty of space. No bubble invasion this time.

"How was practice?" Tim asked.

"Fine. How was football?"

"Fine."

Awkward. He pulled his knees up and crossed his arms over them. Sweat glistened on his forearms—darker than ever after a summer of tanning. His eyes reflected the clear blue sky, and I sank into them. I had to work to catch my breath. I tucked a loose strand of hair behind my ear and looked away.

"Hey, I joined that *Skadi* game you're always talking about."

"Really?" I focused on him and tried to read his mind.

"Yeah, I searched for your character, but it seems like you're never online when I am. Janie said I should ask you if you are accepting new members in your guild?"

"No. I'm having trouble keeping up with *Skadi* and homework and volleyball practice. So, I haven't been on much lately." I didn't want Tim in the same guild with Derek and me. That would be weird.

"Homecoming is next month," Tim said. When I didn't respond, he put his chin on his arms. "Do you want to go to the dance with me?" he asked.

Crap. I closed my eyes, unable to block out the image of dancing with him. He's so tall. My head would rest perfectly against his chest. His muscular arms would wrap around me. His heart would beat in my ear.

And then a car honked.

Mom pulled up to the curb next to us.

"Tim," I whispered, "my parents won't let me date until I'm sixteen."

"What about that guy on *Skadi*?" Tim's jaw muscles flexed, and my breath caught.

A strange sense of déjà vu flooded through me, and I almost pulled out my phone to compare the picture of Derek to Tim. Their jawlines—

Mom honked again. I stood and grabbed my bag.

"Is he why you can't go with me?" Tim prodded.

"I have to go."

I got into the car and watched Tim as we drove away. His head settled face-down on his arms, and I wondered where Josh and Taylor were. The three of them were inseparable.

"How did practice go?" Mom asked.

"Fine."

"That's it?" she prodded.

"The coach made us run stair laps, because we couldn't serve the balls over the net." That was true. Mostly. My cell vibrated in my pocket, but I ignored it. I was exhausted, but Mom insisted on her usual car banter, and I complied the best I could.

"Do you have homework?" Mom asked.

"Yes."

"A lot?"

"No."

"What was the best thing about your day?"

"Seeing you." I glanced sideways at her.

"Right," she said sarcastically. "Then what was the second best thing about your day?"

"I got a 98 percent on my math test."

"Great job! I'm so pleased with how well you're doing in school." She paid attention to driving and turned left into traffic. "So what was the worst part about your day?"

"Not sure."

"Yes, you are."

I dreaded coming up with a story, because I wasn't going to tell her the worst, second worst, or even third worst thing that happened today. So, I changed the subject.

"I'm starving. Can we go out for dinner?"

"Maybe."

"Really?" Shocked, I twisted toward her in my seat.

"Really. Maybe we could go out to eat as a family and go see a movie tonight."

"That'd be great."

"Will you have time to finish your homework, though? And will you be too tired if we stay out for a movie?"

"I'll be fine." Of course I'd be wasted tomorrow, but it'd be worth it. Even if it meant no *Skadi*. Not that I actually played anymore . . . Derek and I used it as a place to chat.

Once we got home, I dropped my bag on the stone floor of the entryway and headed down the hall to my room.

"Thea, the entryway is not your closet. Pick up your things," Mom hollered after me. I pushed the Power button on my computer and went back to grab my bag. I returned to my bedroom, tossed my stuff on the bed, and plopped down at my desk with my phone in hand. One text from Derek asked where I was. I dashed off a reply:

*online!—Thea*

Mom poked her head through my doorway. "Will you be ready in less than an hour?"

"Sure thing. I just need to type up a paper real quick and change."

My computer finished booting up, and I opened the word processing program. I hopped up and closed my door. With some privacy, I logged onto Yahoo! and opened my e-mail account. Five messages from Derek. My heart swelled. In the first three, he wrote sweet romantic things, but the last two e-mails were different.

*Thea, where are you? I need to talk to you! D.*

*I haven't heard from you! Can I call? D.*

Before I could reply to his e-mail, my cell vibrated again.
*Where RU? U said online, but ur not—Derek*
*I can't get online after all.—Thea*
*But I need to talk to u—Derek*
*Won't be able to talk. Sorry.—Thea*
*I am going to dinner & movie w/fam. Is something wrong?—Thea*

I plunked my phone down on the desk and rubbed my forehead. His tone had changed. Did I make a mistake giving him my cell number? Now he could reach me anytime he wanted; that should be okay, considering we loved each other. But my chest tightened.

My bedroom door swung open. I jerked the mouse, and in a flash I minimized the window for Yahoo!

"Hey," Mom said.

"You scared the crap out of me." I hadn't heard anyone coming down the hall, and there was no knock at the door.

"I'm sorry I forgot to knock," Mom said, "but the rule remains. When I come in you cannot collapse screens on your computer." Mom inspected my monitor more closely. My head swam, and I feared she'd notice the Yahoo! bar at the bottom of the screen. I reached over and started clicking menus in the word processing program, attempting to distract her.

"I thought you had a paper to type up?"

"I do."

"Were you online?"

"Yes."

"Doing what?"

"I had to update my status on *Skadi* otherwise my account would go inactive." Mom didn't know enough about the game to recognize my lie. I hated lying, but she would never approve of my relationship with Derek, even though we weren't doing anything wrong.

"I figured you were too busy with school and sports to have time to play *Skadi* anymore."

"I don't have time. That's why I need to update my status every once in a while. I don't want to lose my characters that I worked so hard to level up."

My cell vibrated continuously, indicating an incoming call. I snatched it off the desk top and read the screen. Derek. I hit the

Reject button and slipped the phone into my pocket. He wasn't supposed to call . . . and he picked now of all times.

"Who was that?" Mom asked.

"Janie."

"Why didn't you answer?"

"We're in the middle of a conversation."

"Okay," Mom said. "So, do you still talk with that Kit character all the time?"

I tried to not roll my eyes. "He doesn't really play *Skadi* anymore."

"I thought he was the Guild Master?"

"Guild Leader, and no, he's not anymore. He promoted me to Guild Leader. That's why it's important I check in. I have to respond to questions from my guild members."

Mom remained motionless but said, "Hurry up so we can get to the movie."

"I need a lock for my door."

"Don't use the Internet with the door closed." She walked out and closed the door behind her.

I checked to see if Derek had left a voice mail. Nothing. I texted him.

*We agreed no phone calls. My mom was standing right next to me!—Thea*

He didn't reply. I changed my clothes and took my homework out to the kitchen table. I hoped Derek was okay.

# CHAPTER 11

To trust or not to trust? The question repeated in my mind. I knew I could count on Janie, beyond a shadow of a doubt. I told her everything. Well, almost everything. I didn't divulge all the little details of my private chats and e-mails with Derek. Could I trust Derek? I believed so, but he was still ticked from when I ditched out on him the other night for dinner and a movie. Seemed childish to me. But, I guess if I were him, I would've been upset, too. I should try harder to be more dependable for him.

I wished I could talk to Mom about my relationship with Derek and about his alcoholic dad, but I doubted her reaction. I wanted her to listen to me and then offer objective advice on how I could help him, but I was sure she'd freak out if I revealed the truth about the e-mails, texting, and the fact that Derek and I knew each other's real names.

Mom was driving us to our first yoga class, finally, and we were alone. Safe within the confines of the car, I knew this was an ideal time to talk to her because no one could hear or interrupt us. She checked the rear view mirror and then smiled at me.

"Did you want to discuss something?" she asked.

I considered it. But when I didn't answer, she poked the buttons on the radio, found a station she liked, and sang along with the song. Her face brightened and her chin lifted. She wasn't a great singer, but that never stopped her.

I had lost my opportunity.

My stomach twisted, and I realized I needed my life to slow down so that I could have more time to figure out this mess. I gazed out the side window at the trees, people, and buildings sliding by.

The objects moved too fast for me to focus on them. If I looked ahead I could see the images clearly, but they blurred when they sped past—or when I sped past them. I closed my eyes and tried to shut out the world for a moment.

The car slowed and turned. I opened my eyes at the same time Mom pulled into the parking lot of the rec center. As usual, she drove past a gazillion open spots and parked at the far end of the lot.

"Why don't you park closer?"

"I like to walk."

"But we'll get exercise in the class. Why park so far away?"

"It will give us more time to chitchat."

"We didn't talk in the car. Why would we now just because you parked in another county?" Mom put the key back into the ignition, backed the car up, and relocated to the spot nearest the entrance. Why couldn't she just ask me questions about what's bothering me? I dropped my chin to my chest.

"Better?" she asked and yanked the key out of the ignition. She tightened her lips, and we stared at each other for a moment.

"Much." I grabbed my water bottle and hopped out of the car. We didn't say anything to each other while we walked to the entrance. Mom checked us in at the front counter, and we headed upstairs to Studio Four. It was weird to be back in that room. I recalled the final night of our self-defense class, and my throat tightened. A lot had happened since then.

We were early, so I set my water bottle down and told Mom I needed to use the restroom. When I returned, Mom was on the other side of the room speaking with Jackson. Great. I walked over to them.

"You're out of uniform," I waved my finger up and down at Jackson's attire. I'd never seen him in anything but his skin-tight, black macho clothes, and tonight he was wearing baggy shorts and a loose T-shirt. His feet were bare.

"Yoga clothes." He held his hands out in a "ta-da" kind of pose. Bulging veins traveled the length of his arms, hardly any hair covered his finely sculpted legs, and how he could be that tan . . . I had no idea.

"You don't approve?" he asked.

"The hairy toes are throwing me off."

He wiggled his feet and clasped his chest, a feigned broken heart. "I'm so hurt."

"Whatever!" I shoved his shoulder and laughed.

His perfectly groomed mustache bounced while he chuckled in response. "So, your mom tells me volleyball is going well." I nodded. After an awkward pause, he asked, "Are you in Coach Gavyn's Health class at Skycrest?"

What a weird question. "No."

"He asked if I would loan some equipment for a personal-safety demonstration this winter for his classes. I thought I might see you there."

"Nope. Not me."

"Is he working you hard in volleyball practice?"

"I suppose." My thoughts turned to the day we ran stair laps, and how he singled me out when he yelled at us. "Why?" I asked.

"You kicked the snot out of him in that final self-defense class." Jackson clasped his hands behind his back, but the pose was less intimidating in his baggy T-shirt and shorts.

"Coach Gavyn was the guy in the padded equipment?" I asked.

Jackson nodded with a smile. "Don't worry. He's a good guy. He won't hold it against you. Plus, he told me he couldn't wait to work with you in volleyball because you're so determined to win."

My mouth hung open as I processed this information. Coach never said anything to me about it. I had no idea who the padded guy really was.

"Your mom also says you're spending a lot of time on that *Skadi* game with someone named Kit," Jackson said.

I whipped my head toward Mom. "Seriously?" Her cheeks reddened.

Jackson released his mercenary stance and placed a hand on my shoulder. "She cares about you. Don't be mad. She just wants you to be safe."

"I am safe," I said too loudly. People gawked at us, including Keith who had just entered the room.

"It's just a game." I clenched my teeth together. How could they gang up on me right before class?

"Well, if you ever need to talk, I'd be happy to listen," he said. I didn't know how to respond to that. And I didn't have to, because Keith came over to say hello.

"Welcome to yoga," Keith said. "I'm so glad you came."

I bit my lips together and said nothing.

Keith's smile faded. "All right then, let's get started." He moved to the front of the class and welcomed everyone.

The three of us set up our mats together, and Jackson showed off his physical skills during the class. Yoga was way harder than I ever imagined.

■

After class, we put our shoes back on, and Jackson said, "It was nice to see you both tonight. Thea . . . make smart choices and stay safe."

"I always do," I said. He waved and headed out.

"I can't believe you talked about me before class again," I said to Mom.

"I didn't talk about you—"

"You told him about Kit."

"I merely said I was concerned." Her mouth opened like she was about to say more, but then she closed it.

"What?"

"Not here." She glanced around the room. I did, too, and found Keith staring at us. He gave us an awkward little wave and jutted out his chin. Mom took my elbow and steered me out of the classroom. We talked while walking.

"What else did you say to Jackson about me?" I asked.

"I told him that our relationship wasn't as strong as it used to be. You used to talk to me. But ever since you started playing that online game, you don't listen to me. There are dangers out in the world that you can't imagine—"

"You don't listen to me."

"There's no way to get through to you. I'm afraid your hormones are influencing your decision-making process—"

I accidentally huffed. She stopped speaking.

"What?" I asked. I'd had enough. She didn't reply but continued walking.

We got in the car, but before inserting the key, she asked, "Is there anything else you want to discuss, Thea?"

"Nope." I had enough discussion, and I had my answer. The answer was no. I could not trust Mom with the information about Derek. She would overreact.

■

After school the next day, our volleyball team loaded up for an away game. I climbed onto the bus and clutched my cell next to my hip. We weren't supposed to use our phones while traveling to games, because the coaches wanted us to build team camaraderie. But I needed to text Derek. We didn't connect at all yesterday, and I was worried he was still upset with me. I took a seat at the back of the bus where the coaches wouldn't see me, and I pulled out my phone.

*RU still mad?—Thea*

Relief flooded through me when he replied immediately, which reaffirmed my choice to give him my number after all.

*I needed to talk 2U the other night & u weren't there for me.—Derek*

*Sorry—Thea*

*Where RU now?—Derek*

*Heading to an away game for vb—Thea*

*So . . . can I call right now?—Derek*

*No. I am on bus & not supposed to be using phone—Thea*

*RU going to get in trouble?—Derek*

I peeked to see if the coaches were nearby. The assistant coach stood outside talking to a player, and Coach Gavyn was distracted with his own phone. More girls clambered onto the bus, and a teammate plopped onto the bench across the aisle from me.

"You're not supposed to be texting," she whispered and pointed at my phone.

"I know," I said and started to put it away.

She shook her head. "I'm not going to tell. Who are you texting anyway?"

I considered how to answer. "My boyfriend." I tried to make it sound natural and normal.

"Sweet!" She slid onto my bench and threw her arm around my shoulders. "Take our picture and send it to him. Guys crave that kind of stuff." She waggled her eyebrows.

"Okay . . ." I figured she was right. Derek would love it. We posed, cheek to cheek, and puckered our lips. I snapped the picture and sent it to him. We huddled and waited for his reply.

*NICE! Does this mean u have permission to use ur phone? LOL—Derek*

"Ha! Tell him we need a photo back!" she said, but before I could send another text, the assistant coach started down the aisle, counting heads. I slipped the phone under my shirt, and my teammate hopped back across the aisle to the other bench. My cell vibrated, but I ignored it until he returned to the front of the bus. While the girls around me joked about the science teacher's new haircut, I hunched forward and pulled out my phone.

*Love the pix!—Derek*

*BTW, UR gorgeous with your hair loose around your face today!—Derek*

My heart skipped. He said the sweetest things. Joy flooded through me. I didn't want the conversation to end, but I needed to put the phone away before one of the coaches caught me.

*I can't text more. But thanks for the compliment. I needed it!—Thea*

*Luv U. Have a great game. Text me later!—Derek*

*I will as soon as I can! Luv U 2—Thea*

*And, BTW, I need another pix of U!—Thea*

I slipped the phone into my bag and sighed.

# CHAPTER 12

Found it. I pulled back from the recesses of the pantry and blew the dust off a box of chocolate cake mix. I hollered, "Mom?" and heard a mumble from her bedroom. I headed that direction. My parents' bedroom took up the back left corner of the house; mine took the right. We both had big windows that opened to the backyard, but I did not have an awesome walk-in closet or private bathroom like they did. But I guess since they paid the bills, they should have the better room. I leaned into the open doorway. "Mom?"

"In here," she said from the depths of her closet.

"What are you doing?" I asked.

"Cleaning. Letting go of the old stuff makes space for new and better things to come in."

I did a mental head slap. Whatever. "All right—"

"It wouldn't hurt you to clean out your closet. You most likely have dirty dishes in there from five years ago."

"I do not!"

She came out. A dumb smile crept across her face while my cheeks started to burn. I took a deep breath. "I didn't come in here to talk about messy closets. I came in here to ask if I could make a cake."

Mom brushed her fingers across her cheek. "Go for it."

"We don't have any frosting. Can we go buy some?" I asked.

"We have powdered sugar and milk. You can make some."

"From scratch?" I asked. "Will you help me?"

"Sure." She straightened her pants. "Why are you making a cake?"

"Oh . . . it'd be fun for dessert tonight." Things had improved between Mom and me over the last couple of weeks. We talked more, and she lectured less.

We headed back to the kitchen, and Mom helped me with the cake. She taught me how to make the frosting, and I added red and yellow food coloring to turn it orange—it was almost Halloween, after all. She left me to finish on my own. It was a plain square cake, but the orange frosting and colorful sprinkles made it fun.

A great cake for a birthday.

I grinned and took a deep breath. The fragrant vanilla made my mouth water. I took a finger and scraped some of the remaining frosting from the mixing bowl. I licked all of it from my finger and savored the sweet flavor. Life was good, and Derek would love that I did this for him. I texted him.

*I'm going to e-mail u a bday surprise!—Thea*
*What is it?—Derek*
*Check your e-mail in a few min—Thea*
*K! LuvU—Derek*

Out of habit, I deleted the texts from my phone. I slipped it into my pocket, and I went through the archway to Mom's desk in the family room. I borrowed her digital camera and a cable from her computer and ran back to the kitchen to take a picture of the bright orange cake. Perfect! I darted around the corner and down the hall to my bedroom and downloaded the photo. I deleted the picture from the camera and returned both it and the cable back to Mom's desk. The connector on the cable clicked when I pushed it into the slot on her computer. I glanced around to see if anyone had noticed, but I was alone in the family room and Mom's bedroom was too far away for her to hear me fiddling with her stuff.

I ran back to my room and opened my private e-mail account. I could have sent the picture via text, but it'd be bigger and easier to see in an e-mail.

*Dear Derek,*
*Happy Birthday! Twenty! WOW!* ☺
*I wish I could be there to help you celebrate.*
*But at least I made you a cake! Haha . . . picture attached*
*Have fun. Love you!*
*Thea*

I knew he wanted me to call and wish him a happy birthday, but the idea of speaking to him on the phone unnerved me; I would sound like a complete dope. Typing words came more easily with Derek. Besides, I could edit what I wanted to say before he read it.

I clicked Send on the e-mail, and Mom called my name from the hallway. My heart leaped from my chest.

She stepped into my room and waved her camera in the air. Its strap swung back and forth. "Did you use my camera?"

"Yes." Sometimes the truth was easier than a lie. "I figured it was no big deal."

"You hooked the cable up wrong to my computer. What'd you take a picture of?"

A high pitched buzz flooded through my ears. My private e-mail account was still displayed on my monitor. Maybe she wouldn't notice. My chest constricted, and I fought for each breath.

The camera clanked when she set it on my desk. We stared at each other for what seemed like an eternity. Gunslingers at the O.K. Corral. Who would draw their gun first? Mom. She was the fastest gun in this fight.

"I asked you a question," she said.

"I e-mailed Janie a picture—"

Mom's gaze drifted toward the computer screen.

She didn't seem to breathe. Her face tightened, as though someone pulled plastic wrap across it, dragging her features back toward her ears.

"You have a Yahoo! e-mail account?" she asked.

My head bounced ever-so-slightly, like a sappy bobblehead, and I couldn't seem to make it stop. I reached over and closed the window before she could see any of the details. Things went blurry, and I tried to refocus.

"Thea!"

I rubbed my face and shot out my explanation. "It's no big deal. I took a picture of the cake. I used your cable to download it to my computer, and I e-mailed it to Janie. Yahoo! is easier to navigate than our other e-mail." Fact was, the family e-mail account wasn't hard to use, but my parents controlled it. They received a copy of every e-mail I sent or received, claiming it fell under the umbrella of wanting to keep us safe. I dropped my hands and studied her. She wasn't reaching for my throat to kill me, so I was pretty sure my life was safe for the moment.

"No more computer until I talk to your dad." She said it too calmly. Her facial muscles didn't even move.

"Do you understand me?" she asked, but her words were distorted like I was submerged underwater and Mom was at the edge of the pool. I could almost make out her words, but they were far away and muted. I struggled toward the surface, trying to escape from the suffocating pressure, but I couldn't seem to get there. Mom picked up her camera from the desk and stepped toward the door, but then she turned and glared at me.

I tried to convince myself that everything would be fine. At least I managed to keep Derek out of the details. I wiped my sweaty hands on my shirt and began to strategize a way out of the situation. Did I have time to delete the account before Dad got home? Would that make it better or worse for me?

"Thea, go do the dishes," Mom said.

I ran my finger along the edge of the keyboard and then reluctantly headed to the kitchen.

■

When Dad got home, Mom called him into the kitchen and made me explain to him about the separate e-mail account. I told him Janie and I liked to use it because it was simple.

"Can we take care of this after dinner?" Dad set his briefcase on the counter.

Mom's face was instantly Saran wrapped again. "No. Take care of it now."

He put his hand on my shoulder and led me out of the kitchen. In the hallway, he accidentally bumped a picture off the wall and had to stop to hang it back up. At least it had landed on the forgiving carpet, and the glass didn't break. His jaw clenched, and he pointed me down the hall to my room.

"Show me." He waved his hand toward the monitor. I logged in and opened the e-mail account. His stomach growled in my quiet room, and I squirmed in my chair.

"Cynthia, the reason we don't want you to open random e-mail accounts is because of all the inappropriate spam you can receive." The fact he used my full name was a bad sign. I tried to recall the last time he even came into my room, but I could only remember the time when we redecorated.

"We need to cancel this e-mail account," he said.

"I can do it." I went through the necessary steps. I didn't know how, but I quickly figured it out, because I didn't want Dad poking around on my system. I deleted old e-mails regularly, but I could see three new messages sitting in my inbox, all from Derek.

At first, I thought Dad hadn't noticed them, but as I clicked through screens to delete the account, he asked, "Who's Derek?"

I finished before I answered his question. "A kid from school."

Mom appeared in the doorway. "Did you read her e-mails?"

"No," Dad said. "The account is removed."

"I don't understand what the big deal is," I said. "Most people don't even use e-mail anymore. They text or use Facebook. I hardly use Facebook, and I only text Janie. You can check." I stood and handed them my phone, but neither of them reached for it.

"Thea, the Internet can be a dangerous place," Mom said for the trillionth time.

"Oh. My. Gosh. Mom." I kicked the trash can and crumpled up quotes flew across the floor. "I'm not stupid. Stop worrying about how safe everything is. I could die crossing the street tomorrow, but I won't get killed e-mailing Janie."

"Take the computer away, Robert." Mom crossed her arms and glared at me.

Dad put his hand on Mom's shoulder. "Maggie. Let's go talk about this." She continued to stare at me for a moment longer and then walked out of my room. Dad followed, and in the distance, I heard their bedroom door slam. Their voices were muffled, and I couldn't make out what they said, but I could tell they argued. Over me. Not good. I took the opportunity, closed my door, and texted Derek.

*Trouble w/parents. e-mail acct deleted. not sure when I can get online again—Thea*

*RU ok? Can we still txt?—Derek*

*Don't know gotta go. Don't txt back—Thea*

I deleted the texts to and from Derek, and someone rapped on my door, sending my heart into my throat. I swallowed and opened the door. Seth scowled at me.

"What the crap are you doing?" he asked.

"Nothing. What's your problem?"

"Why do you think the rules don't apply to you?"

"Go away," I said and started to close the door, but Seth's foot blocked it.

"Grow up, Thea." He jerked his foot out and left. I closed the door, leaned against the wall, and then slumped to the floor.

A heavy knock on my door startled me, again.

"Come in," I said without moving. Dad appeared surprised to see me sitting on the floor.

"I need to take away the power supply to your computer, and I need to take your cell phone. You've lost these privileges for keeping the new e-mail account a secret."

"Okay," I said. There was nothing I could do about it. But at least I had gotten a message off to Derek so he wouldn't wonder what happened to me.

■

The next day at school, I asked Janie if she would send a message on *Skadi* to Kit for me. She still didn't know that I knew Derek's real name, so I carefully used his *Skadi* nickname with her. She hesitated and crossed her arms.

"Please, Janie. I need him to know I haven't deserted him."

"This is the perfect opportunity to do just that."

"I can't. Not like this," I said. "Please help me."

"You're my best friend, and that requires me to help you, but I think it's a bad idea."

I linked my arm through hers. "Thanks, you're the best ever."

■

A week passed. My family sat around the kitchen table and ate chicken stir-fry. Through the windows I watched yellow and scarlet leaves float from the trees down to the ground.

"May I have my computer and cell phone back?" I asked.

Mom set her fork down while Dad continued to eat. She began a lecture about honesty, choices, and consequences. Sigh.

"But what do I have to do to earn my stuff back?" I asked in my most polite tone of voice.

"Be honest in all your dealings and clean your room," Mom said and went back to eating. Nice.

"Dad?" I asked.

He raised his fork at me. "Your mom already answered you." He shredded his chicken into tiny little pieces and mashed them into the rice.

I pushed away from the table and went to my room. I started to pick up my dirty socks from yesterday, but then sank on the floor next to my CD player. I popped in one of the CDs Derek had recommended. The lyrics made me picture him in his room all alone and sad about his parents. He couldn't even talk to me now.

■

Over the next couple of weeks, I finished up the volleyball season, my school work continued at its normal pace, and I drudged through the days. Several of my teachers, and even Coach Gavyn, pulled me aside and asked if I was okay. They thought I looked sad, and they were right. My parents kept me so busy after school with chores I barely had time to finish my homework, let alone go over to Janie's house to try to use her computer.

My parents filled Saturdays with yard work and Sundays with family activities. But not yoga. Ever since I violated Mom's trust, we stopped going. I didn't bother to ask why. What was the point? I needed my computer and cell phone back. I even tried to access *Skadi* from school, but Janie explained that they had firewalls to prevent students from accessing unauthorized websites. Great. The whole world was working against my contacting Derek.

I constantly asked Janie to send messages to Derek. She agreed to send him one every week, but Derek's only response was cryptic. He probably didn't want Janie to know how close we were. So, he'd said he'd keep *Skadi* going until I got back. I wanted to borrow Janie's phone to text Derek, but she'd freak if I even asked. I missed him. More than I expected. I was lost.

# CHAPTER 13

I sank into my chair and smacked the side of the computer. Today was the day after Thanksgiving, and it had been a month since my parents took my cell phone and the power supply to my computer. I missed being online. I missed my e-mail. But what I really missed . . . was Derek. What was he doing? Where was he? I picked up the cordless house phone and considered dialing his number, but I feared the long distance call would show up on my parents' bill. Right then, Mom opened my door, and I nearly fell out of my chair. I wish she would learn to knock.

"Janie's here," she said.

"Really?" I hadn't even heard the doorbell. I set the phone down and hurried to the entryway.

"Hey!" I said. "How was your Thanksgiving?"

Janie put her hand to her chest and tried to catch her breath.

"What's wrong with you?"

She held up a finger and took another lungful of air. "I ran . . . over here."

"Why?"

"Let's go to your room." She grabbed my arm and led the way.

We climbed onto my bed and sat cross-legged facing each other.

"You want to take off your coat?" I asked. "You're flushed."

She narrowed her eyes at me and wiped beads of sweat from her forehead with the cuff of her sleeve. "I'm fine," she said.

"Then . . . spill."

"Something happened on *Skadi* . . ." She took a shaky breath and then clutched my hands. "Tim was online with Kit a few days ago. They're in a different guild together—"

105

"Since when? How do you know this? Has Tim said something to Kit I should—"

"Hold up!" Janie squeezed my hands. "I'm trying to tell you. I don't know how they got in a guild together. Frankly, I can't imagine how anyone would have time to be in more than one. But anyway . . . Tim said there are only guys in that guild and Kit spouts off all the time about how he has a bunch of girls wrapped around his finger. Tim pushed him for more information, but Kit wouldn't go into any details, just talked about how gullible girls are—"

"Kit would never say that. It must've been someone else with a similar screen name—"

"Wait! It gets worse," she said.

I yanked my hands free, and Janie recoiled. I doubted the truth of her recycled hand-me-down story.

"Kit is not a good guy," Janie said. "I logged onto *Skadi* this morning after getting back from Black Friday shopping, and he was online. He chatted with me for a while and never mentioned you. I asked him if he'd talked to Red lately because she hasn't been on in a long time. He typed, 'Red's dead.'" Janie stopped talking.

I threw my hands into the air. "And?"

"And?" Janie mocked me. "I asked him why he said that, and he said he was just kidding. That he didn't know anything about Red."

"So, he was joking."

"Thea!" She swatted my leg. "I called Tim right after and told him what Kit said. Tim fished for information in the other guild. He found out Red's real name and did a Google search. She's really dead—"

"Shut up. She is not." My head started to spin. There was no way that Red was dead.

"When Tim asked Kit if he'd ever been to Hawaii, Kit had him kicked out of the guild and posted a message to all Guild Leaders that Tim shouldn't be added to their guilds. He blacklisted Tim from the game. Why would Kit do that if he didn't have something to hide? Maybe Kit killed Red."

"Or maybe Tim made the whole thing up. Did you consider that?" I grabbed my pillow and cradled it in my lap.

"Why would he? Type it into Google yourself. Her name was Lokelani Fisher—"

"You don't know that. There's no proof that's her real name," I said.

"Her first name means 'small red rose.' She told us that on *Skadi*—"

"Maybe we should google how many girls are named Lokelani in Hawaii. It's not her."

"Kit had something to do with this," Janie said and poked my pillow.

"If you are so sure, call the police." She didn't respond. So, I continued. "It's not true. Once I talk to him, he can prove it."

"This has gone too far," Janie said. "You don't even know this guy."

"Yes, I do. I'm in love with him." Janie cringed at my words, and my fingers flinched in my pillow.

"Stay off *Skadi*, Thea. I'm not going on ever again, and I'm not messaging Kit ever again for you."

"You're overreacting." I shook my head. None of it was true. We stared at each other for a few seconds. Stalemate.

"I've got to go. My family's going back out for more Black Friday deals." She hopped off the bed—her ringlets rebounding in the process—and headed for the door. Before she left, she turned and faced me. "I'm sorry it's not what you want to hear, but you need to stay away from Kit."

Then she simply walked out.

I threw my pillow at the door and jumped off the bed. I sat in front of my computer and touched the keyboard. Little bumps on the F and J keys told my index fingers they were properly placed. I traced the edges of the D key and wondered about Derek. I needed my connection back. I needed the truth. I picked up the house phone to call him.

"What are you doing?" Dad's voice scared the snot out of me, and my shoulders jerked backward.

I dropped the phone in my lap and took a deep breath. There he was, in the doorway, holding up my cell phone and the power cord to my computer. He grinned. My gloom began to lift.

While Dad attached the power cord, Mom came in and hammered out the rules, one by one.

"Don't close your door when you're on the Internet." She held up two fingers. "Don't give out personal information." Three fingers. "Don't visit websites we haven't approved." Four fingers, and I had to freeze my eyeballs so they wouldn't roll in frustration. "Don't create secret e-mail accounts." Oh. My. Gosh. She continued on with every rule imaginable, but I kept still and endured it. I'd waited four solid weeks to get my computer back, and I didn't want to blow it now.

Dad patted her on the arm and smiled. Mom took the cue and relented. They both left.

I tried to text Derek, but the cell battery was dead. I plugged it into the charger and logged into *Skadi* instead. My parents couldn't blame me for that. I hadn't been on my computer for a month. I hoped Derek was online. I waited to see what character names popped up on the screen from my friends list—no Kitsuneshin.

I opened another Internet window and pulled up Google. My fingers trembled, and I refused to type in Red's maybe-name, Lokelani. Surely, Tim's jealousy had gotten the best of him; he made up the story. Of course, Janie would choose to believe Tim, because she'd never liked Derek. But it couldn't be true. Instead, I typed *Derek Felton* into Google. I scrolled through dozens and dozens of images, but none of them matched the picture he'd sent me. The various websites listed realtors, broadcasters, and athletes.

None of them were my Derek, and I didn't want to spend hours sifting through pages of irrelevant information.

Next, I typed *Kitsuneshin* into Google. It was a popular name in Japanese anime. I watched some of the videos on YouTube. I found a file uploaded to Photobucket called Soul Eaters. It contained more Japanese anime. When I clicked on a manga game link, an advertisement popped up showing women scantily dressed. It was then that I realized my door was open, and I was risking my computer privileges by doing this search. I closed the manga website and walked over to my door. I heard the television in the distance, and Mom and Dad talking over it. I had a few minutes, at least. I went back to the computer and clicked on the next page of the Google search.

Either Derek played a lot of online games or Kitsuneshin was a common username because the second page of the search listed all sorts of sites with usernames matching Kit's. I didn't bother clicking on any of them. The next page of links took me to an Asian girl's blog, MySpace, and Facebook pages. That didn't help.

About fifteen pages into the search, I discovered an old Japanese legend. First, it explained that *kitsune* meant "fox" and *shin* meant "new." Together, *kitsune-shin*, meant "new fox." But not just any fox, a trickster. The story read:

*One late afternoon, a greedy merchant arrived home and noticed a fox's tail hanging over the edge of his home's roof. He hoped it was only a fox, but his instincts told him it was a trickster. He ran into his home to check for his box of gold pieces hidden beneath the bookcase. The furniture inside the home had been overturned. His heart raced when he saw his young daughter sitting at the table counting the gold.*

*"What are you doing?" he asked. She looked up at him, but the eyes were not her own. Instead the eyes that stared back at him were the eyes of the trickster. It was then the greedy old*

*merchant noticed the ear-like tufts coming out from her hair, where her ears should have been. When the form of his daughter stood, a fox's tail swung up from behind her. The trickster had possessed her.*

*The greedy merchant reached for his box of gold. But she was faster. She snapped the lid down on the box and held it tight to her chest. She smiled and walked out of the house. He followed her, unsure what to do. He did not want to harm his daughter, but he did not want her to take his life's savings either. The fox, the kitsune-shin, that had been resting on the roof jumped down and sniffed the feet of the merchant's daughter. The kitsune-shin pranced out of the yard and down the road. The merchant's daughter followed closely behind. The merchant knew it would cost him less to let his daughter follow the kitsune-shin than it would for him to pursue the trickster.*

The story piqued my curiosity. I wondered if it was the trickster's fault, the daughter's fault, or the father's fault. How could the fox be blamed if the daughter wanted to go with him? Maybe it was the father's fault because he left his daughter alone and didn't guard his money better.

I printed it out and went on to read additional stories. Many more described how the kitsune-shin bewitched the women and girls and played cruel tricks on the samurais and townspeople. According to the stories and legends, kitsune-shin could convince females of any age to do their bidding. And the devoted women were pleased to do it. I printed the stories, so I could read more later. I exited out of the Google screen and closed all of the Internet windows, except for *Skadi*.

Kit was online. Finally. I touched his name that appeared on the monitor, and my heart filled with hope.

# CHAPTER 14

My life had been restored to me, like I'd finished a long hike through the desert and had earned a reward of vanilla ice cream and fresh brownies, except this was better. I opened a private chat with Kit and typed.

**ImmortalSlayer:** hello.

No response.

I waited for an eternity.

**ImmortalSlayer:** hello?

Kit's name disappeared from the list. What just happened? I exited out of *Skadi* and logged in again, hoping it was a game glitch. Still no Kit.

I grabbed my cell and powered it on. I sent him a message and asked him to call or text. I tried to play *Skadi* for a few minutes, but it wasn't any fun without Kit or Janie. I logged off and checked my phone for messages. Nothing. I grabbed the pages from the printer, climbed into bed, and read the stories about kitsune-shin.

"I assumed you'd be playing *Skadi*," Dad said at my door.

"No."

"Why not? You were dying to have your computer back and now you're not using it?" What could I say? Nothing. So I shrugged. "Well, we're in the family room if you want to join us." He left. I figured Mom had sent him to check on me.

Before going to bed that night, I checked *Skadi* again. Kit still wasn't on, and he hadn't replied to my text. I went to sleep with my cell next to me. I had set it to vibrate mode, but I'd be able to feel it if Derek sent a text. He didn't.

■

During the night, I had a dream about a rollercoaster. I stuck my hands in the air and screamed when the car plummeted down the rails. I caught my breath during the boring part of the ride when the cars chugged and vibrated up the steep tracks. But something seemed wrong with the coaster. It crested the top and lingered on the precipice, about to rocket down the other side, and that's when I saw there were no more rails. The cars flew off and plummeted toward the earth. I couldn't breathe. I couldn't scream. I needed someone to save me before I hit the ground. The car trembled beneath me, but the shaking was out of place, and everything became foggy in the dream. I never hit the ground. I woke up instead. My phone was vibrating, and I was sweating.

I grabbed the phone and pushed the Talk button but too late. The missed call log showed Derek's number. I listened for a phone message. Nothing. A text buzzed through.

*I am on Skadi right now.—Derek*

I hopped out of bed and started my computer. While I waited, I texted Derek back.

*I was worried. U didnt reply last night. RU ok?—Thea*

I logged onto *Skadi* as fast as I could. There was his name: Kitsuneshin. I let out a breath I didn't even realize I was holding. Kit opened a private chat box with me.

**Kitsuneshin:** Hi
**ImmortalSlayer:** Hi.
**ImmortalSlayer:** RU ok?
**Kitsuneshin:** Ya
**ImmortalSlayer:** Why didn't you answer me last night?
**Kitsuneshin:** Not feeling well.
**ImmortalSlayer:** RU sick?
**Kitsuneshin:** No
**ImmortalSlayer:** What?

**ImmortalSlayer:** Tell me.

**Kitsuneshin:** Just got home from hospital

**ImmortalSlayer:** What?!

**Kitsuneshin:** I saw u online last night but I couldn't talk yet.

**ImmortalSlayer:** What RU saying?

**ImmortalSlayer:** Why were you in the hospital? Why couldn't you talk to me last night?

**Kitsuneshin:** My dad took me to ER to get my stomach pumped.

**ImmortalSlayer:** What for?

**Kitsuneshin:** I took a bunch of pills with a lot of wine—they had to pump it out of my stomach.

**ImmortalSlayer:** You told me you would never do that again!

**ImmortalSlayer:** Why would u?

**Kitsuneshin:** I can't live without you.

**Kitsuneshin:** I realized your parents were never going to let you talk to me again and I couldn't bear to be alone.

I leaned back in my chair. What if he killed himself because of me? My cheeks burned with anger, and my jaw tightened. I heard footsteps in the hall. I typed:

**ImmortalSlayer:** brb

I closed the private chat box and jumped up to open my door just as Mom began to knock.

"Hi," I said.

"Good morning." Mom peered over my shoulder. "Are you using the computer with your door closed?"

"I barely turned it on. I'm trying to follow your rules."

"Keep the door open."

I agreed, and she left. I angled my monitor away from the door, and I reopened the private chat box.

**ImmortalSlayer:** Sorry. Parents are enforcing rules. I don't want to lose computer and cell again.

**Kitsuneshin:** See? That's what I mean. Your parents are going to do everything they can to keep us apart. I can't live without u Thea. I love you too much.

**ImmortalSlayer:** You can live without me, but u don't have to. I'm right here. I'm not going anywhere.

**Kitsuneshin:** Do you still love me?

**ImmortalSlayer:** How can you ask that? Of course I do. But, I'd be very mad if u hurt yourself. You have to promise never to try that again. I can't handle that stress. Please promise.

**Kitsuneshin:** I'll promise if you promise to never leave me again.

**ImmortalSlayer:** I didn't leave you. I had Janie send you messages on *Skadi* every week.

**Kitsuneshin:** She sent me one right after you lost your computer. I wanted so badly to talk to you, but I thought you were ignoring me.

**ImmortalSlayer:** RU saying she sent you only one message in the entire four weeks?

**Kitsuneshin:** Yes

**ImmortalSlayer:** That's not what she told me.

**Kitsuneshin:** And she was never on *Skadi* for me to ask her if you were ok.

**ImmortalSlayer:** She said she sent u msgs & you two talked on *Skadi*.

**Kitsuneshin:** Did you see her send the messages?

**ImmortalSlayer:** No, but I can't believe she'd lie to me.

**Kitsuneshin:** She was trying in her own way to protect you. Don't blame her. Don't even tell her you know. You can't always trust people. They lie. My dad lies to me all the time. I hate it. I feel like UR the only one who tells me the truth. The only one I can trust. I hope u know u can trust me, no matter what. I love you.

**ImmortalSlayer:** I love you too. I know I can trust you. I am mad to think Janie lied to me.

**Kitsuneshin:** Don't be mad. Forget it, and let's just focus on us for a while.

**ImmortalSlayer:** Ok. I've missed u.

**Kitsuneshin:** Me too. Please never let us go this long without talking again. I can't take it.

**ImmortalSlayer:** I promise if you promise to never hurt yourself again.

**Kitsuneshin:** I promise. I wish we could touch. I need to be near you. Hold you

**ImmortalSlayer:** We could talk on the phone and at least hear each other's voices.

**ImmortalSlayer:** But I'm still worried my parents will catch me

**Kitsuneshin:** What can you do?

**ImmortalSlayer:** I'll just tell them I'm going for a walk.

**Kitsuneshin:** Do it! I can hardly wait to hear your voice. Love U!!

**ImmortalSlayer:** Love u too. Talk to u soon.

I logged off *Skadi* and drummed my fingers against my desk. First things first. I had to pick out an outfit, and then I had to take a cute new picture to send him. I rummaged through the clothes hanging in my closet and chose a bright pink top. I ran to the bathroom and took a super fast shower, but before I could finish, Seth yelled and pounded on the bathroom door. At least this door had a lock on it.

"Just a minute," I hollered back at him.

"Hurry up. Other people need to use the bathroom."

I finished in the shower and decided to take my time fixing my hair, because I knew Seth was waiting impatiently. Oh well. While I ironed my hair straight, I contemplated the possibility of Janie lying to me. Why would she? But why would Derek lie? He wouldn't have attempted suicide if she had sent the messages. He must be telling the truth. Janie always wanted me to leave Derek and hook up with Tim. It made sense that she never sent the messages. Plus, she made up that crazy story about Derek killing Red. Seriously? How could a twenty-year-old guy even afford to fly clear to Hawaii and manage to kill someone with no witnesses? I was sure that Janie and Tim concocted the story to convince me to leave Derek. Once my hair hung perfectly, I snapped a couple of pictures with my cell phone.

Seth pounded again. I gathered my things and opened the door.

"What took so long?" he asked. "And why do you have your phone? Can't you go five minutes without talking to Janie?"

"Shut up." I moved past him, and once in my room, I texted Derek the newest picture of me and asked him to send me a new one of him. I knew he worried that I'd be disappointed with what I saw, but I wished he'd just send another picture. I loved him, no matter what he looked like. Derek didn't reply right away.

I found my parents at the kitchen table reading the newspaper.

"I'm going for a walk."

They both gawked at me.

"Okay," Mom said, and they went back to the newspaper.

Once out of the house, I wrapped my fuzzy pink scarf around my collar twice like a turtle neck and zipped up my coat to protect me from the cold. I walked down the sidewalk, and after I rounded the corner of our block, I pulled off one glove to dial Derek's number. I'd wanted this for so long, but I was still apprehensive. What if I said something stupid? I stared at the glowing numbers on the phone, knowing that when I tapped the Talk button, I'd connect with someone who loved me. I was sure he did. Finally I pressed it, wiggled my hand back into my glove, and held the phone up to my ear.

"Hello," Derek said in a deep chesty tone.

"Hi." I nearly choked. I was hearing Derek's voice for the first time. It may have been thirty degrees outside, but sweat formed on my spine and butterflies danced throughout my body.

"I can't believe we are speaking to each other." He coughed and cleared his throat.

"Me neither."

"What should we talk about?" he asked.

"I have no idea," I said, proud that I strung more than two words together.

"Are you terribly cold?"

"Yes."

"Well, at least you've got a great scarf to keep your neck warm." I stopped walking.

A shadow fell across a bush at the end of the street. I wanted to scan the area around me, but I couldn't budge an inch. I thought I had been alone, but how could he have known about my scarf? I forced myself to ask.

"How'd you know I'm wearing a scarf?"

He coughed and cleared his throat. "You said it's freezing out. I assumed you'd have a scarf. If you don't, then I need to buy one and send it to you right away."

"Oh." I checked over my right shoulder and then my left. I whirled around and inspected the area behind me. No one. Why was I freaking myself out? Evidently, I'd watched too many creepy late night shows. I shook off the eerie sensation and relaxed.

"Are you going to freeze to death?" he asked.

"No," I said and snickered.

"Why is that funny?" he asked.

"Because the weather here is frigid, but I'm so excited to talk to you, I'm sweating! Oh wait, that isn't a flattering thing to say. Forget that. Oh sheesh. I'm making a terrible first impression."

"You can't make a terrible first impression when I'm already in love with you."

"Really?" How did I ever get so lucky? I could barely contain my bubbling delight.

"Of course, Thea. There's nothing you could do that would ever disappoint me."

"You're so sweet to me."

"I don't ever want to lose you. I'll fight hard to keep you in my life."

"Don't worry. You'll never lose me."

I wanted to ask him about Red, but couldn't muster the courage. Plus, he just got out of the hospital, and I didn't want to upset him. So, we spoke about day-to-day things instead. I moved like a lazy dog around the neighborhood. I kicked rocks and twirled my scarf while we talked. Thirty minutes passed, but it seemed like five. Before we ended our conversation, we agreed to meet on *Skadi* in an hour.

I tucked my scarf back into my coat collar and hurried home.

I finally had what I always wanted. Someone who understood me, confided in me, and loved me. I was complete with him.

# CHAPTER 15

Monday morning arrived, and that meant back to school for me. This had been the best Thanksgiving break ever, but this was going to be the worst Monday ever. Janie had phoned several times over the weekend, but I refused her calls. Even when Mom brought me the house phone, I shook my head. Mom apologized to Janie and said I wasn't able to take the call.

The rest of the weekend had flown by in a whirlwind. Derek and I chatted via *Skadi* and texts. We didn't have an opportunity for a long personal conversation again, because my parents constantly checked in on me. However, after they went to bed, I texted Derek, and he phoned. Both calls Saturday night and Sunday night only lasted a minute or two—he simply wanted my voice to be the last thing he heard before he went to sleep.

Even though Monday morning came too fast, I was up before my alarm went off and got ready faster than ever. I wanted to be gone before Janie arrived. In the kitchen, Mom cleaned up after Dad's breakfast, while he grabbed his things and rushed out the door, as usual. My parents never changed.

The kitchen smelled of orange juice and scorched eggs. Mom had a habit of cooking the scrambled eggs too long. I'd take mine runny over scorched any day. Seth hunched over the edge of the counter reading the comics and finishing off a bowl of Frosted Flakes while Mom continued to wipe the spotless granite counter.

"Hey, Mom," I started.

"Hey, baby-girl. You're up early."

"Yeah, I was hoping you could drive me to school."

She stopped wiping. "Why?"

"I left a project at school that's due today. I meant to bring it home, but forgot."

"I can take you," Seth said. "I'm leaving in two minutes."

Mom and I stared at him in disbelief. "Really?" we asked simultaneously.

"Sure. Marcus and I have to be there early to work on a project for our government class. So, it's no problem, but don't make it a habit." Seth shoved another spoonful into his mouth. Clearly, he was possessed.

"What about Janie?" Mom asked.

"I'll send her a text and let her know I'm going in early."

"Are things all right between the two of you?"

"Yeah, we're fine. I wasn't in the mood to talk on the phone, and you know, once Janie gets going, it can be a long conversation." I hoped she believed both stories.

Seth and I left a couple of minutes later. We stopped in front of Marcus's house and Seth honked. Marcus came bounding out but halted midstep when he noticed me sitting in the front seat. He raised his eyebrows, and then he grabbed the handle of the back door and climbed in.

"Hey, Thea," he said in an usually high sing-song voice.

"Hey." I grinned at him.

"Still playing *Skadi*?" Marcus asked.

I twisted around and narrowed my eyes at him. "A little," I said. "Why? Are you still playing it?" Maybe he had a new username.

"She's on there all the time," Seth interrupted.

"Am not."

"Yes."

"Shut up."

"You want to get out and walk?" Seth jerked his thumb toward the road, and I shook my head. So much for my brother being nice to me for once. I rode the rest of the way without speaking. Marcus and Seth didn't say much either. Seth blasted the radio, and we all ignored each other.

Few people, mostly teachers, were at school so early. I went to the cafeteria, grabbed a free breakfast, and parked myself. The lights hummed overhead. The space appeared much brighter than normal, as though everything had been deep cleaned while we were gone. From where I sat, I could hear the kitchen staff working behind the counter. I never really noticed them before, because the cafeteria usually buzzed and jumped with hundreds of people coming and going, eating and talking, laughing and yelling.

I phoned Derek.

"Hello," he said and coughed twice. My stomach tingled at the sound of his raspy voice. "Sorry, my throat is still sore from having the tube shoved down it last week."

"Every time you mention that, I want to hit you and hold you at the same time."

"Why?"

"I want to hit you because I can't handle the stress of you dying . . ." Especially if it's because you weren't able to get ahold of me, and because attempting suicide is one of the most selfish things a person can do. But, of course, I couldn't tell him all of that. Instead I said, "I want to hold you to show you how much I love you."

"That would be nice," he said. "I'd like to wrap my arms around you and feel the warmth of your body next to mine. I'd never let go." The image lingered in my mind until he spoke again. "What are your plans for the day?"

"Only boring school. How about you?"

"Only boring work." He chuckled and coughed again. I told him how I'd avoided Janie and the bus stop, but I wouldn't be able to dodge her much longer, because we had second period together.

I had intended to leave the cafeteria for my first class before any of the buses arrived, but I had gotten so caught up in the conversation—and the rhythmic sound of Derek's voice—I'd lost track of time. Suddenly, Janie was hovering to my left.

"What is wrong with you?" she asked.

I spoke into the phone to Derek, "I've got to go."

"Good luck," he said. He must've heard Janie's voice in the background. I put my phone away and rotated in my seat to face her.

"The only thing wrong with me is a lying friend named Janie."

"I never lied to you." She plopped down next to me, and I had to scoot over so she wouldn't be in my bubble. Most people gained weight over the Thanksgiving holiday, but Janie seemed to have lost weight. Her cheeks sagged in and her jaw protruded out. I wondered how she could change so much in just a couple of days.

"You said you messaged Derek every week on *Skadi*," I said.

"Who's Derek?"

"Derek is Kit. And he said you only messaged him once."

"You know his real name?" Janie asked.

"He loves me. You need to come to terms with that, or we can't be friends anymore—" I bit my lip, but the words were already out, and I couldn't take them back.

"I'm your best friend. Why would you believe someone you don't even know over me? Think about this—"

"If you can't admit that you lied to me, we're done."

A tear rolled down Janie's cheek. I fidgeted with my breakfast tray.

"Listen to yourself," Janie said. She grabbed my arm, but I jerked it away.

I stood and bent over her. "I am listening to myself. I'm also listening to the crazy impossible stories you've been telling me about Derek. You're trying to make me doubt him, because you are insecure and don't want to share me with anybody. Admit it. You are the liar here. You lie about dieting and eating. You lie about Derek. Who knows what else you're lying about."

Tears flowed down her face in thick black rivers, her mascara ruined. She rose and walked away. I let her go. Halfway across the cafeteria she started running and never looked back. The cafeteria, no longer bright and sparkling, filled with people and noise. I no longer heard the humming of the lights overhead, and the space seemed to darken after Janie left. I just ended my relationship with my best friend. This was the worst day of my life.

I went to the nurse's office and feigned the flu. Mom came and picked me up and put me straight to bed. I took refuge under my comforter and swapped texts with Derek all day.

# CHAPTER 16

I didn't set an alarm, because I had no intention of ever going back to school. I could not face Janie. I wanted to stay in the safety of my room.

Mom opened my door and flipped on the light. "Get up or you're going to miss the bus."

"I don't feel good. Could I have one more day? Please?"

She took a step into my room and studied the mess on the floor. "How can I get to your bed when I can't even walk on your carpet?"

"You don't need to."

Mom sighed. She strategically pushed things out of the way with her foot. She made it to the window and opened my blinds. Then she came closer to the bed and placed her hand on my forehead. "Are you all right, sweetheart?"

"I just don't feel good. Can I please stay home? I promise I'll go to school tomorrow." She stroked my hair and rested her hand on my cheek.

"Yes, but no TV or computer. If you're sick, you should stay in bed and rest. Otherwise clean this room. What happened anyway? Did a tornado strike in here?"

"I was cleaning. I don't want this stuff anymore." Like the soft purple sweater Janie let me wear home one day because I was cold, and I forgot to return it. The T-shirt from Rapid Shores—we had bought matching ones. The dangling earrings we made in arts and crafts. All of these things, and more, reminded me of Janie.

"I'll see if I can find some boxes for you." She tucked the covers in around me and kissed my cheek.

"Will you turn out the light?" I asked as she reached the door. She did, and I cuddled under my comforter. I started to doze back to sleep when my cell buzzed.

*Can I phone you? RU out of the house?—Derek*

*No. Staying home today.—Thea*

*RU OK?—Derek*

*I can't deal with Janie anymore—Thea*

*Forget her.—Derek*

*How will I ever be able to go back to school & face her?—Thea*

*Try to relax for now. Go back to sleep & txt me when u wake up.—Derek*

*Sounds good ☺—Thea*

*Love U—Derek*

*I love you too—Thea*

I tucked the phone next to my pillow, rolled over, and tried to sleep. About an hour later, Mom poked her head in my room.

"Are you awake?" she whispered.

"Yup."

"I'm going out for a couple of hours to run errands."

"Okay," I said and tried to not sound happy about her absence. When I heard the front door close, I dialed Derek.

"Hey, can you talk?" I asked.

"How can you be calling right now?" he whispered.

"My mom left for a couple of hours. If you have time, we can talk while she's gone."

"I always have time for you," he said.

At first, we talked about the weather here and the weather in Georgia. I couldn't believe he lived so far away. He asked me where I lived, and I told him Idaho. He asked where in Idaho, and I told him the southern part.

"Guess what I did yesterday?" he asked.

"I have no clue."

"I downloaded the ringtone for DeathTomb's 'It's Me and You, Eternally.' So, when you call my cell, it plays that song."

"So, is that our song now?"

"Always has been."

My heart floated, and I enjoyed the sensation.

"How old do you need to be before we can meet in person?" Derek asked.

"I don't know. What do you think?"

"Well, if you were eighteen, no one would argue your right to meet me."

"I don't know if I can wait that long—" I choked on my words. I wasn't sure if I wanted to continue this relationship that long, or if I wanted to see him sooner. I knew I loved him, but not knowing if he'd still be alive in three years and not knowing if I'd feel the same way toward him in three years confused me.

"We could meet sooner," he said.

"How?"

"I have money. I could come to Idaho."

"My parents would have a cow."

"Why would they need to know?"

"What do you mean?"

"Well, it's not like we'd be running off together. We could just meet in person, hold hands, and walk through the park, like a normal couple."

I took a slow breath to steady the dizziness that overcame me. "I like the way that sounds." I rolled over in bed and stared out the window. Could it be possible to walk through the park with Derek? I closed my eyes and imagined it.

"We are a couple, Thea. I love you."

"I love you, too." The words came easily. "When would we meet?" I asked and pictured the fantasy in my mind.

"What about after school one day?" he suggested.

"Basketball starts in a couple of weeks."

"Could we meet before practice?" he asked.

"I could skip a practice and be back to the school before my mom came to pick me up. Then they wouldn't know and get upset."

"Perfect!" Derek said.

I sat up in bed and worked out the details. "Tryouts are before Christmas break, and the season starts after. I wouldn't be able to miss any practices the first few weeks, and I can't miss any games—"

"What's the name of your team?" he asked.

"Skycrest Eagles."

"I'd like to watch you play," he said.

"No! I would be so nervous I wouldn't be able to pay attention."

"I could come and not tell you until after."

My vision blurred imagining Derek coming to a game. I wondered if he would, but then I knew he couldn't because he didn't know where I lived exactly.

"Don't worry, I won't," he said.

I breathed a sigh of relief, but my chest remained heavy.

"Whenever you want me to come, I'll be there."

"Promise you won't come to a game."

"I promise. I'm just happy to think that we're going to meet in person."

I put the image of Derek watching a game out of my mind and tried to come up with an easier way we could meet, something like the walk in the park he had mentioned.

Then I remembered Red.

"Have you gotten together with other people you've met online?" The question popped out before I had time to filter it.

"What do you mean?" Derek asked.

"Did you ever meet Red in person?"

"Why would you ask that?" His voice tensed.

"You used to flirt with her, and Janie said that you guys hooked up—"

"I flirted with her to make you jealous," Derek said. "I didn't think you were serious about me, and I had to find out somehow."

"Janie and Tim said you went to Hawaii to meet her." I could hear him breathing into the phone, and when he finally spoke, his words became louder and louder.

"Janie is a snarky little brat, and I don't know any Tim. They're both liars. I never went to Hawaii, and I'm not interested in Red. I'm pissed to think you'd even consider that."

"But once you were interested in Red. I know you were."

"Once, not anymore. She acted like a jealous child, and she got on my nerves."

"Would you have gone to Hawaii if she'd invited you?"

"No."

This was our first fight, and I didn't know how to handle it. How was I supposed to contradict him? "One more question and then I won't ever bring her up again," I said.

"What?" Derek punched the word out angrily. But I had to ask. I didn't know if I'd get the courage another time.

"Do you know why Red doesn't play *Skadi* anymore?"

"She doesn't have Internet access."

"Why not?"

"Her parents split up, and now she lives with her father on a fishing boat off the coast of Alaska."

"That can't be true." No way would a surfing Hawaiian girl want to live on a boat in Alaska, especially in the dead of winter.

"Are you calling me a liar?"

Maybe he was testing my trust with this strange story about Red. Besides, it didn't matter why she didn't play *Skadi* anymore. Better for me that she didn't because then I didn't have to worry about Derek cheating on me with her. How would he cheat anyway? It's an online relationship. I was losing my mind.

"You should get some rest before your mom gets home," he said.

"Are you mad at me?" I asked.

"I don't know." Neither of us said anything for a while, but we didn't hang up either. Finally Derek spoke. "I could never really be mad at you. I love you too much." His tender voice returned, and I wanted to believe him. We said goodbye, and I checked the clock.

I figured I had at least thirty minutes before Mom would return. I scooted out of bed and powered up my computer. I googled Alaskan fishing boats, but that was a waste of time. So, I googled Lokelani Fisher, Hawaii, and got a ton of results.

### Fifteen-Year-Old Girl Found Dead Near Hilo

*Investigators responded to a 911 call when a homeowner reported a young girl's body left inside his vacation rental. Police said the girl matched a missing person's report. Detectives utilized dental records to verify the identification. The girl's parents said she had gone for a bicycle ride two days prior and never returned. Police stated the girl had been sexually assaulted. There are no leads on the perpetrator. The police are asking anyone who knows anything about this young woman or this crime to please come forward. The family is offering a $25,000 reward for information that leads to the capture and prosecution of the murderer.*

This still didn't prove anything about Red, because there was also a link about a fifteen-year-old Hawaiian girl named Lokelani who won an art contest. Maybe that one was Red. Maybe it wasn't. I had to call Janie. It was lunchtime, so I texted her.

*Plz call me asap. I'm sorry! I need ur help.—Thea*

She didn't call, and I can't say I blamed her. All day I worked the details over in my mind. The story Derek told about the fishing boat. The story Tim told about Derek. Whether or not Janie lied about messaging Derek. Who was I supposed to believe?

Three o'clock. Janie should be home from school. I called her cell. No answer. I called the home phone. No answer. I needed to talk to her.

I found Mom sorting socks in the laundry room. "Can I run over to Janie's house?"

"No."

"Why not?"

"Because you stayed home today. If you are too sick for school you are too sick to run over to Janie's house. If you are feeling better, go clean your room."

"Then can I go to Janie's?"

Mom dropped a pair of socks and glared at me. "No, but you can clean your room regardless." Defeated, I walked away.

If Janie had told me the truth, I wanted to keep the things that reminded me of her. I looked through the various items on my floor. I picked up an armful of clothes and shoved them into my hamper. It was full, but I didn't want to make multiple trips back and forth to the laundry room. So, I leaned forward with all my weight and smashed the clothes down tighter into the hamper. Then I scooped up another pile and shoved them in, too. I considered standing on the load inside the hamper and jumping, but instead I stood back and looked around at the work to be done. My phone vibrated. I snatched it hoping it was Janie, but it was Derek.

*I'm on Skadi. Can u get on?—Derek*

*No. I can't do computer today—Thea*

*Bummer. Can I call u?—Derek*

*No. Mom is home.—Thea*

*Ok. I have to work later. Guess I'll talk 2u tomorrow.—Derek*

*K—Thea*

I flopped on my bed and sent Janie another text saying I was sorry and please call me. She didn't respond. I reached over and ripped the next page off my Quote of the Day calendar. I threw it at the trash can. Missed.

*You and I ought not to die before we have explained ourselves to each other. —John Adams*

Seriously? That seemed extreme. I smacked the quote with my hand and grabbed my alarm clock. I set it for early the next day. I had to get to the bus stop and talk to Janie before school.

# CHAPTER 17

The next morning, I walked so fast to the bus stop that I occasionally broke out into a jog. I couldn't run the whole way, because I didn't want to smell sweaty, but I had to find Janie. I needed someone to talk to about my situation with Derek, and she was the only person who knew what was going on. I arrived early, and of the usual crowd, three girls were there. They gawked at me and then moved into a huddle. Whatever. I didn't need them, I needed Janie. More people arrived, but not her. Where was she? A few minutes later, the Three Stooges strolled up to me.

"Thea," Tim said.

"Do you know where Janie is?" I asked. The other guys made snorting sounds, and Tim whacked Josh.

"Her mom started driving her yesterday," Tim said, never taking his eyes off me. "What'd you do to her?"

"Nothing!" But I did. I broke eye contact with him and searched the street for the bus. My throat tightened and my cheeks began to heat up, but I refused to get emotional in front of these guys. I had to keep control. I remembered shoving my dirty laundry into the hamper yesterday, pushing more clothes than should've been allowed, but I kept stuffing until the lid wouldn't close. And now, in the same way, I shoved my anger down harder until it seemed no more could fit. But more could fit, if I stuffed a little harder.

Tim touched my arm and startled me. He hadn't touched me since last summer at Rapid Shores. I realized we were alone. Josh and Taylor had left to go flirt with the girls.

"Janie said you believe Kit over her. She also said you know his real name." I didn't say anything. "Thea, he could be dangerous. If you know his real name we should tell someone."

"He's not dangerous," I said, but then wanted to kick myself. Why was I defending him? Yesterday, I thought he might be. That was the whole reason I needed to talk to Janie.

"You can't know either way," Tim said. He waited for me to respond, but I remained silent. "Janie and I are worried about you."

"Then why hasn't she answered my messages?" My throat tightened more. We had been best friends for years, and the last person I ever imagined discussing this with was Tim.

"Janie told her mom—"

"What?" My stomach knotted.

He gripped my elbow. "She was worried about you. She talked to me first but ended up telling her mom, too. And because of that, her mom took away her cell phone and her computer, and she's driving Janie to school because she doesn't want her around you anymore."

"Why didn't Janie talk to me first?"

"She tried."

"When?"

"Thanksgiving break."

All those phone calls I refused. "I thought she lied about contacting Kit," I said.

"She's grounded because she messaged him for you. Janie's mom even read them."

My mouth fell open. If Janie sent the messages, that meant Derek lied to me. The world was crashing down around me, and I couldn't catch all of the broken pieces.

"Is she going to tell my mom?" I asked.

"I don't know." The bus stopped and flashed its red lights.

"Come on," Tim said. We climbed the steps, and I followed him to the middle where he motioned for me to share a bench with him. I hesitated, but realized I had no better option.

My cell buzzed, and the screen displayed Derek's name.

"Who's Derek?" Tim asked, leaning against me so he could see the phone. I clutched it to my chest, and locked eyes with Tim. The color drained from his face. I'd never seen that happen to him before. Bile burned its way up my throat.

"Is that Kit?" Tim asked. "You gave him your number?" He lowered his voice but punched out each word. "Thea, what are you doing?"

"Nothing. We're just friends." My phone buzzed again, and I held it tighter.

"Just friends? Last summer you said he was your boyfriend." Tim glared at me. Then he faced forward and raked his fingers through his hair. What right did he have to be mad at me?

"She swore she wouldn't say anything. Who knows what else she's lied about—"

"Janie hasn't lied," Tim said. I pulled back from him, too far, and fell into the aisle, dropping my phone in the process. Everyone broke out in hysterics, except for Tim. He picked my cell up from the floor and handed it back to me.

"Thanks," I said. He popped his knuckles and gazed out the window. I watched him for a few seconds, but he didn't move. I hurried and read the two messages from Derek.

*Where RU?—Derek*

*Why aren't U answering?—Derek*

I texted back to tell him now was a bad time. I slid the phone in my backpack and folded my hands across my lap.

"Hey, Thea!" Josh yelled from across the bus. "You should hold onto Tim so you don't fall off the seat again!" I ignored him and the snarky comments that followed. I imagined shoving more laundry into my hamper.

Tim broke the silence after an eternity. "Janie and I are your real friends, not this Derek or Kit or whoever he is."

"Friends?" The word escaped me. Tim and I had never been friends. I had a crush on him a year ago. That's all.

"Yes, friends."

The bus pulled into the lot and people piled out.

"Let's find Janie," Tim grabbed my arm. Why did he think it was all right to touch me so much? And yet, I allowed him to lead me to the cafeteria like I didn't already know where it was. Janie sat at a table in the corner, not our usual table, holding an apple. She bit off a large chunk as we approached. Tim pushed me into the seat across from Janie, and then sat down next to me.

"Thea wants to talk to you," Tim said and waved me on like he was a crossing guard telling me it was safe to go.

"I'm sorry," I said.

"What is wrong with you?" Janie asked. Tears welled in her eyes. She dropped the remaining apple on the tray and shoved it away.

"What are you talking about?" I asked.

"We've been friends forever, and you chose Kit over me. I got my freedom taken away because I cared enough to get help for you. Thanks for nothing." She wiped the tears from her cheeks and started to leave. Tim stopped her.

"Janie, wait. Thea is trying to apologize."

"I'm already grounded. If my mom finds out I'm talking to her, I'll be in even more trouble." Janie lifted her bag and left.

"I'll talk to her," Tim said and ran after her.

Why did he care? I plunked my head down on the table. How could I hold myself together? I clenched my jaw and unclenched it, over and over. The more I thought about everything, the hotter my face became. The first bell rang, and I raised my head. People moved out of the cafeteria, and I heard my phone buzz through the pocket of my backpack. I pulled it out and read Derek's text.

*RU OK? If something's wrong, I need to know, or I will worry all day—Derek*

How should I respond? Everything I did lately seemed like a crime, but I went with my impulse, and texted him back.

*How did you know something was wrong—Thea*

*We r connected. I love u. Can I do anything 4U?—Derek*

☺ *Thanks & yes u can do something—Thea*

*What?—Derek*

*Never lie to me.—Thea*

*Deal. Feel better. Text or call at lunch.—Derek*

*Thanks.—Thea*

Who was I supposed to trust? The only thing I knew for sure was Derek was talking to me and Janie was not. I tucked the phone into my backpack and trudged to my locker.

## CHAPTER 18

Janie ignored me during second period, and I only saw her from a distance the rest of the day. Near the end of the afternoon, Marcus passed me in the hall, which was weird considering it was a big high school and his classes were all in different parts of the building than mine.

"Hey, Thea!"

"Marcus." I hugged my textbooks to my chest and waited for him to say something else.

"How'd things go today?" He took a step toward me and flashed his brilliant smile, but the sparkle was gone.

"What do you mean?"

He took another step forward.

I moved backward and bumped into someone. I pivoted around and found myself face-to-face with a blue dummy.

"Sorry!" A voice rumbled from behind. After setting it down, Jackson looked up. "Didn't see you there. Oh. Thea. I didn't think I'd run into you today . . . no pun intended." He laughed at his own joke, and I grinned.

"Hi, Jackson, it's been a while," I said. His mustache lifted as he smiled back at me, then he turned toward Marcus.

"Hey. Marcus, right? How have you been?" Jackson asked.

"Great." Marcus rubbed up next to me. I wanted to tell him to back off, but before I could, Jackson set his hand on my shoulder.

"Do you miss working at the rec center?" Jackson asked. His jaw flexed while he waited for an answer.

"It was just a summer job," Marcus said. I glanced back and forth between the two of them, and the air around us turned muggy. The hallway closed in, and I shut my eyes for a mere second to control the dizziness. Another voice joined the conversation.

"Hey, what's going on?" Tim asked.

"I have no idea," I sighed.

"Are you going to introduce us?" Tim asked. Both Jackson and Marcus focused on Tim for a moment and then back to me. This was nuts. I'd never received so much attention in my whole life. I bit my lip and held back nervous giggles as these three guys wrestled for my attention.

"Tim, this is Jackson, my self-defense instructor from the rec center." I waved my hand from one to the other. "This is Marcus, my brother's friend. And Tim is one of my friends." I offered a big cheesy grin. "Now we've all been formally introduced."

"It's nice to meet your friends," Jackson said.

"Why are you here?" Marcus asked Jackson.

With his free hand, Jackson pointed across the hall at Coach Gavyn, who was walking toward us. "I've been helping Coach Gavyn with personal-safety demonstrations in his health classes," Jackson said and massaged my shoulder with his other hand. Even though I was getting a slight kick out of this attention, they were invading my space. I wanted to shrug away from both Jackson and Marcus, but somehow they had backed me up against the wall; I had nowhere to go.

"Nice team huddle," Coach Gavyn said. "What play are we running?"

"Okay . . ." I waved my hand in the air. "So . . . Jackson, I hope your demonstrations went well. Marcus, give my brother a big hug from me," I said in the most sarcastic tone I could muster. "And I'll see you later, Coach. Tim, we should get to our next class."

"Right," Tim said. I twisted sideways to move out from under Jackson's grasp, and Tim took my hand. I let him, but only because I needed out. We walked away, and I pulled my hand from his. He glanced down but didn't comment. We continued along the hall toward my locker and stopped in front of it.

"Man, that Jackson dude is freaking huge," Tim said.

"I know! Right?" I widened my eyes to emphasize my words, and I couldn't resist the urge to peek back down the hall. Jackson, Marcus, and Coach all stared back at me. A quiver ran over my scalp and along my neck, and I looked away.

"I tried to convince Janie to talk to you, but she's really mad," Tim said.

"Thanks for trying." I put my books in my locker and grabbed a notebook for my next class. Tim leaned in closer. All day, he'd been in my personal space, and I couldn't understand what he was up to.

"You can talk to me. I'm not Janie, but I'll listen."

"I can't talk to you, Tim. You're a guy." Right away, I realized how foolish I sounded. I'd been talking to Derek. He was a guy. What did I want? I slammed the locker door, and Tim took a step back.

"Okay." Tim's eyes, still bluer than an Idaho summer sky, pulled me in, but I couldn't read anything from them. He took a step closer, and his mouth opened, but he spoke no words. Then he simply walked away. Frustrated, I whirled around and went the opposite direction.

The rest of the school day I stared at the clock. The second hand ticked by, but the minute and hour hands seemed motionless. I reconsidered both Janie's and Derek's stories. A boxing match played out in my mind, and my head pounded with confusion. I needed clarity. Why did Derek tell me that crazy story about Red moving to Alaska? I couldn't figure it out. Maybe he was testing my trust. Maybe I should do the same. All sorts of dumb stories popped into my mind that I could tell Derek. I took a deep breath and sat straighter. It seemed clear now. I needed to test his trust in me.

When the last class let out for the day, I pulled my cell out of my backpack and checked for messages—five from Derek. He knew I couldn't check during the day, because I could get my phone taken away by teachers. So, why did he text so many times? In the first four messages, he said he was thinking of me. A smile spread across my face. I couldn't resist him. The last message was more urgent. He said he needed to talk to me right away. I dialed his number and walked toward the buses.

"What's going on?" I asked.

"I needed to hear your voice." The cold winter air made goose bumps pop out on my skin.

"Is everything okay?" I climbed onto the bus and took a seat.

"I've been worrying about you. How did things go today with Janie?" Not wanting to recap it for him there on the bus, I hesitated to answer. "Thea, are you still there?"

"Yes, I'm here, but I'm on the bus, so it's kind of hard to talk."

Tim plopped down right next to me. There were plenty of open seats, and yet, there he was right in my space.

"Hi, Thea!" he said loudly. "Who are you talking to?" I figured he already knew.

"Who's that?" Derek asked.

"Okay, I can't talk right now. I'll have to call you back." I didn't wait for Derek to respond. I ended the call, stuck my phone in my pocket, and turned to Tim.

"First of all, why are you sitting next to me?"

"Someone has to." Tim opened his eyes wide. Did he know the effect he had on me? I maintained control and refused to be influenced.

"Second, what have you got to be so happy about?"

"Come on, Thea. I know you've had a bad day. I'm just trying to cheer you up." He smiled bigger, and I scowled back at him.

Tim talked a lot on the ride home—enough for both of us. He talked about school, sports, Christmas coming up soon, and every other possible topic, except for Janie.

"When does basketball start for you?" he asked.

"Soon." I think he actually ran out of things to say as the bus stopped at our neighborhood. Good timing. We got off and stared at each other for a moment. Then the rest of the Three Stooges thumped down the bus steps and whacked Tim when they passed by.

"See ya," Tim said to me and jogged off to catch his friends.

"See ya," I said, but he'd already left.

I snagged my phone out of my pack. I wanted to talk to Derek while I walked home. Alone. No Janie. No Mom. No Tim. Seven new text messages from Derek:

*I can't believe u hung up on me.—Derek*

*Call me back.—Derek*

*What RU doing?—Derek*

*Who RU with?—Derek*

*Why aren't u answering?—Derek*

*Why RU ignoring me?—Derek*

*Plz. Call me.—Derek*

I needed some air, which was stupid considering I was standing all alone out on the sidewalk. I needed to start walking or I'd freeze to death. I dialed Derek's number.

"Sorry," I said.

"You ditched me so you could talk to some other guy?" He spoke fast and loud.

"I couldn't talk in front of him."

"Then why'd you sit next to him?"

"I didn't."

"You'd rather talk to him than me."

"Derek, stop. I have a couple of minutes. Let's not waste it on this." But he did. He spent the rest of the conversation questioning my love and loyalty toward him.

"How many other guys are interested in you?" I couldn't help an eye roll. Good thing he wasn't watching. I recalled the way Marcus, Jackson, and Tim had encircled me today, but they weren't really interested in me . . . at least I didn't think they could be . . . not the way that Derek meant.

"Maybe this won't work with me so far away from you," Derek said. I nodded. Maybe it wouldn't work.

"Yes, it will." I conceded, trying to ease his worries.

"I don't ever want to lose you, and I will fight hard to keep you in my life," Derek said. I slowed my pace and considered each of his words. What did he mean exactly?

"I can't live without you, Thea." Images of him at the hospital getting his stomach pumped flew into my mind. I didn't want him to die. Not because of me.

"You don't have to live without me. I'm right here."

"Promise me you won't leave me for one of those other guys."

"I won't." Oh. My. Gosh. I couldn't take this anymore. "Sorry, Derek. I'm home. I have to stop talking or my mom will be suspicious. Text me." I ended the call and finished walking the rest of the way home by myself.

I stayed off the computer. I had no reason to go on it today. I worked on my homework at the kitchen table while Derek sent me text after text. Mom had been making dinner and finally asked, "Who keeps texting you?"

"Janie."

"Why every two seconds?"

"Oh . . . first she had a question about our math homework, and then she had a question about what I'm wearing to school tomorrow, and then she wanted to know if I was going to try out for basketball, and then—"

"All right. I get it." Mom went on with her dinner prep. I went on with my homework and texting. I had to reply immediately to Derek, or he would think I was ignoring him.

■

Later that night, after I'd said good night to my parents and gone to bed, I texted Derek.

*RU Ok?—Thea*

*Yes. I'm sorry I overreacted today—Derek*

*Thanks for the apology—Thea*

*I just love u so much—Derek*

*I know—Thea*

*I need to be near u—Derek*

*It's hard . . . being so far apart—Thea*

He phoned near eleven o'clock my time. I didn't mind the late-night calls, usually. But today he had pushed my patience, and earlier tonight I had come up with a plan for our next conversation. I rolled toward the wall and spoke quietly. It was time to test him with an outlandish story. I asked him what the craziest thing was he ever did.

"I guess I'm a pretty boring guy. The craziest thing I ever did was hook up with you online. My friends still give me crap about the fact you're so much younger than me."

"So, don't hang out with them anymore. Janie gave me crap. And, now we're done." My chest tightened at the idea of going through high school without her.

"You're right. And I spend so much time with you, there's nothing left."

"Is that a good thing or a bad thing?" I asked.

"Definitely a good thing." Even though he was in another state, another time zone, I could hear the smile on his face. Moments like this I knew he loved me, and that fact confused me. How could he be anything but a kindhearted guy? How could he have lied to me and still be able to talk so tenderly to me?

"Your turn," he said.

"For what?" I'd already lost track of what we were talking about. It was late and I was sleepy.

"Tell me the craziest thing you ever did." Oh yeah. My game plan was to tell him a ridiculous story and see if he believed me, but I doubted I could go through with it. "Come on," he said.

"All right . . . the night I snuck out of my room to meet a guy—"

"Nuh-uh."

"Yeah."

"When and who?" he asked.

"Well, it was before you and I got serious. Before school got out last year."

"And?" Derek's voice sounded tighter.

"We played truth or dare."

"Who with?" he asked. I couldn't tell if he was angry or sad. I couldn't finish. I didn't want to hurt him. I changed my mind and changed my story.

"So . . . it was just my friend, Tim. He dared me to jump out of a plane and parachute into a lake."

"Whatever. Now you're lying." His condescending tone pissed me off and gave me the motivation I needed to continue with my plan. "We agreed to tell each other the truth," he said. And, yet, I was sure he'd lied about Red living on a fishing boat of the coast of Alaska.

"Okay. The part about sneaking out of my room was true," I fibbed. "And, well . . . Tim had asked me to meet him at the elementary school near us. He only wanted to talk. So, once my parents were asleep, I slipped the screen off my window and climbed out. It wasn't hard, because our house is a single level, and my room is on the opposite side of the house from my parents' room."

"And then what?" Derek sounded angry. Not sad. Not conde-scending. Which wasn't fair. He expected me to believe his wild story, but he wasn't accepting mine.

"And then Tim and I hung out for a while. It was before you and I were serious, so there's no reason for you to be mad."

"Did he try to kiss you?"

"Yes."

"Did you let him?"

"Yes, but nothing else happened. It was no big deal." I sighed. I'd never been kissed by anyone, ever. Never even gotten close.

"And he sat next to you on the bus today?"

"Yes, but we're just friends now." Derek said nothing. "Are you mad?" I hoped he was, because he made me mad.

"I don't think you snuck out of your room," Derek said abruptly.

"Why not?" I sat up in bed and ran my hand through my hair.

"Because the screen is screwed into your window frame."

I jerked my head toward the window. I expected him to be standing there peering in at me, but my blinds were closed and my lights were out. I jumped out of bed and went to the window. I hesitated for a second with my hand on the drawstring for the blinds. I could hear him breathing on the other end of the phone line, and my heartbeat became louder in my ears. I lowered my hand to the window sill.

"Why would you say that?" I whispered.

"Say what?"

"That my screen is screwed in?"

"Because most are—"

"Then how would people get out if there was a fire?"

"I don't know . . . but I still don't think you did it."

I grabbed the drawstring and yanked the blinds up. It was dark outside, except for a sinister glow coming off the distant moon. My breath fogged against the cold and darkened glass. I had no idea if the screen was screwed in or not. It sounded stupid though, because people would need out if there was an emergency. But I'd never tried to remove it myself . . . I'd only seen it done in the movies.

"I think you'd be too afraid to upset your parents by sneaking out," Derek continued. "So, don't tell me things that aren't true. We agreed to never lie to each other."

"I'm not lying," I said. "It did happen." I leaned my forehead against the cold glass and wondered if anyone was outside hiding under the dogwood and maple trees staring back at me. I could almost see myself from a lurker's perspective: my silhouette against the window; the phone to my ear; my warm breath puffing against the glass.

I dropped the blinds and sank to the floor out of sight.

"Okay. It's late," Derek said, "and I've got to get to bed. I'll talk to you tomorrow." He was dismissing me. He ended the call before I even had a chance to respond.

A knock sounded at my door, and I nearly screamed.

I snatched my comforter from the floor, tucked my phone under it, and hurried to the door. Had my parents heard me talking? I tried to recall the conversation and remember if I had raised my voice. I opened the door. Relief flooded through me when I saw my brother.

"Who are you talking to?" Seth asked.

"Nobody."

"We share a wall, and I could hear you. Mom and Dad will take your phone away if they find out."

"Are you going to tell them?"

He straightened and looked at me for a moment. "No," he said, "but stop talking so late, or I will." He walked away.

I closed my door and leaned against it. My world started to spin too fast, like I was on a carousel of bobbing horses. It spun faster and faster. I couldn't focus on the people around me anymore. I wanted off the ride.

# CHAPTER 19

People kept disappearing from my life. Janie was gone. Derek stopped texting me after our late night story exchange, a couple of nights ago now. And Dad left for a two-week business trip. He was gone before I even woke up.

I should've been relieved Derek wasn't texting, because I wanted to end it with him. Really. I did. I needed to focus on the upcoming basketball tryouts and schoolwork, and not worry about a relationship with a guy in another state. But I couldn't stop myself. I sat on my bed and texted him. He didn't respond.

I went through the motions of the day, dreading every moment of the weekend. At least during the school week I had something I could focus on and somewhere I belonged. At home, without Janie, without Derek, I had nothing.

After school, I climbed into bed with the intention of reading for the rest of the day and into the evening, but I dozed off, and the book that failed to hold my attention slipped from my fingers and fell to the floor. The sound startled me awake.

I leaned over the edge of the bed and grabbed my notebook from my backpack. I reread entries in my diary about Derek. I had a hard time being upset with him when I recalled the sweet things he had said to me over the last several months. I flipped through the pages until I got to the back of the notebook. I contemplated my quote collection and starred my favorites. I sure hoped Mom planned to give me a new Quote of the Day calendar for a Christmas gift.

My phone vibrated with a text from Derek. Before I finished reading it, another one buzzed in from him.

*I miss u—Derek*

*Can we talk?*—Derek
*Yes*—Thea
*Let's do it on* Skadi—Derek
*K*—Thea

We logged on and played late into the evening. We leveled up our characters, something we hadn't done in quite a while, and debated song lyrics.

**Kitsuneshin:** Have you ever googled hidden messages in music?

**ImmortalSlayer:** Nope.

**Kitsuneshin:** You should sometime. It's amazing what some lyrics really mean.

**Kitsuneshin:** Like your story the other night had a hidden message.

**ImmortalSlayer:** What RU talking about?

**Kitsuneshin:** The story about u sneaking out and meeting Tim.

**ImmortalSlayer:** Oh? And what was the hidden meaning?

**Kitsuneshin:** I'll explain when we talk on the phone later tonight.

**ImmortalSlayer:** Tell me now.

**Kitsuneshin:** No. I want to hear your voice. When can I call?

**ImmortalSlayer:** Well . . . my mom and Seth are still up. They might hear us.

**Kitsuneshin:** Go see what they're doing and then call me when u can.

**ImmortalSlayer:** Ok.

I logged off. The clock on my monitor showed it was after ten already. Mom usually went to bed by now, but I heard her and Seth in the family room. I moved to the archway and hovered, like a spy, trying to decipher what they were talking about.

"Hi, Thea," Mom said. Seth scowled at me. His disapproval never surprised me.

"I'm going to bed. Are you guys staying up?" I asked.

"No. We're about to head that direction, too," Mom said and patted Seth on the shoulder. He said good night to her and headed down the hall.

"Janie's mom called me today," she said with no warning. Were Mom and Seth discussing this? Did he tell her about my late night phone calls? I held my breath.

"Did you and Janie have a falling out?" She didn't wait for my reply. "Her mom suggested that you've been a bad influence and that you're involved with a twenty-year-old." Mom rested her hand on my shoulder like this was no big deal . . . like we were discussing what to have for dinner. "I think we should talk about it," she said.

I cleared my throat and plopped down on the couch.

"I know you're a good kid," Mom said, "but I'm troubled by your behavior."

"I haven't done anything wrong."

"I didn't say you had, but what's this about a twenty-year-old?" Mom sat next to me on the couch. "Is she talking about the guy you played *Skadi* with?"

"Probably." Truth.

"Are you still playing *Skadi*?"

"Not really. I played tonight for the first time in a long time."

"Was he playing also?" Mom was too calm. Why wasn't she yelling at me?

"Yes, but we're just friends."

"All right, but maybe you and I could spend more time together while Dad's out of town, and you could spend less time online."

"Whatever." I was done with this conversation, but Mom kept talking.

"When does basketball start?"

"Monday."

"Did you get all of your homework done?"

"Yes."

"Would you like to talk more about this guy or about Janie?"

"No."

"Well . . . know that I love you and you can always talk to me about anything."

"Right."

She gave me a hug, and we headed our separate directions. Her calm attitude had me freaked. Shouldn't she be upset? I texted Derek the details. He suggested we wait another hour before we phoned. I didn't know if I could wait that long to find out what he meant by the hidden meaning in my story.

When our house was as quiet as a schoolyard on a Sunday night, I called Derek.

"So, tell me," I said.

"Tell you what?" he teased, but it frustrated me.

"What you think my hidden meaning was."

Derek lowered his voice to a chestier tone. "I don't believe you ever snuck out." Before I could protest, he said, "I think you told me that story because you want to sneak out . . . and because you want to be kissed." He stopped speaking, and my heart rate increased. Uncertain where this was going, I remained quiet.

"I think you want to be kissed by me," he whispered.

My stomach twisted, and I realized I was breathing through my mouth instead of my nose. I pressed my lips together. Derek continued speaking in his soft rhythmic way, and I struggled to keep up with him.

"I know I want to kiss you. I want to pull you into to me, caress your face with my fingers, and then place my lips to yours. I would linger there, and breathe in your fragrance, before I draw you in closer and feel your body press—"

"Stop." The word carried out on a breath. I wasn't sure he even heard me.

"—next to mine. The taste of our tongues melting into each other. My hands stroking your—"

"Stop! What are you doing?"

"I'm telling you how much I love you. I want to be with you in every way." My stomach clenched, and I considered the possibilities of what he meant.

"Have you ever done cybersex?" he asked.

The question jolted me upright in bed. "No, and I don't want to talk about sex."

"Why not? It's just fantasy. We could—"

"No. We can discuss anything else, but not sex."

"Why not?"

"Because . . ."

"Okay, but understand . . . I didn't mean real sex. Just fantasy."

"No. Neither. Let's talk about something else."

"Sure." Derek's voice was back to normal.

I had to switch the phone to my other hand because my palm had become slippery with sweat. I drew up my blinds and opened the window to let in some cool fresh air.

"What do you want to talk about?" he asked.

"I don't know . . . How's your dad doing?"

"Still drinking," he said. "I don't know what to do about it. He doesn't listen to me or care about what I have to say."

"I'm sorry." I climbed back into bed and clutched my comforter. "My dad is gone for a two-week business trip. He didn't even say goodbye before he left."

We spoke awhile about our dads, and at some point, I fell asleep with the phone next to my ear.

■

I woke up with a start the next morning when Mom swung my door open. "Good morning, sunshine!" she said it too loudly. "Oh my, it's cold in here." She rushed to my window and closed it. I shoved my phone under my pillow.

"Why was your window open?" Mom asked.

I rubbed the sleep from my eyes and tried to remember.

"We cannot afford to heat the entire outdoors. Plus, it's not safe to have your window open during the night." I could feel a full lecture coming on, and I tried to preempt it.

"Sorry, Mom. I was hot and wanted some cold air. I must have fallen asleep before I closed it." I yanked the comforter up around my neck.

"Hey . . ." She tugged at the blanket, but I had a tight grip. "Get up. I want to take you out shopping for some new basketball shoes today and some shorts and shirts for practice."

"Sweet! When are we leaving?"

"As soon as you're ready." Mom switched on my bedside lamp and patted my nightstand. "Where's your Quote of the Day calendar?"

"Finished it last month. I need a new one."

"Finished it?" She barely got the words out before she laughed. "A calendar by nature is supposed to last you three hundred sixty-five days."

"Well, Mom, some things just don't last."

"I suppose you're right." She picked up my dirty shirt and socks from yesterday and threw them into my hamper before leaving. Mom needed everything in its place.

■

While shopping, I set my phone to vibrate in my pocket. Derek texted a lot. I read them and replied in the privacy of the dressing room. Otherwise, I'd have to come up with a new excuse for the constant texts, because Mom knew it wouldn't be Janie. I asked Derek to stop texting for a while, but he didn't.

She knocked on the slatted door. "Hurry up!"

I opened the door and modeled the shorts and a shirt for Mom. She nodded her approval, and I closed the door to change back into my own clothes. While Mom was at the register to pay, I walked outside to read a message. She was faster than I expected and caught me in the middle of replying.

"Who are you texting?"

"A friend from school." I clicked Send and pocketed the phone.

"Who?" Mom blocked my path to the car.

"Emily."

"Oh. I haven't heard you talk about Emily in a long time."

"I've had to reconnect with old friends since Janie isn't talking to me."

"We need to discuss that more," Mom said and started for the car. I didn't think she actually wanted to . . . she just wanted me to be a perfect daughter with no problems. A place for everything and everything in its place. We got into the car, and Mom turned to me.

"Have you been spending more time on the Internet than I know about?"

"I've followed your rules and kept my door open . . . like you've asked."

"What about that Kit character?"

"What about him?"

"What do you talk about?"

"*Skadi.*"

"Really?" she pushed.

"Sometimes we compare song lyrics. Nothing major."

"Can you mend the situation with Janie?"

"I don't know. She's told a lot of lies."

"Like what?"

"I think she's bulimic or anorexic or something. She lies about eating and throwing up." Mom's face went white. I stumbled upon the perfect diversion. If Mom worried about Janie's eating habits, she wouldn't focus on me.

"Does her mother know this?" Mom whispered as if she feared someone might hear us.

"Yeah. I told her because I was so worried, and that's why Janie isn't talking to me anymore."

"Oh, dear. Janie is such a sweet girl."

I nodded and wondered if I really should tell Janie's mom. But I couldn't. She thought I was pond scum and would never believe a word I said.

Mom wrapped her fingers around the steering wheel. "I should call Janie's mom and see if there's anything I can do to help." I raised my eyebrows. That wouldn't work! I shook my head and tried to come up with a quick way to discourage her.

"I say wait. Sometimes people have to solve their own problems."

Mom scrunched up her lips. "I don't know." She started the car, and we headed home. I crossed my fingers she wouldn't talk to Janie's mom.

Once home, Mom went to the kitchen to make dinner and I went to my room to read, mostly a book, but also a lot of texts.

After dinner, Seth went out with friends for the evening and Mom asked me if I'd like to play a board game.

"Uh. No. Why would I want to do that?" I hadn't played one in a long time. They were called board games for a reason. They bored me.

"Fair enough. Would you like to come to my room and read with me?" That I considered. Maybe it would be nice to spend some time together and reconnect.

"Sure," I said. Mom seemed surprised. I ran down the hall to my room and collected my big comforter, my pillow, and my book. I carried the load to Mom's room and piled everything on her bed.

"Did you leave any space for me?" she asked. I flopped on top of it all, and we both settled in for some good reading. Even though I set my cell to vibrate mode, the room was so quiet my phone could be heard a mile away. I ignored it. It vibrated again. I ignored it again.

Mom lowered her book. "Why aren't you checking your texts?"

"I was at a good spot in my book." But I was interrupted now, and I'd have to check. I held it close to my face and read the text messages. All from Derek, curious what I was doing. I replied.

*I am reading a book in bed with mom—Thea*
*Ah. Wish u were doing that with me.—Derek*
*LOL—Thea*
*Seriously! I want to be with you!—Derek*
*Someday . . .—Thea*

"Who was that?" Mom asked. I realized she'd been watching me the whole time, but I was sure she couldn't read the small display on the phone from where she was. I slipped the phone into my pocket and came up with an answer.

"It's Emily. She's watching a boring movie with her family and wanted to know what I was doing."

"Okay." Mom lifted her book. My phone vibrated with four more texts. I tried to ignore it, but the room was too quiet, and the air was becoming thicker. I struggled to take a deep breath and relax.

"I've got to go the bathroom." I set my book down and climbed out from under my comforter.

I didn't want to use Mom's bathroom, because she'd hear that I wasn't truly peeing. So, I walked toward the other bathroom and stopped in the hallway to text Derek.

*U gotta stop texting me so much tonight. My mom will suspect something.—Thea*
*I don't deserve you—Derek*
*Yes u do.—Thea*
*Really. I'm lucky to have u in my life.—Derek*
*Thanks—Thea*
*Love you—Derek*
*Me too—Thea*
*Do you want to play Skadi?—Derek*
*No I need to spend time with Mom.—Thea*
*Come on, please? Just for a while.—Derek*
*Ok. Be there in a minute.—Thea*

I went back to Mom's room and gathered my stuff. "I'm going to bed. I'm super tired."

"Okay," Mom said and narrowed her eyes at me. I expected her to challenge my lies, but she didn't. Once in my room, I closed the door and shoved my comforter behind it. I turned on the computer and logged into *Skadi*. We played, but chatted mostly. Derek tried to bring up the topic of cybersex again. I told him no again.

**Kitsuneshin:** Don't get mad. I was trying to do you a favor.

**ImmortalSlayer:** What does that mean?

**Kitsuneshin:** I feel like I should at least offer to have cybersex with you.

**ImmortalSlayer:** Why?

**Kitsuneshin:** Because I feel guilty.

**ImmortalSlayer:** Why?

**Kitsuneshin:** I did it with Red

**ImmortalSlayer:** When?

**Kitsuneshin:** A couple of days after she joined *Skadi*, and I feel bad about doing it with her when I only wanted to do it with you.

**ImmortalSlayer:** RU kidding me? Have u done it with other girls?

**Kitsuneshin:** Only Red. Sorry. I'll make it up to u.

**ImmortalSlayer:** brb

I needed to walk away. I went to the kitchen for a glass of water and stopped short when I saw Mom at the sink.

"I thought you went to bed an hour ago?" she asked.

"Trouble sleeping," I said and prayed she wouldn't follow me back to my room and see that I was on *Skadi* with the door shut. Worse yet, I couldn't remember if I had taken the time to close the chat box with Derek. Mom would have a heart attack if she read our conversation.

"Do you want to play a game of Scrabble?" she asked.

"What's with you and the board games tonight?"

"I feel like we should spend time together. That's all."

I reached for a glass from the cupboard, and my hand trembled. I made a quick fist and then shook out my hand. I filled my glass with water and started back for my room, but I changed my mind and turned toward Mom. "I'll play Scrabble with you tomorrow."

"Really?" Her face brightened. She knew I hated board games, but I could try. Tomorrow. Once in my room, I closed my door and went to my desk. I had left the chat box open.

**ImmortalSlayer:** Back.

**Kitsuneshin:** Where did u go?

**ImmortalSlayer:** To kitchen for glass of water, and ran into my mom.

**ImmortalSlayer:** She might come & check on me. I should log off.

**Kitsuneshin:** What makes you think she'll check?

**ImmortalSlayer:** She keeps asking me to play a game with her.

**Kitsuneshin:** What game?

**ImmortalSlayer:** Scrabble.

**Kitsuneshin:** Scrabble? Doesn't she know you hate board games? LOL

**ImmortalSlayer:** I know! Right?

**Kitsuneshin:** U should go play it with her so she won't worry about you.

**ImmortalSlayer:** I'm too tired to try to spell words.

**Kitsuneshin:** But if you make an effort, then she won't lurk over u.

**ImmortalSlayer:** Maybe UR right.

**Kitsuneshin:** I am. Go. We can talk later.

**ImmortalSlayer:** Ok. Thanks.

**Kitsuneshin:** Love u.

**ImmortalSlayer:** ☺

I found Mom still in the kitchen. "Do you want to play Scrabble?" I asked her.

"Of course. But you're going to bed."

"Oh. Can't sleep. Let's play." I wondered if a bug might fly into Mom's mouth, it remained open so long, but she hurried to the family room and returned with the game before I could change my mind. Derek texted as Mom set up the board on the kitchen table. My cell vibrated in my hand, and she heard it. There was no point in ignoring it.

*RU playing Scrabble with your mom?—Derek*

*Yes, so please stop texting.—Thea*

*Ok have fun. Love u.—Derek*

*Thanks . . . Me 2—Thea*

"Who's texting this late at night?" Mom asked.

"Emily. She finished the movie with her family, and she wanted to know what I was doing."

"Tell her you're not allowed to text so late."

"Mom, it's a Saturday night."

"I don't care. Tell her." It vibrated again before I could tell anybody anything.

"Okay," I said. "I will right now."

I read Derek's message fast and texted him back. He seriously had to stop. I tucked the phone under my thigh and selected tiles for the game. It buzzed against the hard wooden chair.

"Give me the phone."

"What?" I asked, and Mom stuck out her hand. A six-ton monster smashed his foot against my chest and knocked the wind out of me. She reached for the phone at my thigh, and I pushed it under my rear. The blood pounded in my head, and I gasped for air.

"Give it to me."

"No."

Mom bent over me and grabbed for the cell.

"No, Mom." My throat tightened around the words, and I started to shake. My fingers went ice cold. She pushed past my hands and struggled for the phone. "No!" I snatched it, and it vibrated again. "Stop!" I yelled both to Mom and to Derek. He had to stop texting.

"Give me the phone!" Mom yelled. Her face blazed crimson red.

"No," I whispered.

"Now!" She spit the word. "Don't doubt me. I will get that phone even if I have to take it by force!" I'd never in my life seen Mom so angry. Heat radiated off her body, and her eyes widened. I surrendered and gave her the cell. My entire body shook with fear.

Mom pinched her reading glasses and studied the phone. "Who the hell is Derek? And how the hell do I read the text he just sent?" I stuck my hand out to show her, and she jerked the cell away. "I'll figure it out." She did, and she read his last two messages. I didn't know what they said. Plus, I hadn't deleted any of the texts from today. Lately, I'd only cleaned them out before I went to bed. She read more messages, and my body trembled violently against the wooden chair.

"Who is Derek?" she asked in a shaky voice. When I didn't answer, she looked at me with a blank face.

"It's Kit." Defeated.

"The character from *Skadi*?" she asked, surprised by the revelation.

"Yes."

"You gave him your cell phone number?" Her voice rose to a new pitch, and her neck flushed red. I never before imagined that she would hit me out of anger, but I feared she could now. Mom walked out of the kitchen. The phone buzzed again, but she seemed to ignore it. I jumped up and followed her.

"What are you going to do?" I asked.

"I should call the police . . . I'm trying to think. Of all times for your dad to be out of town." Mom stopped at her bedroom door and read the incoming text. Her thumbs started to move across the keypad.

"Why are you typing?"

"Shh." She struggled with the keys, but she managed to press the Send button.

Anger blazed inside of me. Heat rose from the pit of my gut, burning my lungs and lighting my throat on fire. "What did you type?"

"I told him the text was from your mom and that you are fifteen years old. I told him if he ever texted or attempted to contact you again, I would call the police." The phone buzzed. Mom looked at the screen and scrunched up her mouth.

"What did he say?" I asked and tasted dinner coming up from my throat. Mom wouldn't answer me. I leaned closer hoping to see the screen, but she moved away too soon. She stepped into the bedroom and picked up the cordless phone from the charger on her nightstand.

"Who are you calling?" I begged the answer.

"Your father." The bed creaked as she perched on the edge. Momentary relief flooded through me. She was calling Dad, not the police. I squatted on the floor and listened to Mom's side of the conversation.

"Remember Kit from *Skadi*?" she asked Dad.

"His real name is Derek. He has Thea's cell number. For all we know he's been manipulating her for over a year . . ." I wished I could hear Dad's side. Mom's fingers quivered, and she switched the phone to her other hand. "Yes. I will." Mom ended the call, rose, and walked right past me. She carried the house phone in one hand and my cell phone in the other.

"What are you doing?" I stayed right on her heels. She returned to the family room and pressed the Power button on her computer. My cell buzzed. What did it say? I wanted to grab her and yell at her and force her to answer me. She read Derek's text while she waited for her computer. She set both of the phones next to her keyboard, and her hands shook more noticeably. She googled the phone number for the Nampa Police Department.

# CHAPTER 20

What could the police do at 11:30 at night? And how was chatting online even breaking any sort of law?

"I need to report a possible Internet predator," Mom said into the phone. "No, not an emergency, but I fear this guy has been influencing my daughter for a year, and I need the situation investigated." Mom's eyes darted around the room. "Yes, she's here. That'd be great. Thanks." She gave our names and address, and when she finished the call, she dialed another number. It must've been Dad, and he must've been waiting, because she spoke immediately.

"They said there's an officer nearby, and they'd send him over now. Sure. Love you, too. Bye." She set the house phone down and scratched her forehead.

"Are you all right?" I hated seeing her upset like this.

"Don't." She pointed her finger at me and lowered her voice. "Don't talk." My cell vibrated continuously, indicating an incoming call—not just a text. Mom picked it up, and the walls of the room began to close in around me. What would happen if Mom spoke to Derek? My vision began to spin, and my phone continued to vibrate.

"You've given a complete stranger your personal information." Mom set my phone back down. "You have no idea who this guy is. Or what he's capable of!" she yelled, and the whole house reverberated.

"He's not a complete stranger." My voice trembled almost as much as my body.

Mom balled her hands into fists; her knuckles, white.

"He has your phone number. He knows who you are and where you live. He is twenty and you are fifteen. There are laws in place to protect girls like you from guys like him."

"He hasn't done anything wrong," I whispered.

Mom grunted, and the stunned look in her eyes made me want to throw up.

Someone knocked at the door, and Mom flinched. She went to the side window and peeked out. I'd never seen her do that before. I hung back, and Mom opened the door and invited a police officer inside.

"That was fast," Mom said.

"I was on patrol nearby," the officer said. He entered and scanned the entryway of our home. His hands rested on the gun belt he wore around his waist, and he was younger than I expected. Plus, I thought cops always traveled in pairs? He introduced himself, and Mom asked him to sit on the couch in the family room. I remained standing, frozen in place. Mom gave him the short version of the evening's events.

"My daughter met this guy during an online game, and I fear he's been pursuing her for a year."

"Join us," the officer said to me and waved me over. I complied and sat next to Mom on the opposite couch facing him. "Thea, what do you know about this guy?" He pulled out a small notebook and a pen, waiting for my answer.

I swallowed and debated how to answer. I chose truth, for now. "His name is Derek. He's twenty. Lives in Georgia with his dad. His mom died from cancer—"

"Do you know his last name?"

"Felton."

Mom slouched forward, which confused me, because I was telling the truth and I hadn't revealed anything shocking.

"We'll check him out," the officer said. "If he is who he says he is, that's fine, but if he has a record of any sort we'll find that out also. We have a detective who investigates Internet crimes. I'll give him your information and have him contact you tomorrow." Then the officer went into a long lecture about online safety and listening to your parents. I tried to appear respectful, but seriously . . . like I didn't already know this.

A click at the front door startled us.

Seth walked in, stopped at the archway, and gawked at the police officer in our family room. The officer rose, and Mom introduced him to Seth.

"Is everything all right? Why is a cop here?"

"I'll explain later. Go get ready for bed, and let us finish here."

"Okay . . ." Seth dragged out the word and then left.

"Is there anything more I can do for you tonight, Mrs. Reid?" the officer asked.

"Could you at least call this guy, and tell him to never contact my daughter again?"

"Do you have his number?"

"It's in her cell." Mom handed it to him.

"I can make the call, but if he's in Georgia, it's two A.M. his time. He probably won't answer."

"He probably will," Mom said. "He called right before you arrived." The officer thumbed through the menu of the phone and appeared to read a few of the texts. He wrote something on his notepad.

"Have you sent this guy pictures?" he asked me.

"Yes." I responded without thinking.

"What?" Mom said.

I realized I had let my guard down. I was tired, and I thought the interrogation had ended. Wrong. I pinched the inside of my arm to wake myself up. I did not want to betray Derek. He hadn't done anything wrong.

"Have you talked about sex with this guy?" the officer asked.

"Not really." My words came out in a whisper. Mom covered her mouth.

"Did you ever arrange a time and place to meet him?"

"Not specifically."

"But generally?" he asked, and Mom started to cry. So, if I withheld the truth to protect Derek, did that mean I was betraying Mom? I didn't want to choose.

"Yes. Generally," I said.

"When?" he prodded.

"After school before basketball practice."

The officer scribbled in his notebook. In my periphery, I could see Mom's hand pressing against her stomach.

"Are you saying . . ." she started low and slow, like each word cut through her, "that you would have met up with him before practice, and I wouldn't have known you were missing until after? He would have had over two hours to get away with you. You could have been dead or long gone by then." She leaned into me and yelled. "How can you not see what a problem that is?"

"Your mother is right. This could have been a very bad situation. You're lucky she stopped it before it was too late."

I said nothing. I still couldn't believe this was happening. I had tried to tell the truth, but they all jumped to the wrong conclusions about Derek.

The officer pushed more buttons on my phone, and then handed it back to Mom.

"You're not going to call him?" she asked.

"I don't want to jeopardize the investigation. We need to let Detective Corbett handle it from here."

Mom rubbed her cheek. "Do you need to take the phone and computer as evidence?"

"The detective will contact you and arrange for that. But, yes, I'm sure he'll need both."

"I appreciate you taking the time to come over." Mom ran her fingers through her hair.

"That's my job. Stay safe, Thea, and do what your mom tells you. She knows best." He shook my hand and Mom's, started to leave, but then looked back at me. "Just because this guy has a cell phone with a Georgia area code doesn't mean he's in Georgia. He could live down the street from you, or he could be someone from your school. That's the thing about the Internet. You don't know who you're talking to. Be extra careful until this is sorted out." He took a step toward me. "Understand?"

I relented. "Yes." He waited a moment longer then reached for the door and left.

Seth came down the hall right away; he'd probably been eavesdropping the entire time.

"What's going on?" he asked.

"Your sister was almost abducted by an Internet predator."

Oh. My. Gosh. She was blowing this all out of proportion. But I kept my mouth shut.

"What?" His jaw dropped. She told Seth her pessimistic version that made me look bad and made Derek look a lot worse. Seth glared at me. Big surprise.

"I'm going to bed," I said, but before taking a step, Mom stopped me.

"Sit down." She pointed at the couch. I collapsed into the cushions.

"Seth," Mom said, "bring Thea's CPU out here." He went without question while Mom and I sat in silence. He returned sooner than I expected, probably because he only had to unplug my computer from the wall and disconnect a few cables. He set it on the coffee table.

"Thea, bring me the charger for your cell phone."

I stumbled out of the room in silence, and when I returned, I found Mom at her desk, her computer on, and my phone in hand.

"What are you doing?" I asked.

"Showing you how easy it is to find information on someone," she said. "Pull up a chair."

"Do you want me to stay, too, Mom?" Seth asked.

"Go to bed, honey."

"Okay. Get me if you need me." He scowled at me, but walked away when I mimicked him.

Mom pulled up Google and typed in Derek's cell phone number with the words *reverse search*.

"Mom," I said, "reverse searches don't work for cell numbers."

"Oh yeah? Watch." She clicked on a website from the Google list and then reentered Derek's cell number. A picture popped up with a map of Georgia and a thumbtack. Then she clicked on a red button that said, "Get Full Details." She typed in a credit card number and for ninety-nine cents the website displayed Derek Felton's name, street address, and approximate value of his home.

She shook my cell at me. "He did this with your number, too. He knows where we live."

My shock transformed into relief, and I tapped the monitor. "But see, that says his street address is in Georgia. The officer was wrong about him being someone we already know."

Mom rubbed her forehead. After a moment, she typed his name inside quotation marks and his full address into Google. It pulled up different results than when I had googled him. She clicked on the Facebook link. Derek's senior picture from high school displayed on the screen with basic information about him.

"That's him," I said, and I felt like an idiot for not doing a more efficient Internet search than my own mom.

"You know what he looks like?" Mom asked.

"He sent me that picture."

"Are you kidding?" Mom yelled. "I thought you were smarter than this—" She bit her lips together as though she wanted to stop herself from speaking, but she said more anyway. "Where's the picture?"

"On my phone."

Mom pulled the picture up on my cell, squinted at it, and then compared it to the one on the computer monitor. "How can you think this looks like a current picture of a twenty-year-old boy?"

I didn't understand the question.

"Look at his hair," she said. "That's a mullet from decades ago, and how can you even think this boy is cute?"

"I don't care if he's cute. It's his personality that matters."

Mom threw her hands in the air and turned back to the computer. She read aloud the basic information displayed about Derek. Hometown: Statesboro, Georgia; Music: DeathTomb; Studied at: Southern Georgia University; Birthday: October. This was him. Mom scrolled down further on his profile page.

"It says here that he is an alumnus of Southern Georgia University," Mom said.

"So, he's going to college."

"No. Alumnus means he graduated from there." She moved down further, and then she pointed at the monitor. "This says he graduated from Statesboro High School, class of 1986 . . . That puts him in his upper forties now."

My heart shattered. Was this proof? Was I required to believe it? Maybe it was some sort of typo. I rarely used Facebook, because my parents monitored our accounts. And since Derek never even mentioned Facebook, it hadn't occurred to me to search for him there.

Mom's chair squeaked when she leaned back and mumbled to herself, "How could a forty-seven-year-old man be interested in a fifteen-year-old girl?"

It made no sense.

"You've made a huge mistake here." She rubbed the edge of the desk. "I don't think I can talk about it anymore tonight. It's late. Go to bed."

"Can I have my phone back?"

"Are you nuts?" she yelled. I must have been. Mom pocketed the phone and pulled the power cord from her computer. Then she disconnected the cord from mine as well.

"Why are you taking those?"

"Because you can't be trusted. And you're more sneaky than I ever imagined. I'll keep these with me."

"When will I get them back?"

"Never. Don't ask again. Go to bed. And . . . don't close your door. When I come to check on you, I had better find it wide open."

"Why?"

"Thea . . . do you not get it? We had a police officer here tonight. This Derek guy knows where we live."

"But he's in Georgia. He can't do anything to us."

Mom winced and flung the power cords on the couch. Then she grabbed both of my shoulders. Her spittle hit me in the face. "How do you know he's in Georgia? He could be anywhere right now with his cell phone and laptop."

"But Georgia is still pretty far away."

She shook me twice, not hard, but slow. "Thea! If he's not already in Idaho, he could be on a plane and be in here in a matter of hours. A middle-aged man has financial resources that would allow him to do that." My body went numb, and I could no longer feel Mom's hands on my shoulders. She said something else to me, but her voice was muted, like I had a bunch of cotton shoved in my ears.

"Go to bed," she said. "I can't deal with this anymore tonight." She picked up the power cords, and my phone buzzed in her pocket. I needed to know what Derek texted. I was desperate to know his side of the story. Shouldn't he get a chance to defend himself? A fire pulsed through me. Earlier, I had worried about betraying him, but if he was in his forties, then he had betrayed me. Mom left, and I stood alone in the family room, more alone than ever before in my life.

# CHAPTER 21

Sunday was pure torture. Mom paced the house with the cordless phone, waiting for the police detective to call. But he never did. I stewed and replayed the previous night's events over in my head. I struggled to believe it all. I needed to talk to Janie, but that wasn't an option. I needed to talk to Derek, but that wasn't an option either. No one could help me.

Mom made another pass through the family room, and I asked, "Where did you put my cell phone?" It seemed like an innocent question, until she angled her head at me.

"None of your business." She went back to her pacing, and I stayed out of her way for the remainder of the day.

■

Monday morning was worse.

"Get up." Mom flipped on the overhead light and stood in my doorway with one hand clutching the doorknob. Red lines crept through the whites of her eyes, and shadows darkened her lids.

"Don't cause any trouble today, Thea. Go to school and come straight home . . . You know, I bought that cell phone to help keep you safe. So you could call me anytime you needed me, and now, a day you truly need one, I can't give it to you. I can't trust you. You'd better hope Derek stayed in Georgia. Get your butt out of bed and get to school. Don't talk to any strangers. Especially ones named Derek." I imagined him at my bus stop, and my hands clenched. At my school. At basketball. I looked at Mom again.

"What about tryouts?"

She wrung her hands together and sighed. "I forgot about that. Go, and I'll come watch. But you had better be where you are supposed to be. Do you understand?"

"Yes." I swung my legs over the side of the bed. "What about the detective? I thought he was supposed to call yesterday."

"I thought so, too. I'm going to call him this morning. I'm also calling a counselor—"

"Why?"

"Thea, you need something I can't give you—"

"There's nothing wrong with me!"

"Get ready for school," she said.

"If you're worried about me, why don't you drive me to school?" I asked.

"You made these decisions that led to today. You chose to lie. And while I would prefer to drive you, I can't do it. I'm so pissed. You have to be more responsible. You have to choose safety."

"I do choose safety. I am responsible. Please—"

"No." Mom left.

How could she do this to me? I played a game on the Internet and met a guy. I tried to help him and be his friend. I cared about him. I still do. This was some sort of cruel misunderstanding. Derek wouldn't lie to me, not about this. Would he? I needed to talk to him, but not in person. What if he did show up today? The thoughts and images flooded my mind.

"Thea!" Mom had returned. "It's been five minutes. Stop standing there and get ready for school."

"Okay." I stepped forward and reached for the door to close it, but Mom prevented me.

"Leave it open."

"How am I supposed to change?"

"In the bathroom."

"You're being unreasonable. What can I do in here with the door closed? You've already taken everything away."

"Do you want me to take away your door, too?"

"Go ahead. What difference will it make?"

"Get. Ready. For. School." Mom left again.

Unbelievable. She'd popped her cork. I grabbed some clean clothes and went to the bathroom.

Fifteen minutes later, I entered the kitchen, and Seth and Mom stopped talking. Great. I was an outcast in my own home.

"Seth's agreed to drive you to school today," Mom said. I eyed him suspiciously. I hated that he was the favored good child.

"Don't rush to thank me," Seth said.

"Don't worry, I won't." I moved past them to grab a banana. Mom sighed and left, making me rethink my words.

"Actually, I'm glad you're driving me," I said to Seth. Although I wanted to believe Derek was still in Georgia, the possibility of him lurking somewhere along my path freaked me out.

Seth and I didn't talk during the drive—at first—but when we drove past Marcus's house, I asked, "Are we picking up Marcus?"

"No. He's sick today."

Coincidence?

"How old is Marcus?" I asked.

"What difference does it make to you?" Seth asked.

"Just curious . . . I heard he was held back in kindergarten—"

"Shut up."

I reconsidered the conversations I'd had with Marcus over the last year and the information I knew about him. His dad was awful. His mom was dead. He was around twenty years old. He loved winter skiing. He had multiple usernames on *Skadi*. I wanted Marcus to be Derek. It would solve everything. Mom could call off the police. And better yet, I could talk with him and be with him. It could all work out.

Seth continued the drive in silence, but after a while he kept glancing at me.

"What?" I asked.

"I'm trying to figure out how you could be so gullible. And how you could torment Mom and Dad like this."

I pulled the seatbelt away from my neck and faced him. "Let me get this straight, you and Marcus introduced me to *Skadi*, and I'm the one to blame?"

"You're so immature," Seth said.

"Thanks." I wanted so badly to ask Seth if there was any chance Marcus could be Kitsuneshin, but instead I turned away from my brother and looked out the side window so he wouldn't see the tears welling in my eyes. He parked in the student lot at school. I got out, and we went our separate directions. Seth's words echoed in my head. I wanted to shout to the world that I was not gullible, but I feared he was right.

"I heard the police were at your house."

I whipped around and found Tim behind me.

"I was worried when you weren't on the bus," he said. "I thought maybe your mom or brother dropped you off. So . . . were the police at your house?"

"Yes. How did you hear about it?" I wondered what secrets Tim kept. The officer said Derek could be someone at school. And Tim had often acted strangely around me. I examined his familiar features and decided there was no way it could be Tim. He had tried too many times to convince me to drop Derek. He wouldn't have done that if he was in fact Derek.

This must be what insanity felt like.

"Word travels fast," Tim answered. "Janie was worried. She thought an Internet predator got you or something."

"He is not a predator." What was I saying? I didn't know that. I scanned the lot for anyone who resembled Derek. Problem was . . . I was looking for an old-fashioned hairstyle from the eighties. I didn't really know what he looked like today. And . . . maybe the picture Derek sent wasn't even him. I had no way of knowing for sure. Tim's blue eyes locked with mine. "I don't know what to do. I don't know who to believe," I said.

"Come on." Tim motioned toward the school, and I walked inside with him. He led me to the cafeteria and over to the table where Janie sat. She glanced up as we approached, but I couldn't decipher her expression.

"Janie, I'm sorry. For everything." She hopped up and threw her arms around me.

"Me, too!" Janie's black curls smothered me, but I didn't mind. She held on, and so did I, but even through her multiple layers of clothes, my fingers found the channels between her bony ribs. She pulled back. "I was so scared when I heard police went to your house!"

"Sit down. You're causing a scene," Tim said. We huddled around the table, and I looked at him and then Janie.

"Since when are the two of you best friends?" I asked. I made myself smile so I wouldn't appear rude. I just got Janie back, and I didn't want to lose her again because of my sarcasm.

"Since we were both rejected by you," she said and didn't bother with a fake smile.

"Sorry." I took a deep breath and tucked my hair behind my ears. "I don't know what to do." I put my face in my hands and leaned on the table. Janie stroked my back.

"Spill," she said.

I filled them in on most of the details. "I think if I could call Derek, he'd be able to explain everything. I can't believe he's as old as my mom thinks."

"You cannot call him," Janie said. I looked at her in time to see her finish her angry head sway. She put her finger in the space between us and said, "I'm serious. Promise me you will not contact him." Could I make that promise? I didn't want to lie to my friend, and I didn't want to lose her ever again.

"You have to believe your mom," Tim said. "Plus, you have to tell the cops about Red. He's probably done this to other girls, and I bet they weren't lucky like you." My stomach twisted, and my hand flew to my mouth.

"How could I be so stupid?" I asked. Janie put her hand on my arm.

"You're not stupid. You were tricked. We all were."

"I wasn't," Tim mumbled.

Janie stuck her finger back into the air and said to him, "You do not have to be here."

"Sorry," he said. He pretended to zip his lips and throw away the key. I wanted to go home and curl up in my bed and never deal with the world again.

"So what's going to happen now?" Janie asked.

"I don't know. Some detective is supposed to be investigating the case." The first bell rang, and people started moving out of the cafeteria.

"Hopefully, they'll arrest him and throw him into jail," she said. How could it be that simple for her? Part of me still hoped Derek had told me the truth all along, but the other part of me feared it was all a lie.

"It should be easy," Janie said as we rose from the table. "I mean, the dumb guy gave you his real name. So, it's not like the detective has to solve some sort of mystery. We already know who he is. They can simply call up the Georgia police and arrest him."

I imagined my Derek behind bars, alone.

"Right?" Janie asked.

"Right," I said.

We headed to our separate classes. The day moved slower than a slug across dry pavement. My stomach ached during my last class. Even though I knew Derek would not be at basketball tryouts, I couldn't stop imagining him showing up.

The bell rang, and everyone rushed out of the room and into the hall. I headed for the locker room to change, and found the school resource officer, Officer Ford, waiting. He spotted me and moved forward. My heart skipped a beat, and I couldn't swallow. He closed the distance between us.

"Hi, Thea." He stuck out his knuckles. "I'm Officer Ford."

"I know." I bumped my knuckles against his.

"I spoke with Detective Corbett today about your situation."

"Okay."

"I'm going to keep an eye out, but you need to be careful. You never know who is prowling on the Internet. This guy could say he's in Georgia, but for all you know, he could be your next door neighbor. You don't know who he is."

If one more person tells me I don't know who Derek is, I'm sure my head will explode into a million pieces. I nodded at the officer. Seemed like adults only wanted me to agree with their opinion anyhow.

"Thanks," I said. "I've got to go. Basketball tryouts." I could hardly breathe, let alone put a complete sentence together. I needed fresh air, but the last thing I wanted to do was go outside right now. I preferred the safety of the girls' locker room to venturing out in the unknown world.

Tryouts bombed. I couldn't focus on anything but the situation with Derek and the police. And to make things worse, Coach Gavyn was there helping the basketball coaches keep stats. Every time he filled a sheet with tryout statistics, he pulled it off his clipboard and taped it to the gym wall.

The basketball coach yelled at me, "Thea! Get your head in the game!"

Right.

Mom walked into the gym and caught my eye. She moved toward the bleachers and inspected the crowd. I was surprised she didn't carry a mug shot of Derek with her to compare more precisely. I was certain he wasn't there, and that he wasn't coming. I decided they were all making a big deal out of nothing.

Afterward, Mom and I walked to the car together. I was too lazy to change out of my practice clothes, and I nearly froze to death when the cold air hit the perspiration on my skin. I moved faster to stay somewhat warm and to get to the car sooner.

"How'd you do today?" Mom asked.

"Fine."

"I talked with Detective Corbett. We have an appointment with him at seven A.M. Wednesday morning."

"Why so early?"

"Well, it was either first thing in the morning or right after school, and I didn't think you'd want to miss two days of basketball tryouts."

"Two days?"

"Tomorrow you have an appointment with a counselor."

I stopped walking. Mom took a few more steps before she noticed, and then turned and held a hand up to shield her eyes from the bright December sun.

"I don't need a counselor," I said, "and I can't miss tryouts. I'm a sophomore. I have to work harder to impress the basketball coach to make the team."

"Well, you should have thought of that before you started lying to me so many months ago. My choices did not put us into this situation. You made the choices, and now, you get to deal with the consequences. And so do I." Without another word, she continued toward the car. I gave up and followed; I was too cold to stand there and argue. Once we were settled in the car, I tried one more time.

"Please don't make me miss basketball."

Mom put the key in the ignition, but didn't turn it. "You need to see a counselor because of this long-term grooming. We need to find out why this happened and make sure it never happens again. And you've shut down. You've hardly shed a tear or expressed any emotion whatsoever at this situation. It's unhealthy for you to bottle it up. You were deceived, betrayed, and hurt like I can't even imagine, and yet, you're not crying, not yelling, not anything. I want you to express your emotions."

"Long-term grooming? What does that even mean?"

"It's when an adult makes an emotional bond with a child for sexual gratification. This guy has manipulated you and gotten you to trust him."

"I'm not a child."

Mom tightened her fingers around the steering wheel.

"Please don't make me miss basketball," I whispered.

Mom started the car. "I'll see if I can change it, but I can't promise." Mom drove the rest of the way home in silence. She didn't ask me what my favorite thing about the day was. She didn't ask me what the worst part of my day was.

## CHAPTER 22

Tuesday. Another day of trudging through the motions. But at least the day didn't start out with Mom yelling at me. This time, she flipped on the hall light and then came over to my bed.

"Thea . . ." She placed a hand on my shoulder. I rolled over and looked up at her. "How'd you sleep?"

"Better."

"I've decided I'll call the counselor today and reschedule the appointment for next week but under one condition." Her change in attitude made me wonder if this was a false calm before the next storm. I kept up my guard just in case.

"What's that?" I asked.

"When we talk to the detective tomorrow, you have to answer all of his questions."

"I will."

"I mean . . . no vague answers. You can't even answer with an 'I don't know.' I want you to be truthful. Promise?"

"Yes."

I sat up and raked my fingers through my hair. Pushing the counseling appointment out gave me more time to breathe, and think.

■

At lunch, Janie and Tim wanted updates, but there were none to give. I let them know we were meeting with the detective Wednesday morning, and hopefully I'd have more information then.

Tim and I wolfed down pizza and tater tots while Janie pecked at her dry salad. She had lost even more weight. Her hair was thinner and had lost its shiny bounce. Her face sunk in deeply beneath her cheekbones. I set my fork down and twirled a strand of my hair. I considered different ways to bring up the topic with her. We had just started speaking again, and I didn't want to jeopardize our friendship. Plus, it didn't help that her mom still forbade her to associate with me, because apparently I was the plague.

"Hey, Janie . . ." I started. She cocked an eyebrow and waited for me to continue. "Does your salad taste okay? You want some pizza?"

She pushed her tray away. "No. I'm not hungry today." What was I supposed to say to that? I'd been walking on eggshells around this topic for months, but I cared too much about her to let it drop.

"I don't think you should lose any more weight," I blurted out.

"Who are you to set a weight loss limit for me?" she asked and hopped up, but I grabbed her tiny wrist to stop her.

"Wait. I want to help you." I didn't want to make her mad, but what if I didn't get another chance to talk to her about this? She yanked her wrist away from me.

"Help me with what?" Janie narrowed her eyes at me. "I'm fine."

"Are you anorexic?"

"I. Am. Not. Anorexic," she said in her deep angrier tone of voice.

"All right, forget I said anything." We stared at each other for a few seconds more, and I wished I'd never opened my big mouth.

The bell rang.

"We should go to class," Tim said. He'd been so quiet I'd almost forgotten he was at the table.

"Are we still friends?" I asked Janie. She crooked her lips to one side like she had to think hard about it.

"Only if you stop acting like the weight police."

"Deal," I said, but there was no way on earth I could let this go. I just needed a better game plan to help her. Maybe I should still try to talk to her mom. Janie and I exchanged weak smiles, and we all went our separate ways.

■

Once again, I struggled during basketball tryouts. Officer Ford walked into the gym right when someone passed me the ball, and instead of landing in my hands, the ball hit the side of my head.

The basketball coach yelled at me even more. "Take a break, Reid!"

Great.

I jogged over to my water bottle and took a swig. Coach Gavyn, who had been lurking by the bleachers, shifted over next to me. "Are you okay?" he whispered.

"Nope."

He set his hand on my shoulder. I jerked away and spilled water onto the floor.

Coach Gavyn held up his hands in an apology. "Thea, take a deep breath. Focus on the task at hand. You have the ability to make the team. Put everything else out of your mind for now." He took a step back and gave me my space.

"Thanks," I said.

"Now get back in there." He pointed to the court. I set down my water bottle and rejoined the drill in progress.

Mom showed up early again. We drove home in silence again. I asked where my cell phone was again, and she said it was none of my business again.

■

I went to bed after dinner. I didn't read. I didn't write in my diary—how could I? Derek lurked on every page of it. I just stared up at the ceiling until I fell asleep. In the middle of the night, I woke to the sound of a phone ringing. I reached for my cell, but then remembered I didn't have it. I rolled over and tried to go back to sleep but heard a phone ringing again. I realized it was the house phone. The clock read three A.M. Who would call at this time of night? I decided it must be Dad, and I dozed back to sleep.

The next morning when I entered the kitchen, I found Mom at the sliding glass door looking out.

"What are you doing?" I asked. She turned toward me at the same moment Seth walked up to the door from the outside. He slid open the door and came into the kitchen.

"I didn't see anything unusual along the fence," Seth said to Mom. "But that chair is not ours. I think it came from the house behind us."

"What are you talking about?" I asked.

"Come here." Mom motioned to the back patio. We stepped outside onto the cold concrete, and she pointed to a white plastic chair that sat on the lawn about five feet away from the house. The chair couldn't have been ours because we didn't have any patio furniture.

"Where'd that come from?" I asked. Mom's forehead wrinkled.

"Have you ever seen it before?" she asked.

"No. What's going on?"

Mom walked over to the chair but didn't touch it. She pointed down. "Do you see how the feet of the chair have gone down into the lawn?"

"I guess, yeah." She took two fingers and lifted the chair. It was obvious the bottom inch of each foot had sunk into the cold hard ground.

"If the chair wasn't here yesterday, how do you suppose it went into the ground like that overnight?" I shrugged. How was I supposed to know?

"It's probably nothing," I said and plopped into the chair.

My breath caught in my throat.

The white chair sat at the perfect angle to see directly into Mom's bedroom window; her blinds and curtains were wide open. What did that mean? My eyes began to burn from staring so long without blinking. I closed them and tried to think this through. Surely, some teenager left the chair here as a prank . . . but why? I hopped up and ran to Mom's room to see the view from inside. Mom followed.

"Thea, you need to be aware—" She crossed her arms as I looked out her window. "The phone rang in the middle of the night and startled me awake. Since Dad is out of town, I'm especially on edge. I flipped on the light, but since I didn't recognize the caller ID I didn't answer. I decided to ignore it and use the bathroom. Before I finished, the phone rang again. Same number on the caller ID. I still didn't answer. I checked for messages, but there were none."

"So, a wrong number," I said. "What does that have to do with the chair?" Mom hung her head and sighed. "What? I don't get it."

"Derek could have sat in that chair," Mom said. "He could have been confirming this was the correct house, by calling in the middle of the night and then seeing the light come on at the same moment. Either that or he wanted to scare us. I don't know. But I think it was Derek."

"That's crazy."

"Yes, but I believe that's what happened. I'm just thankful we're seeing the detective this morning. Hopefully, he can help." I heard my cell phone vibrate, and I looked around the room.

"You have my phone in here?" Duh. Of course she did.

"Yes, but we're giving it to the detective, along with your computer, today."

"Who's been texting?"

"Who do you think?"

"What's he saying?" I asked.

Mom walked toward the door. "Head out, Thea. I need to shower, and we need to leave in thirty minutes."

I didn't budge. I remembered a conversation with Derek when he told me he would never give me up without a fight. The once-endearing statement now took on a whole new meaning. "I want to know how many times he's texted and what he's saying."

"Fine . . . He has texted about nine times a day. He texts that he loves you, that it's a misunderstanding, that he can't live without you. He's said that he wants to talk to you in private . . . that he could come here, to the house, and talk to you. He even sends texts addressed to me on your phone. He has to be crazy to continue texting after I already threatened to call the police."

Part of me was scared that he wouldn't give up. Another part of me was thrilled that he wouldn't give up. Didn't that mean he loved me? Or did it mean he was crazy? Maybe it meant I was crazy.

"Mom?"

"What?" she said, the word on a puff of air.

"You honestly think Derek sat in that chair last night?"

"What other explanation makes sense?"

"But why would he set the chair outside your room? Wouldn't he be afraid of being caught?"

"Well, how would he know it was my room? Did you ever describe where your room was in the house?" I thought about it for a moment and recalled a conversation I'd had with Derek.

"I told him my room was in the back and to the side of the kitchen."

"Sweetheart . . ." Mom shook her head. "Based on that description, he could've thought he was at your window last night. He could've hoped you had a phone near you and that you'd answer it. Maybe he even hoped you'd go out your window to meet him."

Shivers traveled up my spine. I tried to take a deep breath, but couldn't catch even a small gasp of air. Mom was over to me in an instant and wrapped her arms around me.

"We have to be extra vigilant to make sure the doors and windows are locked until this guy is arrested. We don't know where he is or what his intentions are."

"Can we have the chair dusted for fingerprints?" I asked.

"I don't know. We'll ask the detective. Go and get ready. We need to leave soon."

I headed for my room, but Seth waited for me in the hall.

"What?" I asked.

"Do you have any idea the stress you've caused Mom?"

"Shut up." I tried to move past him, but he stepped in front of me.

"You've lied to everybody. You brought a stalker into our backyard." Seth reddened, and his volume increased. He started to say more but then closed his mouth and sneered at me. His shoulder slammed into mine as he walked away. I knew it was my fault, and I didn't need him to tell me. I'd hurt Mom in a horrible way.

I took a shower and thought about the chair. Whether it was Derek or not, why would the person who brought the chair into our yard leave it there? Because he wanted me to know he was there. That was the only reason I could come up with. Could Derek have been in my backyard last night? No. Surely it was a neighbor kid playing a prank.

Seth loaded the computer into the back seat of Mom's car then headed to school while Mom and I drove to downtown Nampa. Mom circled the block a couple of times, driving past the police department.

"What are you doing?" I asked.

"Watch your tone."

"I just asked a question." I took a deep breath and tried to find the nicest tone of voice possible. "I'm just curious why you're going around the block when the police department is right there." I pointed as we drove past it again.

"Because the detective's office isn't at the police department. It's in the Family Justice building. I can't remember the address so I'm trying to find the sign." I started searching also and spotted it just as we drove past, too late to pull into the lot. Mom circled once more, and then pulled in. Another car came in behind us.

I hoisted the computer out of the back seat, and we headed toward the entrance. A tall slender man stepped out of his car and hustled to the door before us. Dressed like a businessman from head to toe, his hair was short and freshly combed, and his lightly tanned face was clean shaven. He wore a long sleeve shirt tucked into his dark brown slacks, and at his waist he wore an equipment belt with a holstered gun.

"We keep the door locked at all times," he said and pulled out a key. He opened the door for us, and we entered a small reception area, but no one was within sight. The man came in behind us and stuck out his hand to Mom.

"I'm Detective Corbett."

"Maggie Reid." Mom shook his hand. "This is my daughter, Cynthia." He smiled and pushed some items out of the way on the reception desk.

"Cynthia, you can set that here," he said.

"I prefer to be called Thea." I set the computer on the desk, and he stuck out his hand. What was it with adults and shaking? I felt compelled to extend my hand as well.

"Thea, then," he said and smiled again.

"Do you want her cell phone, too?" Mom asked.

"Yes, let's set it all here together."

She handed over my cell, and I wanted to reach out and grab it. I missed my phone. I missed texting, and I wanted to read the messages from Derek.

"Let's go to the conference room," Detective Corbett said and motioned for us to follow him. Mom waved me in front of her, and she followed behind. We walked down the hallway, and other people began to appear. They all greeted us. Most of them wore equipment belts around their waists; however, no one was dressed in a police uniform.

Detective Corbett waited at an open door, and we moved past him into the conference room. Mom and I sat near the head of a long wide table. He grabbed a chair at the same end, but across from us. He had left the door open, and next to it was a large window with slatted blinds.

"Now then, before we begin, let me tell you a little bit about myself . . ." He went on to explain how long he's worked with the department and how many predators he's investigated and how dangerous the Internet is. I tried not to sigh.

"Thea," he said, and I looked up at him. "Tell me what's going on."

"Like . . . what do you mean?" Why couldn't he just ask a specific question?

"Tell me why you're here today."

"Because my mom thinks I'm in danger." Mom rubbed her face, and my neck stiffened.

"Are you in danger, Thea?"

"I don't know. I didn't think so until this morning, but I'm still not sure."

"What happened this morning?" he asked Mom. She told him about the white chair and the phone calls.

"Can you dust for fingerprints?" I asked.

The detective's smile was replaced by a clenched jaw. He sat still for a moment, and then he said, "We'll look into it."

Mom took a piece of paper out of her purse and slid it across the table to the detective. I caught a glimpse; it appeared she had written the phone number from the caller ID on it. Detective Corbett rose, went to the door, and closed it. Then he turned on me.

"Thea, what's it going to take for you to understand that you are in danger here?" He collapsed into his chair and used his feet to roll it around the corner of the table closer to me.

"Who do you think this guy is?" he asked. Panic welled inside me. The detective scared me more than the idea of Derek in the backyard. While I was pretty certain Derek wouldn't hurt me, this detective was in my face and could reach out and grab me right now.

"Derek is my friend—"

"Really? How would you define your relationship?"

"I guess we're boyfriend-girlfriend." I hated having this conversation, especially in front of Mom. The detective popped up from his chair and paced the edge of the room.

"What makes you think he's your boyfriend?" the detective asked.

"Because we have conversations, we trust each other—"

"Do you love each other?" He jutted out his chin and wedged his thumbs into his equipment belt.

"Yes." I peeked at Mom. She slouched back in her chair. I couldn't believe she was remaining quiet.

The detective bent over the table and raised his voice. "He is not your friend, Thea." He pulled back and asked, "Do you have friends at school?"

"Yes."

"Do they go online and play *Skadi* with you?"

"They have . . ."

"They are your friends. Do you know why?"

"Derek was my friend, and I also have other online friends."

The detective straightened. I couldn't understand why he was so upset. I waited. He sighed.

"Thea, no one online is your friend unless you know them in real life as well. Kids at school can be your friends. People online are not. None of them. You don't know where they live. You don't know who their family is. You don't know the color of their hair."

"I know who Derek is—" The detective propped himself on the edge of the table and crossed his arms. "He lives in Georgia with his dad. His mom died from cancer. He hates that his dad drinks alcohol. His friends give him crap for being with me. We like the same music—"

"She doesn't get it," Detective Corbett said to Mom. He slapped his hand on the table and leaned in toward me. "Thea! Wake up! No one online is your friend. No one. This guy, Derek, he could live down the street from you. He doesn't have to be in Georgia . . ."

From the moment his hand slapped against the table, his voice faded from my hearing. I was tired of being lectured and yelled at. In my head, I cocooned myself and distanced myself from his words. It was working until Mom tapped the table to get my attention. Then his words came flooding back into my head full blast.

". . . He could be a pedophile in prison. He could live around the block. You. Do. Not. Know. Him." The detective paced to the end of the room again. I was being attacked, and I needed to figure out how to defend myself. I'm not as stupid as he's making me sound. I'm not.

"Thea, what would have happened if you'd met Derek after school? That is what you were planning, right? To meet him before basketball practice?"

"Someday. Not right away."

"What would that someday look like? How would the events unfold?"

"I don't know—"

"Answer him," Mom said. Her tone of voice sent daggers through my heart. She was on his side.

My chest tightened, and tears threatened to fall. I lifted my eyes to the ceiling. "We would've talked. Gone for a walk. Gotten something to eat. Nothing major. Nothing wrong." The officer sighed again. Seriously? He was supposed to be helping, but he was ticking me off.

"Thea, he would have gotten you in his car and taken you to another location."

"Okay," I said. What was I supposed to say? The officer shook his head.

"He would've taken you to another location, and if you were lucky, he would have only abused you and left you alive. If you were unlucky, he'd leave you dead."

My chest rose and fell noticeably. I didn't want the officer to see that he was upsetting me, but the idea that Derek may have wanted me dead ripped apart my soul. I folded my arms across my stomach and tried to hold myself together.

"Thea, we're going to investigate him. We're going to get in touch with the Georgia police and have them investigate him also. We're going to go onto *Skadi* and pretend to be you and engage him in conversations. We're going to arrange a time and place to meet, posing as you. Do you understand?"

"He'll be able to tell it's not me. You won't know the answers to certain questions he might ask."

"We know what we're doing, Thea. We've been doing this a long time, and we've caught a lot of predators. But, please, tell me what questions you think he might ask that we won't know the answers to."

"Well, our friend Red lives in Hawaii, but she hasn't been online in a while."

"Your friend?"

"Yes." He made it impossible for me to give him this information, but I needed him to listen. My breathing quickened, and I continued. "I've been worried about her because she hasn't been online in a while. What if Derek is a predator, and he's done something to her?" I pulled a folded piece of paper from my pocket. "This is the article from the Internet. Could you find out if this is my friend Red and see if she really is dead?" He stared at me without responding for a few seconds, and then he reached out for the paper.

"We'll check into it. But she is not your friend. How do you know she isn't Derek's partner? Maybe she helps set traps to lure kids in, like you."

I shook my head.

The detective leaned forward and raised his voice even more. "Thea! No one online is your friend. Your friends are the ones you see in person on a regular basis. You've got to understand that. You were fortunate here. Your mom stopped this before you were violated, raped, abused, or killed. You are one of the fortunate ones. But now you have a responsibility. It is your job to tell others— your real everyday friends that you go to school with—tell them what happened to you, so nothing like this can happen to them. Do you understand me? Is any of this sinking in?"

I found the courage to ask one more question. "What will happen to Derek?"

Detective Corbett shoved away from the table, disgusted with me. "If we're lucky, we'll be able to find a law he's broken and arrest him."

"You know his name and where he lives," Mom said. "Why can't you arrest him now?"

"It's not that simple. We'll search through Thea's phone and computer, and we'll pose as her online, but unless we can find a law he's broken, there won't be much for us to do. If he resided in Idaho, it'd be easier for us to pursue him, but since he lives in Georgia, that complicates the matter."

"What would he have to do in order for you to be able to arrest him?" Mom asked.

"He would have to cross state lines and initiate sexual contact with Thea before any law would be broken."

Mom paled. "So, are we wasting our time here?"

"No. Like I said, we'll go through her equipment, and we'll try to catch him with something online, but he's smart. He'll be on guard." The detective turned back to me. "Thea, you understand, you can never use your old usernames again. We'll be using them. So, never create another character with any of your previous online aliases. Got it?"

"Don't worry," Mom said. "She's never going online again. Period."

The officer glanced at her and then back at me. "Whether you go online or not is between you and your parents, but I'm asking you to never go on *Skadi*. And never utilize your old usernames. Can you agree to that?"

"Yes."

He rose and extended his hand to me. "Thea, I'm glad to meet you in person and alive, rather than finding your body somewhere. Stay safe and make smarter choices. And tell me, who are your friends?"

"The people I see in person on a regular basis."

"That's right. Now go tell them the same thing." He shook Mom's hand. "I'll call you when we're done with the phone and the computer. It'll take us a week, and then you can come back and pick up the equipment."

# CHAPTER 23

Mom dropped me off at school after the appointment with the detective. I handed the attendance slip to my second period algebra teacher. Janie squirmed in her seat, but since there was no empty desk near her, I sat on the far side of the room.

I tried to focus on the math, but my mind kept drifting back to the detective. Once the class ended, Janie bolted over to me.

"Are you okay?" she asked.

"Yeah."

"That's all you're going to say?" I looked into the undernourished face of my best friend and fought to control my emotions.

"I'm okay if you're okay," I said.

"This isn't about me." She stiffened with each word. I linked my arm through hers, and we walked to the hall. Her shirtsleeve seemed to be the only thing covering her bones.

"You're too skinny, and I don't know what to do about it."

"Don't criticize me. You promised . . . How'd the appointment with the detective go?" The bell rang and the hall cleared as fast as cockroaches running from the daylight. We stayed together a moment longer.

"I'll tell you later," I said. "We need to get to class."

"I want all the details," Janie said. She removed her arm from mine and headed in the opposite direction.

■

At lunch, Tim and Janie had a million questions about the police detective. I wanted to answer their questions, but my mind faded away to conversations Derck and I had with each other, especially when we quoted song lyrics. Lauren Harper's words played over and over in my head. We were supposed to make history. Sing and dance. Because this was supposed to be more than just a short romance.

"Thea, did you hear me?" Janie asked.

"What?"

"Did the detective find out anything about Red?"

"I told him about her. But he was pretty upset with me."

"Why?" Tim asked.

I chewed on the inside of my cheek. "He kept going on and on about who your real friends are." I rubbed my eyes. "Can we talk about something else for a while? I can't deal right now."

"Sure," Janie said. "What do you want to talk about?"

"When's your dad coming home?" Tim asked.

I threw my head down on my arms. My breath rebounded from the lunchroom table and spread warmth across my cheeks.

"Sorry," Tim said.

I lifted up and asked, "How am I ever going to fix this with my parents? They are so disappointed in me."

"Do everything they say with a smile on your face," Tim said.

"Speaking from experience?" Janie smirked.

"And I've lived to see another day." Tim waggled his eyebrows.

The bell rang.

We separated for classes. The rest of the afternoon went quickly, and I headed to the locker room to dress down for basketball. I laced up my shoes and gave myself a pep talk. I could do this. I needed to concentrate on my basketball skills.

I listened to the basketball coach and paid attention, but halfway through practice a guy who resembled Derek peeked in through the gym doors, and I stifled a scream.

Surely, it wasn't him, but I couldn't tell because he didn't come all the way into the gym. I had to stop for a second and take a deep breath, but that made it worse. My gut hurt like someone had taken a sledgehammer to it. I was overreacting. I ignored the pain and ran back into place for the drills.

Mom showed up and watched the end of practice. I grabbed my gear and walked out with her.

"How'd your day go?" she asked.

"Fine."

"Really?"

"Really." We got into the car and headed out of the lot.

"So, what was the best part of your day?" Mom asked. My mouth dropped in surprise. Was she not angry with me anymore? Her sympathetic tone made me wonder if the danger was over. "Well?" she asked.

"Seeing you?" I accidentally said it as a question rather than an answer. She picked up on it immediately.

"You don't sound certain of that. Let's try again . . . What was the best part of your day?" I remembered Tim's advice to smile and do what she wanted.

"Seeing you," I said with confidence.

"What was the second best thing?"

"Well, basketball went better today."

"What was the worst?" She kept her eyes forward on the road.

"Disappointing you." At first, she didn't look at me or say anything, but then a tear slid down her cheek, and she wiped it away.

"Thanks," she said.

We rode the rest of the way in silence.

■

After dinner, Mom handed me a wrapped box.

"What's this?" I asked.

"An early Christmas gift." She surprised me.

"I figured you'd returned all my presents to the stores. Only coal for me this year."

"Never." She placed her hand on my arm. "I love you, Thea . . . Open it."

I did. It wasn't a Quote of the Day calendar. Instead, the box said, Positive Daily Affirmations. I looked to Mom for a clue, because I wasn't sure how to react.

"I don't get it," I said.

Mom opened it and showed me that the calendar was similar to my old favorite; however, instead of quotes, each day said things like: *I can positively influence my life, and I deserve love.*

Just. Great. Tim's words from lunch echoed in my mind. I smiled and said thanks.

"Don't worry . . ." Mom said as she fussed with a ring on her finger. "Your Quote of the Day calendar is still wrapped for Christmas morning. I just thought you might like this one also."

Or not.

She hugged me, and I headed for bed.

# CHAPTER 24

As I packed my backpack the next morning, I picked up the new Positive Daily Affirmations calendar, tore off a couple of pages, and shoved them into my backpack. I had to show them to Janie, because I knew she'd get a good laugh out of them.

When I set the calendar back on my nightstand, a cold chill ran up my neck. I flashed back to the self-defense class and remembered Jackson's warnings. Pay attention to your instincts, he had said. I jerked around expecting to find someone behind me, but no one was there. I checked my window. Still locked. But goose bumps covered my arms. I pulled up the blinds all the way and opened the window. I peered out. Nothing. I poked at the screen with my index finger to see if it would come loose. It didn't. I couldn't tell from the inside if it was screwed in like Derek had suggested that one night. Why had I never checked it before now? I gathered my courage and examined the screen.

Two black plastic tabs stuck out on the right side. With a hand on each one, I tugged, and the screen moved a bit. I pulled harder and then wiggled it upward. The screen popped out of the frame, slipped from my fingers, and fell to the ground outside. I leaned through the window, and my hands grazed a bunch of nicks in the outside framework of the window. With the tip of my index finger, I traced the gouge marks. I glanced outside, but I needed a better view. I shut the window, hustled down the hall, ran through the kitchen, and rushed out back.

The screen lay on the ground, bent. Dad would kill me when he found it. I lifted it and tried to straighten it back to its original shape. No luck. I only made it worse. I propped it against the house and studied the nicks on the window frame.

Had someone tried to pry open my window? No. That was insane. Those marks had probably been there for a long time. I fiddled with my lip and tried to come up with a reasonable solution. But I couldn't think of one.

As I turned to head back inside, another shiver ran through my bones. I scanned the backyard for anything unusual. The naked branches of the large dogwood tree squirmed after a short gust of air blew through the yard. My imagination was playing tricks on me. I swallowed hard and realized it was official. Not only was I alone, but I was also going crazy. I assured myself Derek was still in Georgia. He'd made up the stuff about my screen being screwed in, and I was worrying for nothing. After a few deep breaths, I went back into the house to finish getting ready for school.

■

I jogged into the cafeteria and searched for Janie, but I didn't see her. A hand seized my arm from behind. I tugged away and spun around. Tim stood frozen, apparently confused by my sudden action.

"You scared me! Give a girl some warning before grabbing her!"

"Sorry," Tim said. His perfectly straight teeth distracted me.

"Where's Janie?" I asked.

"I was about to ask you." We checked the room once more. No Janie. The bell rang. We headed for the hall and walked toward her locker, but she wasn't there.

"Maybe she's sick," Tim said.

"She was fine yesterday."

The tardy bell rang, and Tim said, "I'll see you at lunch." We went separate directions for our first period classes. Where was Janie?

∎

Tim waited by my locker before lunch. "What are you doing here?" I asked.

"Watching for you."

"We could have found each other in the cafeteria."

"Sure, but this way we can go together." Strange. It was one thing when Tim was helping Janie and me get back together, but it was odd being here alone with him. Well, as alone as two people could be in a herd of high school students.

"Where are Josh and Taylor?" I asked. I hardly ever saw Tim hanging out with them anymore. Tim pointed down the hall. Josh and Taylor huddled with a couple of cheerleaders. The two guys proudly wore their wrestling T-shirts. I glanced around the hall at the other students and spotted several more guys in their school spirit wrestling shirts, and then realized the cheerleaders were wearing their uniforms.

"Is there a wrestling tournament today?" I asked. Tim nodded.

"Where's your shirt?"

"I'm not on the team."

"Did you try out?"

Tim shook his head, and then without warning, he grabbed my hand. "Come on, let's go to lunch." He dragged me away from the locker and down the hall.

"Wait!" I pulled back. "The coach promised to post the rosters by lunch time. I want to see if I made the team."

"Sure thing," he said and dropped my hand. But before I could breathe a sigh of relief he placed the same hand on the small of my back to lead me down the hall. Pretty sure I didn't need to be led.

"What are you doing?" I stopped in the middle of the hall, and a girl bumped into me. The stream of students flowed around us.

A bit of pink colored his tanned cheeks, and his blue eyes were duller than I remembered.

"Why are you hanging out with me? Touching me?" For as long as I could remember, Tim always invaded my personal space. I wasn't a hugging kind of girl, and I didn't understand why he needed to be so close to me all the time.

"Why aren't you on the wrestling team?" I asked.

Tim sighed and evaded my questions. "Let's check the list," he said and reached for me, but I swatted him away. "All right," he said. "No touching. Sorry."

"Why aren't you on the wrestling team?" I asked again, determined to find out the truth. "Why aren't you hanging out with Josh and Taylor?"

The color on his cheeks darkened. "Don't push this. Let's check the list and then eat lunch."

What was wrong with him? I'd never seen him act this way before. I hated that he wouldn't answer my questions. But considering how patient he'd been with me, I decided to cut him some slack. I had no idea why he'd stuck with me through all this crap with Derek. He even stuck with me when Janie hadn't.

"You promise to tell me later?"

He gave a slight nod and said, "Sure."

We made our way to the gym. Tim moved shoulder to shoulder with me. His hand brushed against mine, but he didn't try to take it. I wasn't sure if I was relieved or sad. I looked up at him and smiled. He slowly smiled back.

A crowd of girls surrounded the list posted on the gym wall. I maneuvered my way to the front and searched for my name. It wasn't there. I scanned the sophomore team list, the JV, and the varsity, but my name was nowhere. I read through the lists once more. A girl to my left screamed and jumped. She made varsity. Two girls leaned into the list and found their names on the sophomore team. They held hands and squealed. Somebody bumped in front of me, and I could no longer see the roster. Another girl squeezed past me, and I stepped backward. My eyes burned. I blinked, hoping to fight the tears pushing against my will. I looked down at my white-knuckled fists and shook them out.

"I'll be all right," I whispered to myself and took a deep breath.

I walked back to where Tim waited. "There's always next year," he said.

"How'd you know I didn't make the team?"

"The expression on your face," he said. "Let's eat." He pointed to the cafeteria.

We got our food and found an empty table. Famished, I inhaled my taco. Tim pushed his food around.

"I was on *Skadi* yesterday," he said out of the blue. I stopped eating. He popped a carrot into his mouth and chewed.

"And . . ." I said.

"I was curious if you missed it. Missed him. If you're doing okay."

"Did you see him on there?"

"Yes, and . . . I saw your username on there." Tim locked eyes with me. "Were you on *Skadi* talking to Kit?"

My heart beat faster at the idea. I shook my head but couldn't form the words.

"Then why was your character listed in the game?" Tim's voice cracked at the end of the question. Before I realized what I was doing, I reached across the table and touched his wrist with my fingertips.

"Is that why you're acting weird today? It wasn't me. It was the cops. They said I could never go on *Skadi* again, and I could never use my old usernames again. They are trying to trap Derek or trick him. I don't know. But I swear it wasn't me on *Skadi*. The police have my computer and my cell phone. I have no way of contacting Derek."

"Would you if you could?" he asked.

I pulled my hand away. "Not sure. But I don't have the option anyway. Otherwise, I might be tempted, but only because I want to find out his side of the story."

"Thea, promise me you will never contact this guy."

"I won't. But if I am making promises, you have to tell me why you've been acting so strange lately. Why do you keep touching me? Hanging out with me? Why aren't you on the wrestling team?"

Tim opened his mouth to answer, but before he could say anything, Josh, Taylor, and their two cheerleader girlfriends stumbled over to our table laughing uncontrollably.

"Hey, Thea!" Josh said. "I heard Janie's in the hospital. Did she choke on a marshmallow or something?"

"What?" It took most of my strength to not jump up and strangle him.

Taylor's expression changed from a giant smirk to somberness. He stepped forward. "Sorry, Thea. We thought you'd know the details. We heard she was taken to the hospital last night in an ambulance."

I stood up before he finished the last word, and my heart plummeted. I reached into my pocket for my cell phone, but my pocket was empty. Tim handed me his before I could even ask.

"Who do I call?" I asked Tim.

Josh repeated my words, mocking me.

Without thinking, I dropped Tim's phone, spun around, and shoved the heel of my hand into Josh's chin. I was sick and tired of his stupid antics. Enough was enough. Josh stumbled off balance and massaged his jaw.

"You stupid girl!" He lunged for me, but Tim stepped in and blocked him.

"Get out of my way!" I yelled. "I don't need you to save me!"

Tim clutched my wrist. "Stop," he said to me.

"Walk away, Josh," Taylor said. But Josh tensed with anger. When Tim turned toward him, Josh bumped his chest into Tim's and started to lift his hands. Tim was faster and shoved Josh.

Taylor grabbed Josh's arm. "We're leaving." Then he pointed a finger at Tim. "Back off." Taylor coaxed Josh into walking away with a friendly slap on the back with his left hand and a tug of his shirt with his right hand. Their cheerleaders followed behind.

Tim waited, motionless, for a few seconds. Adrenaline pumped through my veins, and I wanted another shot at Josh. They had stopped me before I had a chance to finish. Students who had gathered around to watch, broke up, realizing the action was over. A teacher entered the cafeteria, but he'd already missed the fight. Tim turned his attention back to me. His cheeks were flushed.

"I can fight my own battles," I said.

He bent down and picked up the two pieces of his phone from the floor and snapped them back together. "Call Janie," he said.

But I couldn't. I had become so used to speed-dialing her on my phone that I couldn't remember her number off the top of my head.

"Call your mom, then," Tim said, seeing my hesitation.

I dialed home. With my free hand, I reached up and pulled at a strand of hair. I wrapped it around my index finger and waited for Mom to answer. Tim pulled my hand from my hair and laced his fingers through mine. I didn't stop him this time. We were locked together in that moment, but the spell was broken when Mom answered the phone.

"Mom," I started, but had to pause when my voice cracked. Tim squeezed my hand gently. I glanced at him, and my chin quivered. He reassured me with a small smile. "Mom, Janie's in the hospital."

"What?" she asked, and I repeated myself.

"Can you find out what's going on?"

"Of course, sweetheart." She was silent for a few seconds and then asked, "Are you all right?"

"I need to know about Janie," I said. Tim's thumb stroked the back of my hand.

"I'll find out. Everything will be okay," she said. Then without missing a beat, she asked, "Whose phone are you using?"

"Tim's."

"Don't use it again. If you need to call me, use the school office."

"Why?" I couldn't help but sigh in frustration.

"Because I almost didn't answer. No name came up with the number on caller ID. And, I told you not to use cell phones right now."

"Fine." Seriously? My friend is in the hospital and Mom is upset about whose phone I'm using? Before hanging up, Mom asked if I had practice today, and I told her I didn't make the team.

"I'm sorry," she said. "Can you ride the bus home?"

"Yes," I answered, and we said our goodbyes.

"Are you riding the bus home?" I asked Tim.

He stared at me. "Yes," he said, and I wondered what he wasn't telling me.

The bell rang.

"Are you going to be okay for the rest of the day?" he asked.

"I'm worried about Janie, but what can I do?"

Tim released my hand and touched my shoulder. He said nothing. And in that moment, I heard Detective Corbett's words. "A real friend is someone you associate with on a daily basis. You know where he lives. You know his parents." Standing in the school cafeteria with students heading out for their classes, I knew I would always remember this moment. I would remember the warmth of his hand on my shoulder, but, I hoped I would forget the sadness in his eyes. What had he given up for me?

"She'll be fine," Tim said. "And so will you." Before I could respond, the principal walked through the cafeteria.

"Get to your classes, kids."

Tim squeezed my shoulder, and we went our separate directions.

∎

As soon as the bus reached our neighborhood, Tim and I bolted for my house. I couldn't wait a moment longer to hear the news about Janie. Mom and Dad sat waiting in the family room. I dropped my bag and threw my arms around Dad.

"I'm so glad you're home!"

"Me too, honey." He loosened his grip and motioned for me to sit. That's when they noticed Tim in the archway.

"Hello, Tim," Mom said. "Come on in." He glanced at me, and I nodded. I knew he wanted to hear the news about Janie as much as I did.

"Thanks." Tim sat on the couch opposite from my parents and me.

"What did you find out about Janie?" I asked.

"She may be in the hospital for a couple of days. But she's doing better."

"And?"

"Apparently—" Mom covered her mouth and tears ran down her cheeks.

Dad continued for her. "She had a heart attack."

"What?"

"A complication of anorexia," Dad said. "Her mom will check her into a recovery program when she's released from the hospital." Dad put his hand on my forearm. "Did you know she had anorexia?" I couldn't respond fast enough; Mom spoke up first. "Janie's mom said you never told her anything about an eating disorder." Mom wiped tears from her cheeks.

"I wanted to," I whispered. Were they trying to say this was my fault for knowing and failing to speak up? Maybe it was.

"It isn't your fault, Thea," Tim said. "We all saw how skinny she was. We tried to tell her to eat more."

I rose and started to leave the room.

Mom gripped my elbow. "Where are you going?"

I yanked back. I was tired of being touched today. I wanted to be alone but Mom blocked my path.

"You can't ignore this," Mom said. "Your friend needs you, and you lied about helping her. You need to accept what's happening around you and stop burying everything."

"Tim, you should go," Dad said. Tim moved to the entryway but glanced at me before walking out. Mom grabbed my arm again, and I didn't jerk it away this time. I did my best to comply and conform to what she wanted.

"Sit down."

I sank on the couch opposite of my parents.

"Is there something going on between you and Tim?" Mom asked.

"We're friends. That's all."

"Thea, you've lied to us . . ." Mom started and stopped. I gave in and looked at both of my parents. Dad put his hand on Mom's knee and encouraged her to continue. She turned her attention back to me, but she started crying again.

"What's the deal with Derek?" Dad asked abruptly.

"He needed a friend."

Dad ran his fingers through his thinning hair.

"I tried to help him. He would've committed suicide if I hadn't been there for him."

"Really?" Dad huffed.

"Yes."

"Well, maybe he still will. Then there'd be one less predator in the world."

"That's horrible!" I said.

"Thea, you're smarter than this." He turned to Mom and asked, "When is her first counseling appointment?"

"Monday."

"I don't need counseling. I'm fine. Can we just go visit Janie?"

Mom wiped her eyes. "She can't have any visitors until tomorrow. But Thea . . . Janie's mom doesn't want you there."

My throat tightened. "Why?"

"She said Janie stopped eating to impress boys, and she blames that on you."

"That's not true. I did not cause this." I needed to escape. I ran out of the family room, down the hall to my bedroom, and slammed the door. This couldn't be happening. My best friend had a heart attack and could be dying . . . and her mom won't let me see her? How does that make sense? I needed to be there for her. She needed to know I cared. But I didn't know how to make it happen.

# CHAPTER 25

The next morning, the mere idea of getting out of bed overwhelmed me. Mom shuffled down the hall, and I scooted up in bed. She turned on the overhead light and then handed me another Christmas gift, but I was too surprised to reach out and take it from her.

"It's not Christmas yet," I said.

She set the present in my lap. "Open it."

I removed the green striped paper and revealed a brand new Quote of the Day calendar. I lifted it out of the box, and the top page said *From Mom & Dad, we love you.*

"I thought you could use it early," she said.

I reached out and wrapped my arms around her. "Thanks, Mom."

"You're welcome," she said and walked away.

I removed the top page and set it on my nightstand. The first quote read:

*Rare as is true love, true friendship is rarer.—Jean de La Fontaine*

I traced the edge of the calendar. I needed Janie to be okay. I peeled off the page, but I couldn't bring myself to crumple it and throw it away. Instead, I sank to the floor near my trash can and let the paper float inside. My chest rose, and I read the next quote.

*Education is the path from cocky ignorance to miserable uncertainty.—Mark Twain*

Seriously? Was the universe against me today? I removed the page and set it in the trash can on top of the previous one. I held the calendar closer and read the new quote:

*Truth, like a torch, the more it's shook it shines.—William Hamilton*

Better. This could even be the first quote to write into a new notebook. Maybe. I wasn't sure I was ready to start fresh yet. I tucked the page into the pocket of my backpack.

When I set the new calendar on my nightstand next to the Positive Daily Affirmations calendar, I noticed the wall by my bed was bare . . . except for a small piece of tape that held a torn edge of paper. I lifted my hand to the spot where I had previously posted my August 10th quote, which I knew from memory:

*Love has nothing to do with what you are expecting to get, only with what you are expecting to give, which is everything.—Katharine Hepburn*

A chill ran through me. I was no longer willing to give everything for Derek. I pulled the mattress away from the wall to see if the page had somehow fallen down, but there was nothing. I searched my memory. Was the quote on the wall last night when I went to bed? What about yesterday before school? And why did it appear to have been ripped from the wall, with the tape still there? Could someone have taken it?

My heart hammered inside my chest.

"Mom!"

I scanned the room. Was anything else missing? Uncertain at first, I noticed my jacket hanging on the back of my chair—and my favorite fuzzy pink scarf was gone. My mind raced a million miles per second. I always hung my scarf on top of my coat. I always kept them together. This was not my imagination playing tricks on me.

"Mom!" I yelled again. But no response.

"Dad!" I screamed even louder. Nothing. No one.

Where were they?

I reached out and lifted my jacket, praying that my scarf was tucked underneath. Right then, the house's heater kicked on, and warm air blew from the floor vent. Every hair stood up on my body, and I caught a whiff of a familiar odor . . . but it was faint and

disappearing. I couldn't recall where I'd smelled it before. My heart froze. I couldn't take another breath.

My jacket slipped from my fingers and fell to the floor. No scarf. No quote. Panic swelled inside of me. I imagined Derek in my room, touching my scarf, holding it up to his face, lingering there, and breathing in my fragrance.

A bead of sweat rolled down my forehead. What if I wasn't alone? What if Derek was somewhere inside the house? What if he took the scarf and the quote? Our quote. My breaths jump-started and then came faster and faster. I seemed unable to control myself.

A door slammed.

I shrieked and sank to the floor. What was I supposed to do?

"Mom!" I yelled once more, but not as loud this time. What was the point?

But . . . she came . . . and I stared in disbelief when she stepped through my doorway.

"What is it?" she asked.

"Where were you?" My throat tightened with each word.

"Taking the trash out." Mom's forehead wrinkled, and she knelt next to me. "What's happened?"

"I needed you . . . but you didn't come."

"I'm here now, baby-girl." She caressed my hair. "What's wrong?"

I leaned into Mom's arms and asked, "Did you take my August 10th quote off the wall?"

"No."

"Did you take my scarf?"

"No." Her back stiffened, and she, too, scanned the room. "Are they missing?" While she said the words, she got up and moved to my window, touched the lock, and peered outside. Her face paled. "Did you leave your scarf at school? Or in the laundry?"

I shook my head.

She came back and wrapped her arms around me. "Everything will be all right. I'm sure there's a reasonable explanation. The police

are involved. Derek is probably still in Georgia. Our minds are just playing tricks on us."

I pulled back from her. "Then where's my stuff?"

"I don't know." We both looked at my nightstand.

"Should I drive you to school today?" she asked.

"Yes," I said, but then thought about it longer. "No . . . a lot of people will be riding the bus." The idea of getting there alone petrified me, but I knew Tim would be waiting. I could just walk really fast to the bus stop and be fine.

■

After a hot shower and a quick breakfast, I settled my nerves and headed out of the house. I paused at the sidewalk and studied my surroundings. No one jumped out from behind any bushes. No lurkers hung down at the end of the street. I figured if I paid attention, I couldn't be taken by surprise. But as I walked, my mind wandered, and I focused on Janie and how I could possibly see her or talk to her again.

I heard footsteps and looked up to see who was approaching. My shoulders relaxed when I recognized Tim coming down the street. I could identify him a mile away with his height and plaid winter bomber hat.

"What are you doing here?" I asked.

"Thought you could use a friend this morning." Tim's words created puffs of white air in front of his lips, and his cheeks were red from the cold morning. We walked together.

"Janie's mom won't let me visit or talk to her," I blurted out. Tim asked why, and I filled him in on what Mom said the night before.

"That's crazy," he said. "You've always been the one to stand up for Janie. Remember last winter when Josh and I were about to ask you two to the Winter Solstice dance and Josh screwed it all up by calling Janie a marshmallow?"

I stopped midstep. "You mean you were going to ask us?"

Tim spun around and came back to me. "Of course. I thought you knew that?"

"Well . . . I guess we assumed . . . but then Josh was such a jerk and I . . . well, I got so mad—"

"Do you think things would've been different for Janie if we'd just asked you two to the dance?"

"Different for Janie?" Dang. I stumbled over the words, and my throat closed in. My heart pounded in my chest. I bent forward trying to calm down.

"Are you okay?" Tim asked and moved closer. I felt his hand on my back. Different for Janie. Did this all start with the marshmallow comment? Different for Janie. I couldn't get the words out of my head. What about different for me? Everything would've been different for both Janie and me if Tim and Josh had just asked us to the dance that morning. I could've spent the last year getting to know Tim better, not Derek. I would've never been introduced to *Skadi* if I'd been going to the dances with Tim. I wouldn't need to be worrying about Derek lurking in the bushes, or worrying about seeing a stupid counselor, or worrying about Janie dying. All over a stupid marshmallow comment. I caught my breath and straightened. My cheeks heated with fury, and I started speed walking toward the bus stop.

"Thea!" Tim reached for me, but I jerked away. I did not want to be touched. "Wait a second!"

I slowed my pace just short of the bus stop and scanned the group. Josh wasn't there yet.

"I can't do this today," I said. "People will ask about Janie. What am I supposed to say? Josh will be a jerk for sure."

"He won't be at school. So don't even worry about him."

"Why?"

"The wrestling team left this morning for a tournament on the other side of the state."

"Why are you not with them?"

Tim turned away. I enclosed his bare red knuckles with my mitten-covered hand. He took my other hand and gripped them both.

"Tryouts happened while I was in the guild with Kit," Tim said. "I had joined *Skadi* to have something in common with you, but then Kit started saying stuff about girls online. I was scared for you. What was I supposed to do? I couldn't wrestle knowing this jerk was out there lying to you. I would die if anything happened to you. So, I talked to Janie about you and about Kit. You know the rest."

"No, I don't. What are you not telling me?"

"It would be such a disgrace, if I fell short and you were not safe."

"Don't quote song lyrics to me," I said. "Tell me the truth."

"It's the truth, Thea. I've loved you since the fifth grade." His cheeks reddened even more, and not from the cold morning. He lifted his hand and wiped a tear from my cheek. I didn't even realize I was crying until then. I bit my lip, and his cold smooth fingers rested against my face.

The bus grumbled to a halt at the stop. We waited for everyone else to board, and then I asked Tim to go before me. I still hated riding the bus, but lately, with Tim, it was bearable. He'd find us a seat, even if that meant he had to ask someone to move. But today the bus wasn't crowded since so many people were gone for the wrestling tournament. Tim found us an empty seat in the middle.

We sat in awkward silence for what seemed like an eternity, and then Tim set his hand palm up on his knee, an invitation. I pulled off my mitten and intertwined my fingers with his.

"It's going to be okay," he said. "We don't need to talk about what I said at the bus stop. Let's just worry about Janie and get through the day."

I nodded with relief but then asked, "How am I going to talk to her?"

Tim handed me his cell phone. "I programmed the hospital's number into speed-dial number one for you," he said. "You can use my phone to call her anytime."

"What if her mom answers? She'll recognize my voice." Tim pressed the buttons on the phone and put it to his ear. He asked for Janie's room. Then he asked someone for permission to speak to Janie. Tim mouthed the words, "her mom" to me. My lips pulled downward as I pictured Janie in the hospital room.

"Hey, Janie," Tim said, and I grabbed the phone from him.

"Janie?" More silent tears spilled down my cheeks. "How are you?"

"Alive," she said, but her voice was faint. "Sorry—" Janie choked on the word.

"What are you possibly sorry for?" I bent forward so the other kids wouldn't see my tears. I used my knuckle to wipe them away, but more fell.

"Everything," Janie said.

"I want to see you, but I guess your mom doesn't want me to."

"It's true."

I could tell she couldn't say more. Her mom must be right there.

"How long will they keep you in the hospital?"

"Not sure, but then they're sending me to a clinic for treatment. They say I'm anorexic."

"Are you?"

"No. I don't know. Maybe."

"Will you be able to use your cell phone? I could use Tim's phone to text you at lunch or something."

"I can't use my cell in the hospital, but I might be able to in the clinic. I don't know yet. My mom says I have to get off the phone now."

"I'll try to call at lunch. Okay? Hang in there."

"Okay." She disconnected, and I handed the phone back to Tim.

"Keep it."

"I can't. It's your phone."

"Keep it. That way if you want to text or call Janie you can."

I was tempted. "No . . . but we can call her at lunch." Tim pocketed the phone, and the bus pulled into the lot. We made our way to the cafeteria, and without talking we went through the line for breakfast. We sat at our usual table, and Tim broke the silence.

"Did I damage our friendship this morning?"

Surprised by his question, I hesitated before answering. After I set my food down, I said, "Not at all . . . I feel so stupid for all the dumb choices I've made over the last year."

"You're not stupid. You were tricked." He started to reach toward me, but stopped himself. "Sorry," he said and shook his hand. "I forget that you don't want me to touch you."

"Why do you always want to anyway?"

His cheeks didn't blush this time, and his eyes bore deep into mine. "If I can touch you . . . your hand, your shoulder, your back . . . I'm connected to you, and I know you're all right."

"But I'm not."

"You will be."

The bell rang, and we reluctantly headed to our separate classes.

■

Tim waited for me again before lunch. The sight of him leaning against the row of lockers relaxed my tense muscles.

"Is this becoming a habit?" I asked him.

"Easily," he said through his warm grin. He moved out of the way so I could throw my books into my locker. He seemed to be surrounded by a renewed energy force—his own personal bubble—and when I stood close to him, it seemed as if gravity pulled me in even closer. I took a step back from my locker to shut the door and bumped into him. His hand went to my shoulder to steady me. Without a thought I looked up into his eyes.

His smile faded, and we remained transfixed until he cleared his throat and took a step backward. He glanced down at the floor and then back up to me.

"Let's grab lunch and call Janie," he said. I agreed, and we headed toward the cafeteria, side by side.

We found an empty table near the wall, and Tim fished his cell out of his pocket. After he had Janie on the phone, he handed it to me.

"They're transferring me to the clinic this afternoon," Janie said right away.

"Already? Have you healed enough to be moved?" I asked.

"I don't know. I just have to do what they tell me."

"I know the feeling," I said. "Is your mom right there?"

"No, so we can talk, but she could be back any second. How are you?"

"I'm worried about you. I'm sorry you have to go through this."

"Oh, Thea. I don't want to go to the clinic by myself." Janie hiccupped, and her voice changed pitch. "I don't want to do this alone."

"You can call me whenever you need me," I said.

"What if I can't get a hold of you?" Her sobs became louder.

I glanced at Tim. He listened while he ate his lunch, his eyes glued to me. I watched him as I spoke the next words to Janie.

"Tim said I could keep his phone." I waited for a reaction from Tim. He nodded confirming his previous offer. I mouthed a "thank you" to him and continued speaking to Janie, "So, you can call or text me any time you need to."

"Thanks. When I find out where they're sending me, I'll let you know." I could hear Janie's mom in the background.

"Do you have to go?"

"Yes. Bye," Janie said and disconnected the call. I pushed the End button on Tim's phone and handed it to him, but he shook his head and finished chewing a mouthful of food.

"Keep it. You told Janie you would."

"What if your parents try to reach you on your phone?"

"Answer it if you think it's Janie, and every time we're together, I'll check for messages. Easy." Tim grinned. I slipped the phone into my pocket. We enjoyed the rest of our lunch with simple conversation about schoolwork, and then we went our separate directions.

I headed for my locker to grab the textbook I needed for my next class, and as I approached, I noticed a square piece of paper on the door. I quickened my pace to see it more closely, but then stopped in my tracks when I realized someone had duct taped my August 10th quote to the front of my locker:

*Love has nothing to do with what you are expecting to get, only with what you are expecting to give, which is everything.—Katharine Hepburn*

Dread, like a thick black sludge, welled up inside of me. I scanned the hallway left and right to catch someone watching me, but the students all hurried to get to their next classes. No one paid any attention to me.

I ripped the quote off my locker, crumpled it up into a tiny ball, and threw it along the hallway. One guy turned and glanced at me as the wad whizzed past him, but he said nothing and kept on moving. I opened my locker, expecting to find my pink scarf hanging inside, but it wasn't there. I leaned my head forward and rested my shoulders against the metal frame. Who stuck the quote to my locker?

The image of Coach Gavyn taping up the basketball stats during tryouts flashed into my mind. I didn't think much of it at the time, but he'd used gray tape. It could have been duct tape. And the padded equipment he wore at the final self-defense class had been patched with duct tape. Could Coach Gavyn be Kitsuneshin? Had he been in my house? I gasped.

Should I tell Officer Ford?

No.

There was no way it could be Coach Gavyn.

Besides, everyone had access to duct tape. For all I knew Seth could have played a cruel joke on me. He was certainly angry enough to do it. But I still debated if I should tell anyone. What was the point? They'd all think I was crazy.

I took a few deep breaths, hoping to get a grip on the situation. I convinced myself that Seth had taped the quote to my locker. He had access and opportunity. And I would not give him the pleasure of seeing me freak out. I simply wouldn't acknowledge it at all. I firmed up my determination to remain strong. Besides, I still had another class to endure.

I pulled Tim's phone from my pants pocket and slipped it into the side compartment of my backpack, leaving it in my locker. I did not want to be caught with someone else's cell in my possession. Not with Officer Ford constantly checking on me. I grabbed the textbook I needed and slammed the locker door.

"Hey, Thea!"

I dropped the book.

Marcus stooped down and picked it up for me. Instead of thanking him, I hauled off and whacked him on the arm.

He scrunched up his forehead. "Sorry. I didn't mean to scare you . . . I just wanted to see how you're holding up."

"I'm fine." I wanted to ask him how long he'd been standing there watching me, but I didn't have the strength for much more today. I started down the hall toward my class, and Marcus trailed me.

"Seth mentioned you were in trouble, and the police are involved."

I walked faster toward my class.

"Anything I can do for you?" he asked.

I twisted around and studied him. Maybe Seth had dared Marcus to tape that quote on my locker. Could Marcus be that cruel? "Why are you talking to me?"

He didn't flash his usual drop-dead-gorgeous smile. Instead, he pulled back as though I'd slapped his face.

"Are you Kitsuneshin?" I asked.

He said nothing and gawked at me.

Surely, he would've told me if he was. My cheeks lit on fire. I had overreacted, again. Marcus was only trying to be nice to me.

"Sorry," I said and darted into my classroom before he could say or do anything.

■

Later that evening, I sat in the family room finishing up my algebra homework when Dad walked past the front window. I hopped up and met him at the door. His hands were full carrying his briefcase and my computer.

"Why do you have my stuff?" I asked. He set the heavy load on the coffee table, and Mom came into the room with a kitchen towel in her hands.

"Did Detective Corbett have anything else to say?" she asked.

"He wasn't even there when I stopped in," Dad said. Mom scrunched the towel.

"Will someone please tell me what's going on?" I asked.

They slumped onto opposite couches. I sat with Mom and looked back and forth between them.

"The police finished with your computer and your cell phone," Dad said.

"Does that mean I get them back now?"

"No!" They said in unison.

"When can I?"

"Never, and stop asking or I'll make it even longer than that," Mom said. I couldn't tell if she was joking or serious. Probably serious.

"So, if the police gave the equipment back, does that mean they've arrested Derek?"

"They're not arresting him." Mom threw the wadded up towel on the coffee table. "The Georgia police went to the address listed with his cell phone registration and no one lives there. The place was abandoned and falling apart."

"So where does he live?" I asked.

Dad leaned forward. "The detective said they tried to back trace his computer's IP address from *Skadi*, but he used something like the Tor network and Privoxy software, which hindered their investigation. They even tried to find him through his cell usage, but he must've used VoIP or some other Internet phone service to mask his location. They don't know where he is. There was no forwarding address from his Georgia property. For all we know, he changed his name and left the state years ago." Every fiber of my being froze. Where had Derek been during our hours of chatting online? During our phone calls? I knew the Georgia time difference by heart. Was it possible he'd never been there at all?

"And besides all that," Mom said, "the police say he hasn't broken any laws. There's not much more they can do to help us."

"What about fingerprinting that white chair?" I asked.

"The detective said it wasn't necessary," Dad said.

"Why?" I asked.

Dad rubbed his jaw. "The police know what they're doing."

"What about Red in Hawaii?" I asked.

"The Hawaiian police department is still investigating her death."

"Did they confirm that the girl in the article was my friend Red from *Skadi*? Is she really dead?"

"It appears so, but they haven't been able to connect Derek to it."

"So, he didn't have anything to do with Red's death? Maybe he only lied about where he lives. Maybe he didn't do anything wrong." My heart rate increased, not because I hoped to renew anything with Derek, but because I hoped he had told me the truth, or even mostly the truth, all along. I hated the idea of him lying to me, and worse yet, I hated the idea of him hurting Red. I didn't care what the detective said, she was my friend, even if I only knew her online.

"No," Dad said. "Derek lied to you, and I'm sure he was about to lure you away. Mom stopped it before any harm came to you, but because she did, they can't arrest him."

"That's freaking nuts." I rose and stepped over Mom's feet to leave the room.

"Pick up your things, Thea," she said. "The family room is not your closet."

I gathered my schoolwork. "Should I pick up my computer and cell phone, too?"

"No." Mom straightened and folded the towel on the table.

I headed for my room, and once there, I pulled out Tim's cell phone to see if Janie had tried to call or text. Nothing. When I returned the phone to the pocket of my backpack, I felt a piece of paper. I pulled it out and reread it.

*Truth, like a torch, the more it's shook it shines.—William Hamilton*

I taped it to the wall where my August 10th quote used to hang.

# CHAPTER 26

Saturday. The December sunlight busted through the blinds on my window and forced me to wake up to another day in the hardest week of my life. So much had happened that it felt like months had passed, not merely days. The clock showed 9:30 A.M. and I couldn't believe Mom let me sleep in, but before I could finish the thought, she knocked on the doorframe.

"Tim wants to talk to you." She waved the cordless phone and then brought it to me.

Seriously?

I couldn't remember him ever calling me before. I scooted up in bed and took the phone. Mom sat at my desk. Apparently she intended to stay and listen to my side of the conversation. Great.

"Hey," I said in a scratchy morning voice.

"You want to go to a movie today?" Tim asked. Absolutely. That would be a perfect distraction from this miserable day.

I turned toward Mom. "Can I go to the movies?" Tim kept talking while I waited for a response from Mom; he was suggesting I tell her it was with a group, not just him.

"No, I'm pretty sure you're grounded," Mom said.

"Why?" I had never been grounded in my life.

"Are you kidding me?" she asked. "You lied, and we've had multiple conversations with police this week." Valid points. But I hated the idea of spending the entire day locked inside with uptight wardens.

"How long am I grounded for?"

"Forever."

"It's all right," Tim said. "Just tell her okay." I did as he suggested, and he asked if she was still listening.

"Yes," I said to him while staring at Mom. She was relentless.

"Would it be better if I called you on the cell phone?" he asked.

"No point." I knew if he did, somebody in this prison would hear me. I felt like I was the one under arrest. I couldn't talk to anyone or do anything without my parents' permission. They'd taken away my privileges, freedom, and friends. I said goodbye to Tim and handed the phone back to Mom.

"Get up and get ready for the day. There are a lot of chores that need to be done."

Great. She left without another word. I slid off the bed and reached into the backpack for Tim's cell phone. I made sure it was on silent mode, and then with my back to the door, I checked for messages. I hoped for one from Janie. Nothing.

Out of habit, my fingers traced Derek's numbers.

The screen on the cell lit up with an incoming text, and the first five words of the message displayed on the screen. It said it was from Tim. I clicked on View Message and read it. He was using his brother's cell to text me and wanted to know what he could do to help me. I answered.

*Get my freedom back. Get Janie home & healthy. Find out truth about Derek.—Thea*

Tim's reply came, and we swapped texts for a few minutes.

*You did not seriously just list Derek as something u want me to help u with.—Tim*

*I just need to know the truth.—Thea*

*U know the truth.—Tim*

*But the police couldn't arrest him.—Thea*

*Thea, believe your parents and the police. Don't contact him.—Tim*

There was a knock on my open door. I slipped the phone into my pajama pocket and turned around.

"Hurry up. We've got errands to run," Mom said and walked away.

Instead of getting dressed, I sat next to my closet and pulled the cell out again. I sent a quick text telling Tim my mom almost caught me, and I had to stash the phone. He replied with an encouraging "be strong" message. I slipped the cell back into my pocket.

I knew I should agree with Tim, and I knew I should believe my parents and the police, but the detective had returned the equipment in less than a week. They couldn't arrest Derek. Maybe Mom had ruined the investigation before it ever began by warning Derek about contacting the police. Or . . . maybe Derek was innocent. I needed to hear his side of the story . . . but I was relieved that the relationship was over. His unhappiness was too much of a burden for me, and yet I wanted a chance to say goodbye, or something. Maybe I just wanted someone to talk to. Derek and Janie were the ones I talked to everyday, and both were gone . . . but Derek wasn't really gone. I still pictured a twenty-year-old playing computer games somewhere in Georgia. That's who he was to me.

Another knock at the door startled me out of my thoughts. Mom looked down at me sitting on the floor.

"You haven't even moved!"

I didn't answer her.

"Well, since you're nowhere near ready, your dad, Seth, and I will go do errands. We'll be back in less than an hour. Get dressed. We have plans to do things as a family today."

I sat there until I heard them leave and shut the front door. Then I went to the bathroom for a shower, but I didn't get very far because there were no clean towels in the linen closet. After checking the laundry room, with no luck there either, I checked Mom and Dad's bathroom, where I found two clean towels neatly folded.

I began to leave their room, but I heard my cell phone ring. An incoming call. It continued to chime. I listened and tried to zone in on the location of the sound, but it stopped before I found it. What would I do if I found it anyhow? Read the text messages and listen to the voice mail. That's what I'd do. The phone beeped indicating the caller had left a message. The beep came from Mom's dresser. I looked closer and found a cord coming out of one of the drawers.

I dropped the towel on the bed, opened the drawer, and grabbed the phone. I read the list of missed calls. All from Derek. It took me a while to count how many from the last week. Thirty. I listened to the voice mails before reading the texts. Most of the messages were the same . . . asking why I'd done this to him; why wasn't I responding to him; why didn't I love him anymore. The final voice mail, left minutes ago, was different.

"Thea, this is Derek. This will be my last message. I don't understand why you've done this to me. To us. I need to know you're all right. If you want to end our relationship, that's fine. But please talk to me one last time to say goodbye. Please. I won't call or text you again. I hope you will call just to say goodbye."

I held the phone with the tips of my fingers. I wanted to call him. Instead, I scrolled through the text messages. Some didn't make any sense. One said he had to talk to me in private. Several begged me to answer him. I couldn't stand the idea of causing him so much pain.

I unhooked the phone from the cord. Tapped in Derek's number. And let my finger hover over the Send button. Janie's voice rang out in my mind: *Put the phone down and go take a shower!* I could see her swaying her head and shaking her finger at me telling me I'd better put it back or she'd put it back for me . . . I pressed Cancel and pocketed the phone.

I grabbed the towel and headed toward my bathroom. Once there, I set both cell phones—mine and Tim's—on the counter and studied them. I picked up Tim's phone and texted him.

*Call me.—Thea*

A few moments later the cell screen lit up. An incoming call.

"What's up?" Tim asked.

"What time is the movie?"

"Your mom changed her mind?"

"Yup." I needed out of this house. I needed air. Mom would ground me for three lifetimes, but I needed a distraction. I did not want to be tempted to call Derek.

"We're going to leave here in about thirty minutes. Do you want us to pick you up on the way?"

"No. My mom can drop me off at your house."

"Awesome! See you soon then."

"Yup." I set Tim's phone back down on the counter next to mine. Without looking at myself in the mirror, I undressed and stepped into the shower. I tried to keep my mind blank; otherwise, I'd have to think about my actions. I focused on the tasks of washing and scrubbing my body. I started with my hair and lathered it up. I leaned backward under the spray of water to rinse and heard a thud. I strained to listen. Another thud came from somewhere outside the bathroom, but this time it was more like a door closing.

My family must've gotten home. I hurried to finish my shower. When I stepped out, I quickly dried off, slipped my clothes on, and pulled my hair back into a ponytail. I pocketed both my phone and Tim's and wished I had left mine in Mom's room. If she caught me with it now, I'd be dead.

When I opened the bathroom door, I hollered to my family, "Hello!?"

No response.

I walked barefooted down the hall and around the corner to the kitchen. "Hello?" I repeated. Nothing. My stomach tightened. They weren't home after all.

I needed to get out of here.

I headed back toward my room to grab some socks and shoes, but when I started down the hallway, my heartbeat quickened. A framed portrait lay on the carpet. An empty spot on the wall indicated where it should have been. Could one of the thuds I'd heard earlier been someone bumping into the wall and knocking the picture down? My fingers twitched as I bent and picked up the photo. The glass in the frame had cracked. I hung the damaged portrait back on the wall.

The house's heater clicked on, and I jerked my head toward my bedroom door. Had I left it closed? I stepped softly and tried to listen for anything unusual. I turned the door knob and flung the door wide open. It bounced against the door stop. I scanned the room for anything out of the ordinary. My comforter hung over the edge of my bed and extended to the floor. With my bed on risers, it'd be simple for someone to squirm under it. I kicked up the comforter and dropped down on my stomach to look underneath. Nothing. I sat back against the wall and tried to calm down.

After a few deep breaths, I yanked on my socks and shoes and grabbed my winter coat. But before leaving my room, I decided to write a quick note to Mom telling her I went to the movies. She'd be furious, and I'd have to deal with that, but I didn't want her to think I'd run off with Derek. I taped the note to my bedroom door and headed down the hallway. I reached into the bathroom to flip off the light and halted when I caught a glimpse of myself in the mirror. Dark circles shadowed my eyes. I made no attempt to hide them with makeup or mascara. My ever-present freckles no longer bothered me. They were a part of me. I slipped my arms into my coat and moved down the hallway.

I walked toward the front door, and a strange shiver ran up my spine. My hand quivered when I reached for the deadbolt. My finger touched it, and static electricity shocked me. Where could that have come from? We had a stone floor in the entryway; there was no way I could have shuffled my feet to create static electricity. "Never ignore your body's warning signals." The instructors had said it over and over during our self-defense classes. But my body signals had been screwed up the last few days. I wasn't sure I could trust them anymore. I swung the door open and headed outside.

# CHAPTER 27

I walked to the end of the driveway, and hesitated for a moment. Was I being foolish? I searched the length of the street. No one. I inhaled the cold air and reaffirmed my decision. I refused to be locked up in a house all day. The world would not end if I went to a movie with Tim. I turned left toward his house and moved quickly to keep myself warm. About halfway there, I reached the small elementary school that we all attended, a lifetime ago.

I glanced at the time on my cell. Ahead of schedule, I took a detour to the playground hidden at the back of the school. A breeze picked up a pile of dry broken leaves and spun them along the asphalt. A swing set creaked in the distance. I crunched through the fallen leaves and checked the fence line. The frigid day kept kids away from the playground. With my phone in hand, I sat in one of the swings and pushed back and forth, my feet on the frozen ground.

Alone.

I'd disappointed my family. Let down Janie. Lied to Tim. And I had trusted Derek. What now?

I could call Tim and tell him I changed my mind. I could be back inside my house before Mom ever even knew I'd left. There'd be no consequences . . . except for the fact I'd have to live with myself for the rest of my life. Doubting. Wondering. Submitting to the will of the adults around me. The police. The counselor. The parents. My breathing quickened. I tilted my head toward the sky and fought back the tears. I refused to cry. I would not be weak any longer. I could make my own choices for my own best interest.

I could discover the truth for myself. Get my questions answered. Move on. With peace. Knowing.

I could call Derek.

Let him tell his side of the story. What was the worst that could happen? He could tell me more lies. But, maybe, he'd tell me the truth. He'd have a rational explanation for everything that had happened. He'd put my mind at ease. And I could move forward with my life, knowing that I stepped up and took control of this situation. Did he truly love me? The hours we'd spent confiding in each other. The way his voice made my body tingle. I was certain of it. He loved me more than anyone else.

I removed a glove, tapped his number into my keypad, and before I could change my mind, I pressed Send. I lifted the phone to my ear, and along with the ringing, I heard another sound.

Behind me.

A ringtone.

"It's me and you, eternally—" The DeathTomb lyrics.

Lightning struck along my spine. My phone slipped from my grasp and hit the ground below. My world stopped spinning. The breeze stopped blowing. And the swing stopped creaking. Maybe if I stopped breathing, this wouldn't be real. Just my imagination.

"Thea . . ."

I recognized his voice.

I squeezed my eyes shut. I couldn't turn around. A trickle of sweat rolled down the back of my neck. I clamped my hands around the chains that suspended the swing. He stood so close behind me his body heat warmed my hands. Every fiber in me tightened. Run. Get up and run. But fear and disbelief froze me to the seat of the swing. It could not be him.

His fingers stroked my hair, and I flinched ever so slightly. "Thea . . ." He moved to the side of me and then to the front, never removing his hand, but letting it glide from the top of my head to the side of my face.

I reluctantly opened my eyes, and he knelt in front of me.

Truth.

I gasped, and a tear ran down my cheek. He wiped it away, and I trembled.

Sculpted. Defender. Mercenary. Eight-pack. Instructor. Brick wall. Derek. Kit. Jackson.

"Say something," he pleaded. The stench of sour milk from his breath hit me. I coughed and moved to cover my mouth, but Jackson grabbed my wrist and restrained me, his strength undeniable. This was really happening. He was stronger and bigger than me . . . bigger than one hundred of me. I studied him. His hair, limp and greasy. His face, stubbly and tired. He'd clearly not showered in days. His mustache, no longer neatly trimmed, had overgrown his lip and hung in a sad little frown.

"I don't understand," I whispered.

"It's me," he said.

"Derek?" I choked out the word.

Jackson wrapped his massive arms around me and embraced me tightly. His navy wool jacket scratched against my neck like sandpaper. "Yes."

Over his shoulder, I searched the fence line, hoping someone would come. But no one did.

"Can't breathe," I said, needing him to release me.

"Sorry." He pulled back, but his hands still gripped my shoulders.

"You lied." The words escaped my lips before I had time to filter.

Jackson's eyes narrowed, and his hands squeezed tighter. My stomach knotted, and Seth's advice came to mind: *You need to gently say no so you don't crush the guy.* Choosing what I said from this moment on was crucial. Jackson could easily crush me.

"About your age," I added, trying to soften the accusation. His grip relaxed, but not his expression.

"I told you, that if you knew who I really was, you wouldn't want to be with me. I'm too old for you." He released his hold on me and rubbed his unshaven chin. "I'm so sorry." He clutched the swing and pulled me closer to him. "I love you. That hasn't changed."

I needed to figure a way out of this. But my brain was stuck between knowing this was Jackson—the man who looked out for me, defended me to Mom, and taught me—and knowing this was Derek—the guy who said he was twenty, lived with his drunk father, attempted suicide, and loved me. I couldn't wrap my mind around the person in front of me. And, yet, I still needed to find a way to outfox this kitsune-shin.

"Do you still love me?" he whispered. Tears welled in my eyes. I did not want to cry. But the harder I tried to hold it back, the more my cheeks quivered. "Thea, it's okay. You're safe. Everything's going to be fine." He rubbed his bare hands against my thighs. "You look cold . . . here . . ." He reached into his pocket and pulled out the end of my pink scarf; the rest of it wound out like a snake. He draped it around my neck and knotted it close to my throat; his fingers grazed across my skin.

"I needed something of yours," Jackson whispered, "since we couldn't be together." He lifted the end of the scarf and touched it to his lips. My toes clenched inside my shoes, and my knees jerked. I pictured Jackson in my bedroom, fingering my things. I couldn't breathe.

"Thea, I don't ever want to lose you, and I will fight hard to keep you in my life." His eyes narrowed.

I willed my tears to recede and decided not to antagonize him. If I wanted to run, I'd have to free myself from this swing first. He had me pinned on three sides, and I wouldn't be able to get out of it backward quickly enough. Strength. Psychology. Confidence. Jackson taught these traits in his class. Right now, strength was on his side, but I could draw on the power of the other two traits to distract him.

"Please. Explain. Your side." I struggled to speak, but I needed to get him talking.

"From the moment you came into my self-defense class, I was drawn to you. When I heard you played *Skadi*, I realized fate had brought us together. I haven't connected with anyone like you in real life for decades. Thea, you are the whole package—your soul intoxicates me as much as your body does. And sometimes . . . we can't help who we fall in love with. But I worried you'd think I was too old for you. So, I connected with you online and told you I was younger."

"Why didn't you ever tell me who you were?"

"I wanted to . . . so many times . . . I hoped once you got to know me, you could accept my age. But before we got that far . . ." His jaw clenched. "Your friends. Your mother. They interfered."

My vision blurred when I recalled the classes with Jackson. I had to figure out how to make him move away from me. "What about your dad? Your mom? The suicide attempts?"

"All true. But that all happened over twenty years ago. You're the only person I've ever told." I bit the inside of my cheek. He had said he tried to take his life recently because he couldn't talk to me. That must have never happened. I needed him to keep talking until he let his guard down.

"How old are you?" I asked.

"Forty-seven." He fiddled with one end of his mustache, watching my reaction. I held still.

"What about Georgia?"

"I grew up there and went to school there. I even own a house there."

"What about Lokelani?"

"I never touched her."

"But you knew her real name?"

His lips tightened, and I knew he'd made a slip.

"Yes, I knew her name, but that doesn't matter anymore . . . Let's go and talk somewhere else," he said. His words rushed out. "Come with me. My car's out front. We can go anywhere you want.

Somewhere warmer. Or we could take that walk in the park we fantasized about . . ." His hands moved to my waist. I chewed on the inside of my cheek again and tasted blood in my mouth. For a split second, I wondered if I should try to appease him and go with him, but then I remembered all of the "stranger-danger" warnings: never let him take you to a second location. I could not leave with him. Plus, if he did kill Red, if that was true, it meant he could kill me, too.

"Thea, I love you. I always will. My life is nothing without you. Tell me you still love me."

I had to calm him somehow and convince him to move back. And . . . sometimes lying was easier than confrontation.

"I still love you," I said in a breath while setting my hands on top of his.

He grinned, but his mustache still drooped, and I could see each and every one of the greasy blackheads along the rim of his nose. He lifted one hand to my face and cupped my cheek. Then he traced his thumb along my jawline and paused beneath my lip. He leaned in.

No.

Air puffed from my nose.

I did not want this to be my first kiss.

He closed the distance between us; one hand behind my head pulled me closer; the other hand fingered the wretched scarf beneath my chin. He pressed his lips to mine. The coarse wiry mustache stabbed my skin, and I thought for sure I would vomit. But I didn't respond at all. And in that moment he knew the truth. I did not love him. How could I?

Jackson jerked back and belted his open hand across my face. The blow threw me off the swing, my foot tangling in the seat. The world darkened, and I worried I would pass out. I lifted to my elbows. He grabbed me by the front of my jacket and dragged me to the side of the school building, more secluded from view.

"Wait." The word sputtered through a mouthful of blood.

He backhanded me, and I fell on a soft pillow of leaves. He ripped open my jacket and pinned my arms above my head.

"You said you loved me." His eyes flared wide. And I finally knew. This is what ugly looked like.

Jackson held my wrists with just one of his massive hands. With the other, he tore open his wool jacket, and in a flash—before I had a chance to react—he threw off one side of his coat, changed hands, and threw off the other side. He bent down, restrained me again, and worked at the zipper of my pants.

I struggled against him and remembered Mom telling me how she'd been attacked on the college campus. She'd been lucky, saved by other students. No one was coming to save me, and I couldn't recall anything that I'd learned in the self-defense classes.

His classes.

But then I remembered something . . . and went limp.

He paused to reevaluate my actions, and in that second, I rammed my knee into his groin. He loosened his hold on me, and I chopped the edge of my hand into his solid neck. He batted it away like a fly. I shoved the heel of my hand into his chin, but he slapped me with so much force my ears whistled.

He pinned me again and yanked at the waist of my pants.

I closed my eyes, and an image of Mom floated into my mind. The moment the police tell her I'm dead. The agony on her face. I loved her too much to let that come true. It could not happen this way. Not here in the schoolyard. I imagined where Mom was now. At the store? Did she park at the farthest end of the lot? Wherever she was, she was too far away, and I was alone. Somewhere inside of me had to be the strength I needed to save myself. But I wasn't sure I could do this on my own. I said a prayer.

And then I heard a sound. All of the women—mothers, daughters, grandmothers—from the self-defense class yelling and clapping and cheering me on. I focused and drew from their energy and strength. No more intimidation. No more good girls. Our energy combined, we were a tough team to crack. I would not be broken. I opened my eyes and started screaming at the top of my lungs. Shocked, Jackson fought to keep me pinned, but I twisted and kicked and flailed my arms. He moved quickly against my every effort.

"Stop fighting me!" he yelled. He continued to straddle my waist, and I continued to scream. My lungs ached from the cold air. He backhanded me, again, but before he could restrain my hands once more, I shoved my thumbs into his eye sockets. I remembered Mom's strength in her final self-defense test. With my legs, I reached up and wrapped them around his torso. I thanked Coach Gavyn for making me run stair laps. I used all of my lower body strength to try to rock Jackson backward. But he was too big.

I reached deeper and channeled my mother's life force. I needed her help. In the distance, I heard her vicious primal scream—a gut wrenching roar of defiance—and I jerked my head to the right expecting to see her running up behind Jackson, coming to save my life. But she wasn't there, at least not in body. And it wasn't her screaming. It was me. Triumphant energy surged through me like a firestorm, and I realized: I am my mother's daughter. I roared even louder.

Jackson rotated to see what I was yelling at, and in that moment, he tipped off balance. I pulled his torso back with my legs. I threw myself forward, and I pounded my fists into his groin. He let out a monstrous moan and cupped his balls. I pulled myself out from under him and ran for the front of the school.

My shoes pounded against the pavement of the parking lot and kicked up loose gravel bits. I ran even faster when I heard Jackson's feet hit the gravel behind me. Before I could figure out where my steps were taking me, Jackson grabbed my ponytail and yanked me backward. I stumbled and fell to the ground.

Exhausted, I didn't know how much longer I could keep fighting him, but surely he was getting tired, too.

Any passing car would be able to see us fighting in the middle of the parking lot, but there were no cars. He sat on top of me again, and in slow motion, he balled up his fist and cocked it back . . . if he landed the blow, I knew he would knock me unconscious. I wouldn't let that happen. I clutched his other arm and brought it to my mouth. I bit down with all my strength, and my teeth sank into his muscle. My mouth filled with warm fleshy tissue, and the metallic tang of his blood competed with the sour milk stench of his skin. I struggled against my own gag reflex and clamped my teeth down even harder. He still punched me, but instead of hitting my head, he hit my shoulder. Pain shot down my entire arm, and it went numb. I was running out of time.

He grabbed his arm where I'd bit him. A large chunk of flesh hung loosely and blood oozed down his hand. I took advantage of the moment and threw some loose gravel into his eyes. He yelled and bent sideways. I squirmed out from under him and took off running again. I didn't look back.

I knew where my steps were taking me now. The only place they could: home.

I ran faster and harder. Tears streamed down my face, but I didn't care anymore. I knew I wasn't weak, and I gave myself permission to cry. And I just kept running. I didn't want to know if he was following or how close he was behind me.

My house was within sight, and the cars were in the driveway.

My family was home.

The front door flew open, and Seth yelled, "What the hell?" He put his hands out like he was going to touch me, but then he pulled back. I waited there panting, unable to speak. Seth yelled into the house, "Mom! Dad!" A tear slid down his cheek, and his hand covered his mouth.

A car pulled up to the curb behind me, and I freaked. I jerked around to see if it was Jackson. But it wasn't. Tim stepped out of the car. His mouth dropped open when we made eye contact, and he came no closer. My parents burst out onto the porch, but stopped in their tracks and stared. None of them said anything, at first.

Then, Mom said, "Robert, call the police. Seth, get a blanket." She gingerly took me in her arms like she was afraid she'd break me. I sobbed and buried my face in her shoulder. That's when I realized I was a bloody swollen mess, because I ruined the shirt Mom wore with the blood from my face.

Mom guided me to the family room and sat me on the couch, never releasing her arm from my shoulders. My body trembled from the exhaustion and the adrenaline. Seth brought a blanket and draped it around me. I wondered where my winter coat was . . . and noticed my shirt had been ripped wide open . . . and that the horrible pink noose still hung around my neck. I swiped at it.

"Get it off. Get it off!"

Mom untied the scarf and tossed it aside. "You're safe now. You're home," she said and smoothed my hair.

"The police will be here soon," Dad said.

Between sobs, I choked out the words, "It was Jackson."

"What?" Mom asked.

"It was Jackson."

"Who the hell is Jackson?" Dad asked.

Mom covered her mouth and staggered away from the couch. A few feet away, she let out an agonizing scream that dropped her to her knees. Dad ran to her and clutched her face in his hands.

"Tell me," he said.

"The self-defense instructor," she yelled. "I'm the one who told him Thea played *Skadi*." She pounded her fist against her chest. "I'm the one who told him personal things about her. This is my fault." He embraced her.

"I'm sorry, Mom," I whispered.

Both she and Dad turned to me and stared for a brief moment, and then Mom rushed back to my side. "This is not your fault." She rocked me, and we sobbed together. "Everything's going to be okay. We will get through this together," she said.

The police and the ambulance arrived minutes later. Two EMTs cared for my cuts and wounds while the police asked me questions about the attack. The EMTs insisted on taking me to the hospital to finish treating my facial wounds and to x-ray my shoulder.

I rose from the couch, and Dad wrapped his arms around me. "Thea, I'm so proud of you. You are the strongest young woman ever." He escorted me outside and helped me into the ambulance.

Tim pushed past the EMTs and climbed in next to me. He wrapped his hands around mine and opened his mouth to speak, but nothing came out.

"I'm okay," I said, but then corrected my lie. "I will be . . . okay."

He nodded and held my hands tighter, unable to speak. A tear dropped from my eye onto our clutched hands.

The police officer came over toward us. He finished saying something into his radio, and then he said the three most beautiful words in the world to me:

"We caught him."

# EPILOGUE

Some old dead guy once said a journey of a thousand miles begins with just one step. Obviously. I only wish I'd noticed sooner where mine were taking me last winter.

The next year was long and hard, but it was good, too. Janie and I graduated from our counseling sessions. She spent several months in a clinic and then attended private and group counseling. She looks better than ever with her black bouncy ringlets and designer clothes. I went through a couple of counselors before we found one that was helpful, but once we did, I made amazing progress in my own recovery. I still have occasional nightmares about Derek attacking me, but I know that whatever happens to me, I am strong enough to handle it.

Since the police caught him that day, Derek Felton, also known as Derek Jackson, was prosecuted for six different counts of statutory rape and one first-degree murder. When my story had hit the news, other girls came forward and shared their stories. They each thought they were alone. I had not been his first victim, but hopefully, I would be his last.

The police used DNA evidence to connect him to the death of Red in Hawaii.

I still can't wrap my brain around the fact that Kitsuneshin—the guy I'd met playing an innocent online game, the guy I'd debated song lyrics with late into the night, and the first guy to ever tell me he loved me—was capable of something so horrible as murder. My skin crawls when I wonder how I could have been so wrong about him. Red didn't deserve to die. And I still think of her as a friend. We both loved quotes. I knew her real name. I knew where she lived. And her parents took the time to call me. They thanked me for helping solve Lokelani's case, and I apologized to them for not speaking up sooner. We cried on the phone together, and they told me about the daughter they cherished. That could have been me. I came so close to dying. But it helps knowing Jackson will spend the rest of his life in prison.

Officer Ford taught an Internet safety class during school today. I sat in shock while he described Internet predators and how they manipulate kids. On one hand I felt like he was talking specifically about Derek and what he did to me. On the other hand, I felt like I didn't hear a word Officer Ford said because I was too busy floating above my own body remembering the events. I still couldn't believe it happened to me. I couldn't believe how stupid I was. Mom keeps telling me I wasn't stupid, only naive, and that there's a difference between the two.

My counselor said learning from the experience is what matters, because if I grow from it, I can become a better person. But if I don't learn anything, she warned, I'll continue to struggle with the same problems over and over. This was a journey I wish I'd never taken, but I can't change the past. I can only change today, one step at a time.

Tim and I have agreed to be friends and wait a while to date. What's the rush? Of course, we're friends who happen to hold hands when we walk together, and we happen to sit side by side whenever we eat lunch together, which happens to be every day at school.

And, my favorite quote from the last year?

*It would be such a disgrace, if I fell short and you were not safe.—Lauren Harper*

# About the Author

Margo Kelly is a native of the Northwest, and she has enjoyed a career that has included motivational speaking for business people, church groups, and teenagers. Now that her own children are out of the house, she has decided to actively pursue her love of writing. She has written several young adult novels and is plotting the next one. Margo welcomes opportunities to speak to youth groups, library groups, books clubs, and school assemblies. You may contact her at *www.margokelly.net.*